Beach Winds

Emerald Isle, NC Novel #2

Beach Winds
by
Grace Greene

Emerald Isle, NC Novel #2

Kersey Creek Books
P.O. Box 6054
Ashland, VA 23005

Cover Design by Grace Greene

Trade Paperback Re-release: June 2015
ISBN-13: 978-0-9907740-7-5
Digital Re-release: June 2015
ISBN-13: 978-0-9907740-8-2
Original Trade Paperback/Digital Release: November 2013

DEDICATION

Beach Winds is dedicated to those who struggle through disability and illness and to the ones who support and care for them. This book is dedicated to those who recover well enough to make it back home, and to those who don't.

My great-uncle W.E. Ellen was career navy. He served on the USS North Carolina. Many years ago, in retirement, he suffered a serious stroke, but his dignity and courage, despite the disability he struggled with, inspired all who knew him. In the present, my aunt and uncle persevere together through that same adversity. This past year, our dear friends who were married in the same year that we were are now dealing with the challenge of a stroke—and I know they are equal to the job.

Beach Winds confirms the power of love. Love is not a matter of blood or genetics. Love is a blessing wherever you find it and should be tended as if it were the most delicate seedling, yet shared as freely as the most common plant. Like the dune grass that helps the dunes withstand the ocean and weather, so are we to those we love.

W.E., Jane and Billy, and John and Sue—this is for you.

ACKNOWLEDGEMENT

My love and thanks to my family. My gratitude and praise to God.

BEACH WINDS

Off-season at Emerald Isle ~ In-season for secrets of the heart

Frannie Denman has been waiting for her life to begin. After several false starts, and a couple of broken hearts, she ends up back with her mother, with whom she doesn't get along, until her elderly uncle gets sick and Frannie goes to Emerald Isle to help manage his affairs while he's recovering.

Her uncle's oceanfront home, Captain's Walk, is small and unpretentious, and even though Frannie isn't a 'beach person,' she decides Captain's Walk in winter is a great place to hide from her troubles. But Frannie doesn't realize that winter is short in Emerald Isle and the beauty of the ocean and seashore can help heal anyone's heart, especially when her uncle's handyman is the handsome Brian Donovan.

Brian has troubles of his own. He sees himself and Frannie as two damaged people who aren't likely to equal a happy 'whole' but he's intrigued by this woman of contradictions.

Frannie's mother wants her back home and Brian wants to meet the real Frannie, but Frannie wants to move forward with her life. To do that she needs questions answered. With the right information there's a good chance Frannie will be able to affect not only a change in her life, but also a change of heart.

BEACH WINDS

Chapter One

Frannie Denman stood at the sliding doors and stared beyond the glass, the porch and the dunes. She didn't belong here—not at the beach and not in this dreary February world.

Angry crests foamed out of the churning, steel gray Atlantic and rode the waves to a cold shore swept by a frigid wind, the same wind that whipped up the sand and tossed the tall weedy dune grasses. An occasional super gust shook the house. She touched the glass as it shuddered.

A lone man moved along the wooden walkway that crossed over the dunes. With slow, determined steps, he hunched forward as he fought the wind. His jacket and hooded sweatshirt were inadequate, plastered against him by nature. She watched him, wondering if he'd end up at this door, but then he descended the steps and disappeared between the houses. It was where he should've been all along, using the houses as a buffer, instead of taking the wind on headfirst.

This was an inhospitable place and it matched her dark mood.

Why was this house, and Will Denman's life, her responsibility? She couldn't manage her own. How was she supposed to help anyone else?

She turned away from the window to face Mrs. Blair. "I am sorry about this."

"So you said before." The woman gathered up her purse and a bulky tote bag brimming with cleaning supplies.

"I'll get the door for you. Let me help you with that bag."

Mrs. Blair stood taller and scowled. "No, thank you. I've been finding my way in and out of your uncle's house for fifteen years. I can manage one last time."

"Yes. Again, I'm sorry." She clasped her hands together. "What about the broken lattice? You said you had the name of Uncle Will's handyman?"

Mrs. Blair stared with accusing eyes. "On the fridge. Name's Brian."

Frannie followed her out. At the top of the stairs, she clutched the rail. With her free hand, she held her sweater closed at her throat. Cold, salty wind blew her hair across her face and stung her nose and cheeks. She wished it could also blow the self-doubt from her brain.

If Uncle Will ever returned home, what would he say about Mrs. Blair being fired? She was a cleaning lady, yes, but one with a fifteen-year history. If he did come home, it wouldn't be soon. More likely, never.

Back inside, she dialed the thermostat down, leaving just enough heat to keep the pipes from freezing. Had she left anything undone?

No. There wasn't much to the place.

Her uncle's furniture had no particular style or age. Strictly thrift shop. There was no elegance, no shine, not even the customary beachy wicker or white rattan.

It was a retired sailor's home. Captain's Walk, he'd named it. This house was small, only a ranch style, but here it was oceanfront and thus, had a grand name. This house, inside and out, was unremarkable except for the observation deck. The deck was unusual, perched halfway up the roof near the end of the house, but this time of year... Well, with a veritable gale blowing, the idea of sunning herself wasn't appealing.

It's just a house. No interest in dolling it up, Uncle Will had told her a year ago. They'd met for the first time—one meeting out of a lifetime of opportunities—and only then because he'd called and asked her to come see him.

She'd visited him again after that and had meant to return sooner, but she hadn't, and now he wasn't here.

Magnets secured bits of scribbled paper to the front of the refrigerator. One magnet listed local emergency numbers. A smaller green magnet had a bank name and number. Another advertised a pizza delivery place.

There it was. Brian Donovan. His name and phone number were written in large block letters on a neatly torn square of paper.

She disliked talking to strangers, even over the phone, but she got lucky this time because the voicemail answered.

"Mr. Donovan? I'm Will Denman's niece. Grandniece, that is. My uncle is ill and I'm...I mean, he asked me to take care of his house. I understand you do handyman work for him? Would you please take a look at the lattice on the west side of the house? Send the bill to Mr. Denman's post office box." She gave the number and finished with, "I'll see you get paid."

Done.

The lights were off. She gave a last tug on the sliding door to make sure it was locked. Now she could be on her way. It was winter in Raleigh, too, of course, and not exactly balmy, but without the deadly cold ocean and its bitter winds.

She slipped on her coat, wrapped the scarf around her neck twice, and picked up her purse.

The parking area was below and behind the house on the street side. Her car and her uncle's old green van were the only vehicles.

It was freezing inside the car, but the leather seat would warm up quickly. She backed out onto a deserted Emerald Drive. She'd just hit cruising speed when the dashboard lit up and rang.

Laurel Denman, it displayed. Mother.

Frannie let it ring, determined to ignore it, half-expecting her mother to emerge from the caller ID screen like some half-formed specter of guilt and frustration.

There should be tender feelings between mother and daughter, shouldn't there? Like mother, like daughter—maybe their capacity to care about each other had died with her father.

Almost three hours later, and after two more calls from her mother, Frannie drove up the long, curving, blackened asphalt driveway. The tall, straight pines, the bare, sculptured branches of the crepe myrtles growing in the perfectly landscaped yard, always welcomed her, but after these last few years she'd realized that was all it was—an empty offer. She braked to a stop in front of the house. Now, coming home was more a reminder of personal failure.

She opened the front door with as much stealth as she could. It wasn't enough.

"Frannie."

Her mother stood in the wide opening between the living and dining rooms. Her honey blond hair was precisely groomed. Petite and curvy, she was the opposite of her slender, brown-haired daughter.

Frannie's best feature was her dark blue eyes, like her dad's. Dad had called them 'the Denman eyes.' When she fastened those eyes upon Laurel, she knew it made her mother uncomfortable.

Laurel stared back. The firm set of her lips, and her hands held artfully in front of her waist, showed her anger. Unhappy words were imminent.

"Don't do this right now." Frannie shook her head and tucked a lock of her fine, flyaway hair behind her ear.

"Don't do what?"

"I drove down to the beach for the day. I don't need your permission."

Her mother came to stand close to her. She smoothed the remaining strands of hair away from her daughter's cheek.

"I'm sorry, sweetheart. I was worried." She touched Frannie's arm. "Let me take your coat. You'll get overwarm and it's time to dress for dinner anyway. Our guests will be here soon."

"Our guests?"

She stared beyond her mother. Her dad's chair still sat in front of the fireplace, empty for almost fifteen years. The worn chair was lost amid a roomful of newer, more expensive furnishings.

"Don't sulk, Frannie, and don't blame me. Will Denman had no right to ask this of you. I begged you to refuse. You agreed just to spite me."

"I agreed because it was the right thing to do." She shook her head. "The attorney is handling the difficult decisions like medical and veteran's benefits and such. I'm doing the easy stuff."

"It's not your responsibility."

"He's dad's uncle. How can you be so cold?"

"I hardly knew him. I think I met him once in all the years your father and I were married."

"He was in the navy. At sea."

"He's been retired for years." She shrugged and shook her head. "I don't understand how you got pulled into his life at this late date, but he has a lot of nerve expecting you to put your life on hold while he's... sick."

"A stroke, Mother. Bottom line, he doesn't have any other family. His attorney will be his executor when it's time for that. Uncle Will needs me to deal with his house, bills and personal property in the meanwhile."

"A realtor and a low-end auction house is all that's needed. Or just call the Salvation Army."

"There's more to it than that. Besides, he's not ready to sell."

"You're not up to this, darling—that's my bottom line. As for going there today, you know I have a dinner planned and how much it means to me, yet you leave without warning and stay away until the last minute."

Frannie gripped the stair rail, wanting to walk away. "I told you I'd be here. I shouldn't though, because I know what you're up to. You're match-making."

In a low voice, Laurel said, "I'm trying to prevent another disastrous choice on your part. Joel's a fine young man." She mumbled a few more words.

"What?"

Laurel stood taller, her neck long and smooth. "He won't

hold your past against you."

Angry words tumbled in her brain, wrestling for an exit, but Frannie set her jaw and refused to allow them out.

"You're an attractive woman and you have money. Joel might not be exciting, but he has money of his own. He won't try to take yours, and he won't abuse you."

She moved to continue up the stairs, but Laurel stepped closer and rested her hand on her daughter's arm.

"If you don't show up, it will be embarrassing for me, which won't bother you, but it will be cruel to Joel. You may be cold, but you aren't heartless."

Cold, but not heartless. That about summed her up. Frannie hurried upstairs, leaving her mother standing there, her hand suspended mid-air. She ran to her room. Her lifelong room.

"Still living at home?" someone had asked her recently. She'd tried to salvage a speck of pride by explaining, "My mother needs me."

On her dresser, there was no dust but only the usual items, carefully replaced in the exact same spots each time Hannah came through with her feather duster, the lamb's wool duster and her anti-static cloth. A photo of daddy and little Frannie was protected in its glittering crystal frame. The one next to it showed them in the garden. She was maybe two or three? The sun shone on them, both with their brown hair and deep blue eyes and big, happy smiles. Then the trio, her dad, her mother and herself. She'd been almost four, she thought. Back then things had been better between them. She turned that frame to rest face down on the dresser.

Despite appearances, and apparently despite the opinion of some, she wasn't an emotional ice cube. The cold was her protection, her armor. Without the armor she was no more than a shy, awkward, almost thirty-one-year-old woman who'd never been able to make a go of independence.

She knew she was attractive. People told her so and she could see it with her own eyes, but that was on the outside. Inside was a different story. She was good at hiding the mess inside—could almost make it cease to exist—at least until someone reminded her, someone like her darling mother.

****

The light from the crystal chandelier reflected in the high gloss of the china. Frannie spread the linen napkin across her lap. To her right, Joel sipped his wine and smiled. Rather, he smiled at his plate. His short brown hair was unremarkable, but his eyes were sweet, open and honest. He was attractive enough and he was kind, but there was no spark. No electricity. She'd been in love before and though it had ended badly, she wasn't willing to settle for less, even if it meant she'd never be in love again.

She shouldn't have agreed to this. The small group, with only Joel and his father, was too intimate. They were nice people, but under the circumstances, it felt like a lie.

Joel startled her, saying, "That dress is beautiful on you. That shade of blue, I mean. The color matches your eyes. What do you call it? Sapphire?"

Sapphire. In reflex she looked at the ring, deep blue and flashing with light. She refrained from reaching up to touch the drop earrings.

"Thank you, Joel. Sapphire blue was my father's favorite color."

"I remember. He gave you those at your sixteenth birthday party."

She frowned. "That was a long time ago and a lot of people were at that party."

"It was and there were, but it made an impression. Most of our friends got a car. You got the car and the crown jewels." He laughed gently.

She didn't want to go back there, not back to that dear memory while sitting here with these people. Father, beaming, happy to show his love and pride in her—she felt again the warmth of his hands as he'd fastened the necklace. Mother had been far from pleased with the gift.

She glanced up, sensing Laurel's eyes upon her, staring.

Involuntarily, Frannie touched the pendant. The platinum setting was cool against her skin; it reminded her to cool down. Joel's father spoke to Laurel and her mother looked away.

Joel cleared his throat and blushed. "I heard you were down at the beach today."

From Mother, of course. Who else would know or care?

"Yes, I was."

"We have a house at the beach, too. At Hatteras."

"I know."

"Were you anywhere near there?"

"No. Not near. Emerald Isle."

"It's not that far. I didn't know you liked the beach."

Frannie interrupted, shaking her head. "I don't. I'm not a swimmer or a sunbather. I'm helping a relative."

"I see." He looked away. "That's nice of you."

"Sorry. That was rude." She took a deep breath.

He shook his head. "I shouldn't have asked. I didn't mean to pry."

He really was a nice guy. Too nice. It was stressful being around someone who could be so easily hurt or cowed. She felt compelled to smooth it over.

"My father's uncle. He had a stroke and I'm helping to manage, perhaps dispose of, his property."

"How sad. No wonder you don't want to talk about it." He folded his napkin and set it on the table. "If you need anything at all, please let me know. Anything I can do, I'm happy to help. No matter what."

Joel leaned in closer. She tried to relax, but then caught the approving look from her mother. She sat back and glared at Laurel, ignoring Joel's look of surprise.

Laurel said, "Your father told me that you are getting a promotion, Joel. That's lovely and so well deserved. Isn't that marvelous, Frannie?"

"Wonderful."

Joel tugged at the front of his sports jacket as if the fit wasn't quite right. He smiled. "Yes, very exciting. I'm glad of the opportunity."

That was one of the big problems with Joel. Always correct. Always courteous. Not a bad guy, and maybe someone she could spend an evening with under other circumstances, but a lifetime? Not a chance.

Laurel whispered to Joel's father and both looked their way. The beaming expressions they bestowed upon her and Joel were blatant.

Anger flooded her. The noise of it roared in her ears and her hands trembled. Frannie folded her napkin carefully.

"It's been lovely, but I must go." She pushed back the chair and stood abruptly, pre-empting Joel's move to assist her.

Her mother's expression of benevolence didn't change, but it hardened, and her eyes grew large.

Laurel could be counted on not to make a scene in front of her guests. Frannie didn't want a diva scene either, but she didn't have the least problem with a dramatic exit.

Within minutes Frannie heard Laurel's soft footfalls on the thick carpet in the hall.

Her mother stopped in the open doorway and, in a low voice, she hissed, "How could you do that? What on earth are you thinking?"

"I tried. I really did, but you overplayed it." Frannie tossed the last, hastily grabbed items, into her duffle bag. Time apart would be good for them both.

"It's humiliating to make excuses for you. I told them you were unwell earlier today and it might have returned. It's not too late. Come back to the table. If you must go, do so after dinner."

"No." Frannie heard the shakiness in her voice and willed it away. "If it's any help to you, I'll leave by the side door so they don't see me."

"If you thought it would help me, you wouldn't do it." She clenched her fists. "Am I supposed to go back down to our guests and pretend my daughter has taken ill and has retired for the night? All while you're sneaking out of the house?"

"I'm sure you'll do a fine job." She yanked the zipper with finality.

"Then go. Suit yourself. That's what you've always done. You run away." Laurel placed a hand on the door lintel and leaned against it as if exhausted. "No, please don't go. It's too late to drive back tonight. Wait until morning. Don't put yourself at risk just because you want to hurt me."

"I'm ready now." She put the bag's strap over her shoulder. "A couple of hours or so and I'll be there."

"Be where? A house at the beach that means nothing to you? He has no money. All he has is that house."

She drew in a deep breath and held it, then released it very slowly. "It's not about money."

"Well, it's certainly not about family because I'm here, I need you, and that man is a distant relative you hardly know. That doesn't make him family."

Frannie bit her lip. She wanted to scream that it wasn't about close relationships or blood ties. It was about toxic love. However, some words shouldn't be spoken aloud no matter what the provocation, no matter how their sharp edges tore her up inside.

Mother was silent. Her face was still, almost resigned. Finally, she said, "Do as you will. You'll only be hurt and your troubles will start up all over again. Smart people learn from their mistakes. I can't say that for you. Joel might not be exciting, but a man like Joel won't hurt you. You might not recover from your next true love as easily as you did from the last one. When you fall apart again, and you need my help, remember I told you so."

Easily? Recover easily? Had her loving mother really said that? Yes, along with 'when you fall apart again' and 'I told you so.'

"You aren't going like that?" Laurel looked her up and down.

In this case, Mother was right. She was still in her party dress and heels.

"You wore that jewelry tonight to wound me."

Frannie touched the necklace again and ignored the last question. She set the duffel bag down near the door, as if that had been her plan all along.

"No, I'm not traveling like this."

"Good, because the sapphires belong in the safe. In fact, in a better safe than the one you have here." She nodded toward the closet. "I don't understand why you insist upon taking such a risk."

"You'd better get back to your guests."

Laurel gave her a last, icy look. She slapped the door lintel, but left without another word.

Frannie waited until her mother was out of sight and then grabbed the duffel bag. She didn't need her mother or anyone else telling her what to do. She was almost thirty-one, for heaven's sake, and getting older by the minute.

She stopped in the kitchen on her way out, snagged a couple of tins of tea and a steeper, dropping them into one of the shopping bags from the pantry. A maid was cleaning the kitchen and didn't look up. A new maid. Frannie didn't recognize her.

"Where's Hannah?"

The woman shrugged.

Never mind.

It was a long dark road from here to there. From beginning to destination, it was a different trip, a changed landscape at night. The miles raced away beneath her tires, to the rhythm of highway lights or the headlights and red taillights of other travelers. They were her companions. All going somewhere, but separately. Together and forever separate. Alone.

Alone and ungrateful. She had so much. A comfortable life. No financial worries. Yet she felt always alone, trapped, marooned on her own desolate, emotional island.

Keeping the jewelry on was silly and careless. It was jewelry, not her dad, but it felt a little like her dad was here with her.

She'd tried to break away before and failed. Maybe this time she would succeed. It felt possible as she was speeding down the dark road. Many people had worse losses and greater troubles. She should be able to overcome hers, unless Mother was right and the flaw was inside her, along for the ride no matter how far she fled.

Tomorrow she'd drive over to Morehead City to visit her uncle.

When the stroke happened, the attorney had contacted her, and she'd gone to the hospital right away and then again just before and after he moved to the rehab. She blamed the distance for not visiting more often, but honestly, she hadn't been prepared to see him so weak, so changed by the stroke.

Tonight there were no stars, no moon. She drove over the bridge to Emerald Drive. It was a long, lonely road in the winter, especially at night. She slowed way down to pick out her uncle's driveway. A blanket of dark covered all, and when she braked, the wind rocked her car. Her headlights cast a glow ahead, into the parking area behind and below the house, until she turned the lights off.

She shivered. The house blocked the worst of the onshore wind, but the wooden stairs leading up to the side door would be awkward in the dark, and in her heels. She put a finger through the key ring and closed her fist around it.

With her duffel bag and purse hanging on one shoulder, she clung to the handrail. Finally inside, she flipped on the lights, dropped her bags on the chair, stripped off her gloves, and then pumped up the thermostat. She'd keep the coat on for a while.

She'd left this sad place only a few hours ago.

It felt foreign here, alone and at night.

She could pick up that duffle bag and go back down to her car. She could stay in a hotel. That's where sojourners were supposed to tuck themselves in for the night, right? Where there was a comfy bed and uniformed housekeeping and no clutter of personal objects? In the morning, she could behave like a reasonable adult and go back home.

She ditched her coat and threw it across the sofa. Cold or not, removing it put one more step between her and retreat.

Books were stacked here and there. Luckily, the cable TV would be working for another day or two.

Her uncle wasn't much for knick-knacks or bric-a-brac. A few framed family photos hung on the wall. One was of her dad as a boy with his Uncle Will. Another showed Will and his brother and sister in black and white, including starched white shirts for the boys and a starched white dress for the girl. He'd pointed them out to her, telling her about his brother, Marshall, and his sister, Penny. All gone. Long gone.

Most of Will Denman's literary taste ran to non-fiction. Navy stuff, naval history. Books lined the top of his roll top desk with heavy metal bookends to hold them in place. She slid one out noting the dust that marked its place. She thumbed through it and a slip of paper fell out.

The scrap of notebook paper was long and narrow, neatly torn from a larger piece. A hand-written note was penciled on it. She squinted to read the words.

"And he said, I called by reason of mine affliction unto God, And He answered me; Out of the belly of Hell cried I, And Thou heardest my voice." Jonah 2, verse 2.

Well, that was grim. She looked around the room. Not exactly in the belly of hell, thank goodness.

Frannie folded the slip of paper and slipped it back into the book—a book about the USS North Carolina. The verse about Jonah and the whale tucked into a book about a battleship? Really? Was it intended or a coincidence? She smiled, wishing she could ask her uncle whether it was a joke or a confession.

There were three bedrooms. Two had beds. Frannie pulled the coverlet back in the guest room and examined the sheets. They looked clean. The idea of sleeping here felt strange, but not as odd as sleeping in her uncle's bed, as if he were already past tense. That felt rude.

Frannie pulled the drapes across the sliding doors and

closed the window blinds. She got her pajamas and robe from the duffel bag and told herself this was no different from a hotel room, but it was different.

She undid the catch of the necklace and removed the earrings. The sapphires glittered on her palm. She really was foolish.

The dresser in this small room had some of Will's overflow clothing. She found a pair of white cotton socks and carefully dropped the earrings and necklace into one of them. She added the ring, too. She twisted the sock and folded it back over itself, then hid it between the mattress and box spring.

She left the lights burning in the living room and the bedroom door cracked open. She huddled under the blanket and bedspread. In the silence, the house rattled and the ocean boomed. She buried her face in the pillow and tried to shut out images of blown-in windows and collapsing walls. Was there a hurricane she hadn't heard about? This was wrong time of year for that, but not for winter storms.

Frannie checked the doors and locks one last time, then climbed into bed. She held one pillow down over her ears and pulled the blankets up so far they came untucked, but that didn't matter because she was curled up into as small as form as she could make herself.

****

She awoke at dawn, groggy and bleary-eyed. She eased herself upright and stretched. The blankets had fallen to the floor during the night. Her pajamas were twisted and wrinkled.

She pulled on her robe and headed toward the kitchen. She fit the tea holder into the steeper as the water heated. As she waited, she noticed the silence. The bluster and buffeting had ceased. The house no longer shook.

She shuffled over to the front window and grabbed the drawstrings. She tugged and the blinds opened.

Dawn. Puffs of clouds and a lighter shade of dark mixed with threads of morning color near the horizon. She went to the sliding doors and pushed the drapes aside.

A group of large seabirds was flying by. They skimmed the water, diving for breakfast.

She fumbled the lock open and slid the glass door wide.

The air, fresh from the Atlantic, rushed in, cool with a promise of better to come.

The rough wood of the handrail had been a sponge for the night and the deck boards were cold and damp. Sand peppered the rails and planks. She walked along the wooden crossover, over the dunes and wild grasses, to its end where the public beach began. A bench was built into the crossover near the stairs to the beach, but the seat would be too chilly and damp this morning. It would be better when spring arrived.

The rough waves no longer sounded angry, but natural, as if saying Yes, we're loud. We're the ocean.

Facing the east end of the strand, waiting for the full sunrise, the chill crept up through her bare feet. When the sun broke the horizon, it highlighted walkers coming her way. She pulled her robe closer about her and scurried back up the crossover and into the house.

The morning sun followed her inside in bright, but dusty streams that shone through the glass door and the windows. In this light, the furnishings, though old and plain, gained a little dignity, and then her cell phone rang.

She picked it up reluctantly. "Hello?"

"Frannie?"

"Mother. Good morning."

"Is it good? You didn't really drive all the way back to the beach last night?"

"I'm at Uncle Will's house. You know that."

"You have a sharp way with words, Frannie. I wish you'd pause to think before you bite my head off."

She 'paused to think' but couldn't come up with anything helpful to say, so she didn't.

"Now the silent treatment." Laurel's tone softened. "Sweetheart, you're all I have. All that I have left of your father. You're my daughter. I love you."

Frannie drew in a breath and held it for a moment attempting to reset the day. Beyond the sliding doors, the morning, serene and looking almost mystical as light picked its way through the water and the morning mist, called to her.

She breathed out slowly and said, "I'll tell you my plans when I know them."

Laurel was silent. After a long pause, she said, "Whatever you say, but please, keep me informed. Don't leave me to worry until I have no choice but to track you down."

"Bye, Mother."

She clicked off the phone and went back to the kitchen to enjoy her tea.

Mother. She certainly knew how to take the shine from the morning, but this morning, Mother Nature had the better hand.

****

Showered and dressed, Frannie boiled an egg and steeped more tea. She was more than a little apprehensive about going to see Uncle Will.

As she settled at the table to enjoy her little breakfast, she felt a noise more than heard it. It was only a slight vibration, but on this quiet morning, it was enough to get her attention. She threw her coat over her shoulders and stepped out onto the porch. She bypassed the white rockers and looked over the end of the porch.

A man was down below, kneeling by the lattice at the end of the porch. He was wearing a hooded sweatshirt under a leather jacket, but the hood was pushed back to show sandy-colored hair. That was all she could see clearly from above. The jacket and sweatshirt rang a bell.

He pulled and pushed against the latticework and, apparently satisfied, grabbed his tool bag. He started to rise, but then put one hand against the side of the house. It seemed to take him a while to stand. He was tall and moved stiffly.

"Hello, down there."

He stepped backward with a slight limp and looked upward. "Good morning."

"Are you the handyman? You got my message?"

He paused before answering. "I'm Brian Donovan. You're the niece, right?" He motioned toward the lattice. "Yeah, I got your message."

"I'm Frannie Denman." She crossed her arms and hugged them close. He had a nice face, but the stubble on his cheeks bothered her. It seemed a less than professional appearance, but then again, he was the handyman. "Were you out here yesterday?"

He nodded. "Checking around after the storm."

"I see. Well, you'll send a bill? I'll see that it's taken care of."

"Yes, ma'am. No problem."

The timbre of his voice was calm and sure, but his blue eyes grabbed her. She sighed. Blue eyes and a nice smile had led her astray before. Not again. Never again. No third strikes for her.

"Thank you, Mr. Donovan." She nodded and moved out of view.

****

Will Denman had always been a lean man, but his legs and arms seemed outrageously thin. His bristly white hair defied combing. She sat in front of this man she hardly knew, perched on the edge of an awful padded chair with pink vinyl upholstery, and he sat in his wheelchair. His head was tilted to one side, almost in a questioning pose, but he couldn't vocalize words she could understand, except three: take me home.

Faded hazel eyes drilled those words into her. She didn't have any good answers for him.

Did she think he'd ever come back home? No, but he did, so she smiled and nodded. "You'll be better soon."

She stared at the half-eaten lunch sitting on the rolling table next to him. A cloth, like a large bib, was tucked inside his pajama collar. What was she supposed to do? Pick up that spoon? Offer him assistance? He wasn't making any effort himself.

A smell flooded the room as a woman entered. That anti-bacterial dispenser attached to the wall acted like an air freshener every time someone tapped it. Air freshener? Not unless you liked the smell of hospitals and illness.

"I see you have a visitor, Mr. Will. Are you family? The niece?"

"Grandniece, actually. Or great niece. Whichever it is. You're Janet?"

"That's me. It's nice of you to come see him. He hasn't had many visitors."

Frannie slid the chair back a few screeching inches to allow the nurse's aide to pass. Janet pulled her own chair close in order to spoon the soft food into Will's mouth. He choked and Frannie was alarmed. How did you help someone who was choking when their body was so frail? She was glad the nurse was there and the responsibility was hers.

Frannie wanted out. More than that smell, it was the faces, the waiting faces she'd passed in the hallway—the can-you-see-me faces—that weighed her down like she was dragging chains. Add to that, the inability to have a reasonable conversation with her uncle, as well as not knowing what to do, made her feel captive. Yet, she kept her butt in the chair and tried to keep her expression bland so he wouldn't read the impatience that tied her up in knots. Had she taken her stomach medicine? A growing burning sensation, like banked coals not quite extinguished, warned her of worse to come.

"Should I leave? I don't want to be in the way."

Janet looked at her as if the question were nonsense. She didn't waste words on an answer, but instead, turned back to Will with a spoonful of applesauce.

"Have another bite, Mr. Denman."

He sputtered and shook his head. She snuck a peek at her watch. How much longer? She looked up. His keen gaze, sharp despite the faded hazel color, was fastened upon her.

He could afford a dedicated nurse's aide. She hadn't considered correcting her mother when she'd made the remark about Uncle Will's financial state. He wasn't living only on his pension. That was a tidbit of info her darling mother didn't need to know.

"I'll be right back." Janet left the room.

Frannie searched her brain, desperate for light conversation—statements that didn't require a response.

"I remember what you told me about the navy, and why you named the house Captain's Walk."

He lips moved, but his words were garbled.

"Remember that day you called me? I didn't know what to think. I never had much family, except for Mother and Dad, but you know that. Anyway, you told me you had been a chief petty officer. You said you named the house Captain's Walk because it was the only deck you'd ever be captain of, right?"

He gave a small nod, but he looked frustrated and that defeated look returned to his eyes.

Frannie tried again. "Mrs. Blair said to say 'hello'.

No change in his expression.

Try again, Frannie.

"Your handyman, Brian Donovan, made a repair to the house." She saw something in his eyes. He was worried about his home. She added quickly, "A small repair. Nothing big. Loose lattice." She hoped that hearing about his house and his handyman might give him comfort, but how exhausting it was to have this one-sided conversation. She was certain that inside his brain, he heard and responded, but they were powerless to breach the communication wall caused by his stroke.

Desperate for something else to throw into the silence, she said, "I'm thinking of sprucing things up with a little paint. Inside, that is. If you don't mind."

He'd turned away and was now staring at a poster on the wall. A beach scene. Bright shades of pink, blue and turquoise. Typical beach colors.

That smell swirled again.

Frannie looked at Janet and said, "I guess I'll go."

She rose and walked slowly to the door. Will continued

staring at the poster.

"Get better, Uncle Will. I'll come again soon."

He did nothing to indicate he'd heard her, or that he cared.

Driving back to Emerald Isle, she decided it was too soon to sell his house even though, more likely than not, it would need to be sold. In fact, in this real estate market, it made sense to spend some time sprucing it up. A little paint and a tweak to the decor would make it more marketable.

The decision to paint kept her moving forward, but without the risk of irrevocable actions. No commitment needed. Painting mistakes could be fixed easily. She'd hang out here and let Mother stew by herself for a while. Mother would be plenty surprised when she saw that her daughter could handle this and so much more.

Impulsively, she pulled into a home improvement store parking lot. Might as well get the supplies before she crossed back over the bridge to the island.

With the paint cans and supplies loaded in the trunk, she built up such a vision, imagining plans for the makeover of Captain's Walk, that when she actually entered the house, its dreariness almost overwhelmed her, but it didn't keep her down long.

She'd never painted a house before, but really, how hard could it be?

****

The smell of plastic drop cloths, pristine and fresh from the manufacturer's packaging, complemented the sawdust smell of the new stepladder unmarred by use. The paint cans contained nice off-white tones that aligned with what was already on the walls. Those unopened cans held a lot of untried promise. She opted not to tape the trim despite the clerk's recommendation. She had a steady hand and was innately neat.

Frannie put on a pair of navy khaki slacks and, in a concession to practicality, she found an old button-down shirt in Will's closet. She would start in the middle of the wall using the brush. The roller seemed vaguely intimidating.

She pried the lid off and dipped the brush delicately into the paint. There was not yet a drop on the wall when her phone rang, its vibrations drumming on the kitchen counter. Not a ring she recognized. Better to grab it now than after she'd started applying paint. She went for it and answered one-handed.

"Frannie?"

"Mother?" Not her ring. "Where are you calling from?"

"I borrowed a phone. I left mine at home."

Likely story. "What do you need?"

A moment of silence. "Need? Not 'how are you?' but 'what do you need?' I need to know when are you coming back home."

"When we spoke this morning, I told you I wasn't sure. I have obligations here."

"No longer. Good news. I've arranged with an attorney to handle all that for you. He does this professionally and will take care of Will's business affairs properly. You don't need to worry about it."

"He already has an attorney and I don't need help. I'm doing fine."

"Frannie—"

"No, mother." She looked down and saw white blobs of paint on the vinyl floor. The brush.

"I have to go."

She threw the phone aside and grabbed for the paper towels. She hadn't anticipated drips, including the ones she'd stepped in and that now marked her path. Run, she told herself, and headed for the plastic cloth. It slipped beneath her feet and kept moving. As it moved, so did the open gallon.

In horror, in slow motion, she slid toward the can like a runner coming in to home plate feet first. She sacrificed the brush so that she could try to swivel. She needed both hands to save the can. And she did. Or most of it. The top couple of inches of paint sloshed over the rim, but she righted it before the whole gallon spilled.

Hurriedly, she gathered the plastic sheet up around it like

a dam to contain the spreading lake of almost-white.

Painting was easy, or should have been.

Her hands were covered in paint. One leg of her navy khakis was now substantially off-white and sticking to her leg.

The phone began ringing again.

She sat up and wiped her paint-covered hands on the dry leg. Fine. Now, she had a pair of painting pants. Designated painting gear.

In the midst of disaster, she started laughing. Well, as disasters went, this one was pretty minor. Frannie laughed out loud. She laughed until she felt the tears beginning to burn her eyes.

Enough. She gulped in air. Walk away from it. Just walk away. She headed outside to cool down in the brisk February air.

She stood on the porch. The ocean was loud, but its roar was regular in rhythm and the worst of the crashing sounds were borne off by the wind. The sun was nice, but misleading. It promised warmth, but wind from a winter ocean could only be cold.

"Hello?"

She jumped when the man spoke. Brian Donovan. He stood below the side of the porch; his sandy hair and his forehead were barely visible from this angle. Then he moved and she realized he was coming up to the porch. To join her.

He still had the hooded sweatshirt on, but the leather jacket was gone. His jeans looked well worn, or worn well.

She reached up to smooth her blouse and her hair, but caught herself in time. Her hands were a paint-smeared mess like the rest of her. She plucked at the pants leg adhering to her skin, then waved her hands to show him she didn't care.

She tried to laugh it off. "I'm working on a new fashion."

After a pause during which he seemed to assess her, he smiled. Something happened to his face. He jaws and chin were still stubble-covered, but his eyes brightened and his whole face re-shaped into something fresh, someone engaging. She couldn't help herself and smiled back.

"I was painting."

"I see." He frowned. "But what?"

"Funny." She laughed. "Don't take this wrong, but where'd you come from?"

He nodded toward the side of the house. "I was checking that lattice. It needed another screw."

"Of course, you fix things." That felt lame.

He started to speak, then stopped and shrugged. "Yeah."

"What else do you do?"

"Ma'am?"

"Do you paint?"

He gestured at her slacks. "Paint? As in house painting?"

She nodded. "Interior painting."

After a long pause, he said, "I can."

That sounded supremely non-committal. Which actually she liked. Not an overwhelming 'sure let's get it done.' But a more thoughtful approach. She sensed he was also chagrined, probably by his profession. She pretended not to notice. She understood being embarrassed about not feeling good enough.

"I want to give the interior of my uncle's house a facelift. A fresh coat of paint."

Brian looked at the sliding doors as if recalling how the interior was laid out. "I don't guess he'd mind."

She shrugged. "Either way."

"What does that mean?"

"Whether he comes home, or doesn't, he won't mind."

She knew she'd stepped wrong somehow and said the wrong thing. The atmosphere around them soured, and Brian was already turning away. He was leaving and taking his good humor with him. No, scratch that, his good humor had already vanished. So had hers.

It ticked her off. She raised her voice and called after him.

"I'll pay whatever the going rate is. Unless you're not interested." She said it like a challenge, believing he wasn't interested, knowing he was leaving.

He stopped on the step and looked back. "When do you want me to start?"

Chapter Two

What had possessed him to agree to paint Will's house? He could've walked away. It wasn't a big deal, but a paint job? Not his favorite pastime.

It was one thing to do favors for Will, but for this woman? For a brief moment, he'd seen…what? A woman who was full of trouble, that much was obvious. Those two vertical lines etched between her eyebrows were an obvious warning sign. He felt some sympathy figuring she was torn up about her uncle.

Then she did what every woman ultimately did, except this one didn't waste any time. Her true nature came out and her cold practicality outdid even a winter gale on the ocean. What had she said? 'Either way?' Like it meant nothing. As if whether Will Denman recovered or not was all the same to her.

Her own uncle. Will had said he trusted her. For her, this was nothing more than business. To sell the place faster. She only wanted to run back to her soft, convenient life.

It didn't take long for a woman to forget a guy. Took even less time for her to replace him.

Brian grabbed his leather jacket from the handlebar and shrugged it on. He threw his leg over the motorcycle, jammed the helmet down on his head. Not ideal weather for bike riding, but his mood demanded it.

He was almost a mile down the road when he remembered what Will had said about his niece. Aside from his elderly sister, Fran was the only blood relative, or relative of any kind for that matter, who was worth anything. Which, in Brian's opinion, was about the saddest thing a man could admit. The only thing sadder was when Will had also said if a man lives long enough, he outlives his friends and everyone he loves. To Brian's way of thinking, that wasn't all bad. At least, it meant you once had friends and loved ones worth keeping.

He parked his bike in the garage next to his apartment. The apartment was on the back of the garage. Now that was convenience he could appreciate.

His phone beeped. He pulled off his helmet and heavy jacket, and dropped them on the chair by the door. He stripped the sweatshirt over his head and tossed it over the back of the chair. The sudden loss of thermal warmth caused a shiver, yet it was a relief at the same time. One day he'd learn to wear the suit and protect his legs, too, so he could walk like a whole person, instead of limping along like he was still injured. He dropped onto the couch and put his boots on the coffee table, then touched the voicemail icon to retrieve the message. It was his sister, his well-meaning and interfering sister.

"Are you coming to dinner tonight? Mom and Dad will be here and hoping to see you. Let me know. Give me a call. Come whether you call or not. Dinner's at six and I'm making one of your favorite meals. If six doesn't work for you, we can eat a little later. Please come, Brian. It's been a long time since we've all been together."

Unlike Will, he had family that was worth something, but he'd lost the connection. He pulled off one boot and then the other, wincing at the pain in his thigh, and put his feet back up on the table. He laid his head back against the soft sofa, letting loose a groan since there was no one to hear. His back. His neck. His leg. The muscles had tightened up like a board, each twisting the other, even after a year. The cold didn't help. He rubbed his thigh.

Someday maybe he'd get his old enthusiasm back. He would welcome it, and his family, back into his life. There was more to life than what he was doing now. There had to be more. But for a long while now, he couldn't remember what.

Now, apparently, he was a handyman and a house painter. He stood abruptly, jolting his back and thigh. He paced the room, which only took about twenty steps. He was going to paint the inside of Will's house. For this woman. Not for Will. Will was happy with his house as it was. But what would a coat of paint hurt?

He could watch out for Will's interests at the same time. Maybe intervene if she wasn't living up to Will's expectations.

He searched the freezer for the most likely looking frozen dinner. Salisbury steak and gravy? Beef tips and broccoli? He kept digging until he found the least objectionable one. He'd make do.

He was a simple kind of guy and it didn't take much to make him happy. Well, not happy, but content. Enough, anyway. He knew the good and the bad and had learned that you have to be willing to live somewhere in-between.

****

The next morning, Brian stood in the middle of Will's living room and scratched his head. If she'd started painting yesterday, why did everything look so completely in place? The ladder was standing in the corner with a few books stacked on its steps as if that were its true purpose.

Behind him, she cleared her throat and said, "I didn't move the furniture. I thought we might start with one blank wall and then move the furniture around as needed?"

"We?" He was only half-kidding. She was wearing slacks and a soft-looking sweater, not the casual kind, but nice clothes as if she was heading into the office or maybe to church. All she was missing was a string of pearls like his grandma sometimes wore.

"Or we can hire a helper? Whatever you think best."

He nodded. "I'll need some help with the larger furniture. We should be able to manage it." But even as he spoke, he noted she was on the thin side. Probably wouldn't be moving much furniture, after all. Nice looking, though. He unbuttoned his flannel shirt and dropped it on the sofa. He didn't mind risking his T-shirt for the job.

"Maybe you could take the pictures down from the walls?"

There was a cheap print of an ocean scene and another of

a naval battle. She carried them down the hallway and then returned to gather up the framed photos. Next, she carried off armloads of books. He had to admit, she made herself useful and without complaint. When the drapes came down from the sliding doors, dust particles swirled in the light. She had a coughing fit.

She waved her hands to clear the air. "Apparently, Mrs. Blair draws the line at cleaning the draperies." She coughed again.

He gathered the musty drapes and carried them down the hallway himself.

They saw the slip of folded paper on the floor at the same time.

"Did you drop something?" she asked.

Since the answer was obvious, he didn't respond, but reached down to pick it up. He knew what this was. He called them Will's fortune cookies, but without the cookies.

"What is it?"

Brian held it out, but she stayed back, so he left the paper on the counter. "It's Will's. He salts these around the house."

She walked over and picked it. "2nd Corinthians. Why does he do that?"

This woman, Fran Denman, asked a lot of questions. He shrugged and went to move an end table out of the way. He'd already said enough. He wasn't going to discuss Will's quirks, not even with his niece.

When the room had been cleared of stuff, the woman went to stand in the kitchen with the counter between them. After all the running around, now she stood very still, like a rabbit trying to vanish into the background. When he looked at her, she blushed.

"You okay?"

She waved her hands around. "I'm fine. Would you like a cup of tea?"

"Tea," he repeated back to her. "Iced tea?"

"A cup of hot tea. I have several blends."

36

Hot tea? "No, thanks. Not for me." He went to work rearranging the drop cloth and then positioned the ladder.

"Do you have spackling?"

"Spackling? Oh, for patching holes. No, I'm sorry."

She had tea, but no spackling. "I'll bring some tomorrow. I'll start the trim work today. Where's the tape?"

"I didn't buy any."

He frowned and stared. "Was I supposed to bring it with me? I assumed you'd have the supplies since you were already prepared to do the job yourself."

"I didn't think I'd need tape."

Her ready-to-run rabbit stance was changing. He heard a danger warning in her voice. He almost smiled. She was so perfect, so cultured. So ladylike. As if nothing could rattle her. It gave him some satisfaction to shake up that composure, so he didn't answer. He turned his back and began painting, cutting in the corners.

He tried to focus, to keep it all in perspective, but after a while he was dissatisfied. Something was bugging him. He must've given signs of it because she spoke, asking, "Is there a problem?"

He replied smoothly, "Nothing that can't be fixed tomorrow with tape and spackling."

"Should I go get some? I can drive over to the mainland. Or the grocery store might have them."

He grunted. "By the time you get back, I'll be ready to stop for the day. I have to leave by mid-afternoon." He stopped and turned around. "I guess we should have discussed it. I can only paint part of each day. I have other obligations, so this project may take a while."

Was that a look of approval on her face? Did she actually sigh? As if in relief? Odd, since this woman seemed to have more hurry in her than most.

"That's fine. Really, there's no rush."

She'd come around the end of the counter like she was ready to usher him right out the door.

"Maybe I'll wrap up for now. I might as well wait until I have the supplies."

He expected her to object, to ask why he couldn't get more done today using what he had, but she didn't.

"No problem at all. Totally understandable. I'll help you clean up."

He looked around. Clean up what? The work area was only now ready.

"Can we leave the ladder and other supplies out? Maybe fold over the plastic a little so you can walk around?"

"Certainly."

Did she want this place painted or not? "I'll pick up the other stuff later today."

"Thank you. Do you need cash up front or will you bill me?"

"Now that I think of it, I'll roll a couple of the walls first." He couldn't help himself. "I'm already here. It'd be a shame to waste the whole day."

He watched from the corner of his eye as he bent to pick up the three-pack of rollers. He tore the plastic, still watching. He saw her dismay and felt a little guilty. It wasn't his purpose in life to torture this woman. He hadn't meant it as torture anyway. Something about her irritated him. And those two lines between her eyes—yeah, those eyes. They were deepest blue he'd ever seen.

"Yep, shame to waste the day, that is, unless you have something you need to take care of. If so, I'll get out of your way." That was her opportunity. Would she take it?

A moment of stillness, then she spoke, but in a voice that sounded measuring, maybe a little suspicious.

"As a matter of fact, I do have a couple of errands to run, but you can stay here and work if you want to."

Bravo, he thought. Score one for Fran Denman. Did she know there was a game on? Now, he was embarrassed. He didn't recall Will asking him to give his niece a hard time.

"Up to you, ma'am."

"Please call me Frannie."

He nodded.

Her phone rang. "Excuse me." She went straight to it. "Hello?"

Brian heard only her side of the conversation and had no idea who she was speaking with. He tried not to eavesdrop but went ahead and put the roller cover on the frame and got the tray situated.

"Yes, please." She paced a bit, concentrating on the call. "Can he afford it?"

She stopped, standing still while she listened.

"I see. Well, I'm having the house painted." She grimaced at Brian and mouthed, "Sorry". "When it's time to sell, the house will be ready." She paused, listening, and then continued, "Whatever we need to do. I'll be here on and off. Thanks for the update."

Brian pretended he wasn't interested, but it was obvious who and what they were talking about. Ready to sell whenever? That so? He stopped short of taking the lid back off the paint can.

"I'll pick up again tomorrow, after all," he said.

"Whatever you want."

"See you about ten a.m.?"

Leaving so early in the day, he went straight up the road and across the bridge to the hardware store. He was on his bike. He should've gone home first. Should've worn warmer clothes. Should've. By the time he made it home, the wind chill and damp air had worked into his thigh and he could barely walk.

He ran a hot bath and soaked his leg, then got out dripping. He pushed himself to do the stretching exercises, easing into the workout his physical therapist had taught him.

All this for spackling and tape. All this because of his sister's interference. All this because he still hadn't learned to cool down before pressing that accelerator.

Chapter Three

Frannie watched as Brian rolled paint on the wall. Only the second day of the project, but she already felt more comfortable having this stranger in the house with her. She'd tried to hide her tension yesterday, but it had been a shock when he ditched his shirt. It made sense. Practical. He'd kept his T-shirt on, but still it disconcerted her. Likely because he was so tall. He seemed to fill up more than his fair share of the room.

He made the painting look easy. His arms were well-muscled and those muscles moved as he applied a wide strip of paint over another wide strip, angle, angle, then one long roll down. A long roll because he was so tall. Each pass made that squishy sticky wet paint sound. A catchy rhythm began to beat in her head. Each time he did that long roll down, there was a slight hitch in his stance, likely related to the limp she'd noticed. She was anticipating the next roll when suddenly he stopped and turned around.

"Is there a problem?" he asked.

"No. Nothing." Had he felt her eyes on him? "I was watching your technique."

"Technique?"

"How you roll the paint on the wall."

He looked doubtful, but turned back to the wall.

Only the second day, yet, he was moving right along. He didn't need her staring holes in his back. She really did have to find something useful to do. She took the last doughnut from the bag to munch. How many people were lucky enough to hire a painter who brought doughnuts and coffee for two? To be polite, she sipped the coffee. She wasn't really a coffee drinker.

Her attention drifted, remembering how different it had

been to get up this morning with the expectation that someone—someone relatively pleasant—was coming over, even if it was a guy hired to paint the house, and even if he was on the grumpy side. She became aware he'd stopped painting again.

He said, "If it wasn't wet, you'd never know where the paint went on. When it dries, you won't be able to tell at all."

"It'll look fresher. Cleaner."

"The walls aren't dirty. It's the color of the paint. Off-white."

"That's silly." She veered around the furniture piled in the middle of the room and marched over. She stared at the wall and crossed her arms. "Definitely fresher."

"You're wasting your money."

"Have you changed your mind? You don't want this job?" She looked at the paint paraphernalia lying around and her heart sank.

"It's not about wanting the job."

"Then what?"

"It's a waste of time and money to paint over a perfectly good coat of paint with the same color."

"Are you suggesting a different color? Not those tacky beach house colors? Turquoise and hot pink? No thank you."

He shrugged. "Up to you. Have you noticed the house is at the beach and on the ocean?"

"Uncle Will obviously favors neutral colors." She waved her hands at the walls. "Plus, a house with neutral colors is easier to sell." She knew that. Everyone knew that.

Except maybe Brian didn't know because his expression hardened. His jaw tightened. It seemed an extreme reaction over color choices, especially for a house that wasn't his.

"Don't quit, please. I'd hate to have to finish this job myself."

"What?" He frowned.

"You looked so unhappy. Listen, I'll get out of your way. I have to run some errands, anyway. You can continue to paint without me, right?"

"Yes."

"Why don't I bring lunch back with me?"

He stared at her. He looked more bemused than grim now.

"A sub? Pizza?" She hoped a change of topic would allow them to move on, past this disagreement, but judging by the stubborn expression on his face, it wasn't working. She really didn't want this job back on her plate. "Let's compromise. You know my uncle."

"Yes."

"If you find a color, something soft, I'll consider it. I want it to look nice. I don't want to overdo."

He was shaking his head with infinitesimal movements, but he said, "Whatever you want. Never mind lunch. I'll be gone by mid-afternoon, remember? I'll eat later."

"If I'm not back in time, please lock up when you leave? Just hit the thumb lock and pull it closed behind you?" She grabbed her coat and bag and escaped.

There was an old blue motorcycle parked near Uncle Will's van. The finish was scraped up and the fenders were dented. She looked back up toward the house. Must be his.

In winter? Riding a motorcycle? Crazy. She shivered. Maybe, he really was crazy. But he was good-looking, too, and seemed to know his way around a can of paint. It was his business if he wanted to freeze.

****

Two days later, Frannie stood in the middle of the living room, admiring the walls. Brian had chosen well. The soft mossy green color picked up the light streaming in through the windows. It seemed almost translucent. What a shame it would be to let down the blinds, much less rehang those thermal-backed waffle weave monstrosities. Maybe vertical blinds were worth a try?

Brian was right about the color. When she'd told him that, he shrugged it off, saying it was just a color. Not a big deal. Still, it was sad to watch Brian push Uncle Will's old, tattered furniture back into place.

The living room was finished, and Brian was taking the weekend off.

The house phone rang. She answered and a woman said, "May I speak with Frances Denman?"

Her heart did a blip. Who knew she was here? Someone connected with her mother? No, more likely the attorney. Or the rehab home. That thought spurred her to reply. "This is she. Frannie, that is."

"Well, hi there. I'm sorry about your uncle. I hope he's doing better?"

The woman's soft lilting voice had a musical quality, almost like gentle laughter. Frannie felt her lips wanting to curve into a smile.

"I wish I could say he is. How do you know him?"

"Oh, sorry! The Front Street Gallery in Beaufort. Do you know us? I'm Maia."

"I've never been to Beaufort."

"Well, I hope you will very soon. We're a small corner of the world, but not far away. Your uncle placed an order with us and it's ready."

"Oh."

"Mr. Denman wanted these items. I don't want to push if that has changed, but he'll be able to come home at some point, right?"

"I don't know."

"I'm sorry to hear that. You have a lot to deal with, I'm sure. If you think he won't want them I can try to sell them out of the gallery."

"What is it? Or they? If he wanted it enough to order it, then maybe I should pick it up."

"It's a set of beach scenes. He commissioned it."

"Special order."

Maia laughed. "A very special order."

"I can drive over tomorrow. Will that work?"

"Yes, ma'am. That'll be lovely. I'll be here. Do you need

directions?"

Uncle Will had secured the gallery's business card to his fridge with a magnet. The bold lettering said Front Street Gallery.

"I have your address and GPS, so I'm all set."

"See you tomorrow, then. We open at noon on Sunday."

They disconnected. Frannie tapped her fingers on the countertop. A retired sailor who thought it was a waste to 'doll up his house' had commissioned a set of beach paintings?

Curiosity stirred. She placed the card back beneath the magnet.

****

How had she missed Beaufort? She was glad to have found it now.

She'd come back to visit in season. Right now, in winter, many of the stores and restaurants were closed or had reduced hours. The upside was she could stroll along the walk past the marina and through the old cemetery without the distraction of vacationers.

The Front Street Gallery faced the sound. The buildings on the other side of Front Street actually toed right up to the edge of the water.

She climbed the concrete steps. When she opened the door, a bell rang. A short dark-haired woman was busy with a customer at a counter at the far end of the room. Another woman was on her way out. She had a canvas baby carrier attached to her shoulders and abdomen and it was filled with a sleeping baby dressed in blue. Frannie had only a brief peek at the curve of his cheek and the fuzzy hair, before they passed.

The woman smiled. She looked vaguely familiar, so Frannie returned the smile and nodded as she stood aside to let the woman exit. She was certain they'd never met. It was the dark blue eyes that caught her attention.

At the counter, the shop owner was finishing up with her customer. Frannie browsed.

A round table in the center of the room displayed trinkets

like small shells glued together to mimic sea creatures. There were frames with more shells glued on, but on the walls were more classic works of art. There was the expected assortment of seascapes and sunrises and sunsets. Most of the artwork seemed to be from local and regional artists. There were groupings that were obviously local because the artist bio was attached on a colorful card next to the paintings. Next to a series of small landscapes was a card for a lady named Anna Barbour. Next to that grouping was a painting of sand and that wild, grassy stuff that grew on the dunes.

It was a rough painting, both in texture and style. Frannie leaned closer and raised her hand, stopping short of touching it with her fingers. Was sand mixed into the paint? Maybe a few grains from the heads of the weeds, too.

The woman's voice said, "Hi. What can I do to help you?"

Frannie turned to face her and the woman stepped back. The warmth in her eyes and smile quickly changed to something that looked like surprise, which made no sense whatsoever.

"Are you Maia?"

"I am. Excuse me for asking, but have we met?" She chuckled. "I'm sorry. I know we haven't, but you remind me of someone."

"I'm Will Denman's niece. Frannie Denman."

"The special order." She extended her hand. The smile was back and a friendly light lit her eyes. "Frannie, I'm pleased to meet you. Your uncle is a special person and a friend."

"My father's uncle." Why had she felt the need to correct a simple statement?

Maia only smiled more broadly, obviously not offended. She gestured toward the counter. "It's over there."

She lifted a large box and set it on the counter. "It's light," she said. "The paintings are small and already framed and wrapped, but if you'd like to see them first, I can take them out."

"No need. They belong to Uncle Will, after all."

Frannie picked up the box with a hand on each side to test

the weight. "Do we owe you anything?"

"No, indeed. Already paid for. Can I get you to sign here to show they were picked up?"

She wrote carefully, neatly, 'Frannie Denman on behalf of William Denman'. She looked at Maia. "Will that work?"

"It will. Please give my regards to your uncle when you see him. We were all terribly sorry to hear about the stroke. If there's anything I can do, let me know."

"I will." She should go visit him again. How often was enough? She put the purse strap over her shoulder and wrapped her arms around the box.

Maia walked with her to the door and held it open. "Need any help?"

"I can manage."

"Please come back and see us again real soon."

Chapter Four

"It was the oddest thing," Maia said. "Sure I can't get you something?" Then she went silent and her attention drifted. She lifted her mug and sipped the hot chocolate.

Brian ignored the question. They were seated at the lunch table in the back room of the gallery, but he hadn't removed his jacket, had only unzipped it.

He asked, "Odd? What do you mean? She's kind of nervous."

She shook her head. "She didn't seem nervous to me and she wasn't odd at all."

"What do you mean, then?"

"When I saw her, well, she reminded me of someone." She laughed softly. "I heard somewhere that we all have doubles, right?"

He didn't understand her. The words, yes, but not the interest. "What do you want? Do you have some issue with her?"

"Oh, no. Nothing like that. She came in to pick up the paintings Will Denman had ordered."

"Then what's the big deal?" He said it harshly. He had no use for gossips. Always sticking their noses into other people's business. They did a lot of damage.

Maia's face showed every thought that whirred through her brain. Annoyance, hurt, recovery, hope, and they passed over her face like a kaleidoscope. He felt like a bully. Maybe he was, but if you weren't careful, your loved ones would try to 'love' you into living according to their rules—even the rules they should be ashamed of.

"I was just making conversation. I miss you. You're still

angry. How many times should I apologize? Because I will, you know. Over and over. As many times as necessary, plus one."

"I have to go."

She placed both of her hands on his arm. "I'm sorry, Brian."

"It's in the past. It doesn't matter." He stood, moving away from her hands, and picked up his helmet.

"Brian."

"Enough, Maia. You're sorry and I've moved on."

"But you still won't join us for dinner. Won't even sit here and share a cup of coffee or hot chocolate with me?"

He zipped up his jacket. "I won't, because you give me no peace. Can't you accept that I'm fine?"

"No, because you're not."

"Drop it." He walked out and into the alley where he'd parked his bike.

He was angry as he kicked the stand and brought the engine to life. He shouldn't have looked at her. She used those big eyes like weapons.

Need a little coercion? Hire Maia to bring on the tears. Not many could withstand her. She was emotional blackmail personified.

But he wouldn't leave angry. Not on the bike. Never again. He breathed deeply, risking fogging up the helmet. After a minute he looked up and there she was, standing at the door with a hand raised to wave.

He didn't wave. He just rode off.

****

Resentment still drove him the next day. He stomped up the steps and knocked loudly. He heard her light footsteps speeding to answer the door. No need for her to run. He hadn't pounded on the door.

"Yes? Is there a problem?" She looked at him and then stuck her head outside to look past him, as if something might be chasing him up the stairs.

He almost laughed. In a manner of speaking, he did feel

chased.

"Fine. Ready to start the next room?"

His eyes caught on the paint job. Was that satisfaction he felt?

"Looks good, if I do say so myself."

The door clicked closed. She stayed behind him. He tried not to turn toward her too quickly. To panic her. Why? No idea, but she was so skittish. He recognized a damaged person when he saw one. Took one to know one.

As he paused in the living room, he noticed the small paintings lined up along the base of the wall next to the dining table.

"What's that? Do you need help hanging them?"

"Oh, those are Uncle Will's paintings. He ordered them. I don't know where to hang them. Perhaps we should wait until he can tell us."

"They're easy to move."

"So, you think I should go ahead and hang them?" She pointed to a blank wall in the dining area. "Is that a good space?"

"Up to you."

She looked down at the paintings. "Yes, it is up to me."

"They're kind of neat." He tilted his head, looking at them. "Like I'm looking at the same stretch of beach but through different windows of the same house. At different times of year, too. Different seasons."

Frannie stood next to him. "Yes, I see what you mean. I hadn't pulled it all together in my head. Yes, exactly. Well, I think they should hang on that wall after it's painted."

"What's next, then? The dining area and kitchen?"

She looked at the cabinets. They were chockfull and helter-skelter. That didn't matter for the painting, but the appliances and general clutter on the counter did.

"What about the almost empty bedroom? I'm thinking of setting it up like a study or something. Staging, you know. Marketability is mostly in the staging."

Staging. Faking. It all came down to that with women. He walked away without a word. She followed.

"We should save the kitchen until I can move everything out of the way, and I can't stay to help today."

"Okay."

"I have a lunch appointment."

"Okay." He started moving the few items toward the door.

"Unavoidable, I'm sorry to say." She blocked the doorway.

"No problem." He waited for her to move and she did.

"My mother. She called this morning."

Did she actually gulp? Like they wrote in books? He thought she had.

"She's coming to visit. Not to the house. I made sure of that."

He was getting interested despite himself. Fran had family problems, too? He threw out some feelers. "You can bring her here. I'll stay out of the way. I can skip today if that's the problem."

Her already pale face paled still further. Her hand gripped the doorframe. "No. Lunch is enough." She looked away. "I'll get out of your way. I'll be leaving shortly."

She looked in the mirror by the door and said, "I hope I look all right."

Was she expecting an answer? Apparently, no, because she went on, "I didn't bring much with me. I'm running out of decent clothing."

She was dressed in the simple kind of clothes that you knew cost a mint and where dressed down was still dressed up. It looked good on her, but not any better than regular clothes would look. She was slender and on the shorter end of tall, and with that face she'd look good in anything, except she was so tightly wound it spoiled the picture.

She tugged on her sweater and put her coat over her arm. "I should go now."

"Have fun." What more did she want from him?

"Right."

He knew what she wanted—an excuse not to go. Illness? Accident, maybe. Even a minor earthquake would do. He couldn't give her any of them. She was a grown woman. If she had problems, it was up to her to solve them. But then it slipped out.

"Want to borrow my bike?"

Her face went blank, and then suddenly laugh lines bloomed at the corners of her eyes. She laughed out loud. She clutched her middle and then put her hands to her cheeks. "I can see Mother's face!" Carefully, she dabbed at her eyes.

"Thank you, Brian. Maybe next time I'll take you up on that. See you later."

He waited until she was gone, but as soon as the door closed behind her, he returned her smile. It had been hard not to laugh with her. Her face had changed from attractive to...to compelling? As if the tension had washed away leaving something special in its wake. He returned to painting, but with a lighter spirit. It struck him that he'd done a good deed and, in the end, unaware, Fran had returned the favor.

Chapter Five

It was every bit as grim as she feared.

She was grateful to Brian for the moment of laughter he'd given her. She told herself that if she got too nervous, she'd imagine herself straddling that bike.

Laurel walked in like an empress. Frannie watched as her mother spoke to the hostess who then escorted her to the table. She fought the impulse to rise and curtsey.

She cleared her throat. "You look well, Mother."

"I am well." She gave her daughter a long look and then capped it with a smile. "You look different somehow." She managed to seat herself and pull in her chair. "Tell me what you've been up to."

The waitress stood by the table.

"We should probably order first."

"Whatever you wish, sweetheart."

"A salad. A garden salad. Oil and vinegar dressing."

Laurel placed her order. Frannie listened, wishing she could be as cool. It was one of the many traits she hadn't inherited.

After the waitress left, Laurel repeated the question, "Tell me what you've been doing."

"I'm fixing up Uncle Will's house. You already know that."

"So, tell me more." Laurel perked up her eyebrows and leaned forward.

"Not much to tell. It's only been a week." She placed the napkin in her lap. "I'm doing a little painting."

"No. You?" She laughed. "I'd love to see. I didn't know you had it in you."

"I'm painting walls, not a Da Vinci."

"Seriously, Frannie. You could hire someone."

"I could." Not a lie.

"You should put your time to better use."

"Doing what?"

"They are missing you down at the shelter."

"No. That's one day a week and they're covered. The same goes for the other charities. I won't be missed."

"Sweetheart, that's only because you don't dedicate more than the minimum to any of them. You spread your time around like you're afraid to commit." Laurel pressed her hands against the tabletop. "And I need your help with any number of things."

"No, you don't. All you need is someone to run your errands and play secretary."

One manicured hand drew up into a fist. "You are as difficult and argumentative as ever. I believe you practice it. I wish you'd try half as hard to learn civility and respect."

The waitress's smile was too big and bright. Frannie sympathized. No sane person would want to be part of this luncheon party. The girl hurriedly moved their food from her tray to the table.

"Anything else?"

"No."

Her mother whispered, but in a stage whisper that everyone within a few yards could hear. "Is your stomach upset again?"

"No, I'm fine."

"Have you been taking your pills? You have your hand on your abdomen like you do when you're having stomach trouble."

Frannie looked down and brushed her sweater as if that had been the intent. "I'm fine."

"I care about you."

"I know." Frannie tapped the hilt of her fork lightly on the table. "But I'm an adult. I've been one for an embarrassingly long time considering I still live at home and don't have a real

53

job."

Mother shook her head. "No, darling. You had your sadness and so did I. One of the nicest things you ever did was to give up a bit of your independence to keep me from being alone."

She waited to hear more about her personal dark time. Her mother took some kind of perverse pleasure in reminding her of it, but this time she didn't.

Laurel sat up straighter. "You are correct. You deserve time on your own. I've been selfish. Do what you need to do. Remember, I'm your mother and I love you. I'll be here for you whenever you need me."

****

It was so very unsatisfactory, yet she had to admit few people could make an entrance, or accomplish an exit, with Laurel's style. Her mother was who she was. At least, she tried.

Unlike her unfilial daughter.

Frannie sat in the car. With the sun hitting the exterior and no wind to speak of, it was cool, but pleasant. She'd parked in a public beach access lot. There were picnic tables near where the parking ended and the dunes began. There wasn't another soul in sight.

What drove her? Guilt? Over being a bad daughter? Over resenting her father's death and holding it against her mother?

She didn't lie to herself. She knew her feelings were unreasonable.

There was something wrong with her. Something broken inside. Something that nibbled at her nerves and refused to let her be comfortable in her own skin. Refused to let her live her life without guilt.

Brian was gone when she returned to the house. Vaguely, she wondered what he did with his time when he wasn't here.

His business. Not hers.

She was alone at Captain's Walk, but that was okay because there wasn't anywhere else she'd rather be just now.

****

That night she swam up out of sleep, looking for something, seeking frantically and finding only a dark room. A faint memory of soft crying, whimpering, lingered. This hadn't happened in a while and she blamed the lunch date. She'd learned long ago that it was better to get up, have a snack and watch a few minutes of middle-of-the-night TV to break the cycle of restless sleep.

She paused in front of the fridge. She'd bought a few groceries, but it was time to give the refrigerator a real cleaning out and do some serious food shopping.

A real cleaning…the words brought to mind Mrs. Blair. It might be nice to have her in one day a week. She could clean up the fridge and chase the dust bunnies. Maybe some other household duties, too.

The toast popped up from the toaster. She carried it, along with a small glass of apple juice into the living room and snapped on the TV. She snuggled on the sofa, tucking her feet beneath her and dragging the sofa blanket down over her legs. A fascinating infomercial selling a new facial care system played out before her. Not much, but better than a blank screen, and mildly amusing in a cynical way.

Starlight twinkled in through the gaps in the blinds. To cover the glass door, she'd fastened a sheet over the drapery rod.

Too bad it was cold. By the time the weather warmed up, she'd be back in Raleigh. Back with Laurel.

She slid down until her head rested against the back of the sofa and propped her feet on the coffee table. The smell of fresh paint lingered.

Back with Laurel.

No, she wouldn't.

She closed her eyes and tried to imagine where else.

She could get her own place again. Maybe get a real job.

Living with Mother had been a temporary arrangement, something that benefitted them both, but was not intended to last indefinitely. Yet the temporary stay had stretched to five years.

Was she so afraid of being alone that she had allowed Laurel to make her choices? Or was it procrastination?

Waiting, that's what it felt like.

But waiting for what?

Chapter Six

It was morning and her neck ached. She stretched and felt the tug of a pinched muscle near her collarbone. An infomercial had lulled her to sleep. Sales pitches had infiltrated her dreams. Not exactly restful, but still better than the recurring dreams. Like the one about the baby. A searching dream. Or a waiting dream. Sometimes one, sometimes the other, but they both reeked of loss and regret. On this bright morning she thought she might have been wrong. Whether of regret or waiting or searching, those dreams—almost nightmares—probably signaled her failure to move on with her life.

She unwrapped the blanket that trapped her legs. She went over to the front windows and opened the blinds. The morning sunlight sparkled on the water and created mirror-like depths in the wet sand.

Frannie released the sheet from its pins. She slid the door wide and let the morning rush in. The chill air came in with it. She pulled on her coat, wrapped the scarf around her neck and stepped outside. It was cold, yes, but no wind and the sky was a sharp, post-dawn blue. She loosened the scarf.

She stayed well away from the water and walked through mounds of dry sand, watching the sea birds diving for breakfast. On the shore side, rows of colorful houses mimicked the colors of dawn and sunset. The tang of salt and wet sand mixed with the smell of those weedy grasses on the dunes and tickled her nose.

She turned back. After her shower, she'd pay a visit to Uncle Will and make a grocery run. New sheets, too. Uncle Will's bedding was grim. But her first stop would be in Beaufort at the Front Street Gallery to take another look at the painting that had caught her eye.

****

Frannie parked at the marina and walked down the sidewalk toward the gallery. She paused to cross the street and saw Maia standing outside.

Maia was actually with someone, chatting. The woman had longish brown hair, slim, and there was something about the way she held herself. The woman was pretty, but not remarkable until she smiled. She knelt to tuck a blanket around a baby in a stroller. This was the woman who'd been leaving the gallery the other day. Maia bent over the baby, too, and judging by her animation, she was stirring him up as much as his mother had tried to soothe him. Frannie watched as both women started laughing.

No place for her there. A car drove past. She stepped back up onto the sidewalk.

Maia saw her. She waved, but not only in greeting. She motioned for her to join them.

Frannie hesitated, but then the other woman was looking her way, too, and she knew she looked odd standing there and staring. She stepped back into the street and crossed over.

The woman had one hand on the stroller handle. She and the baby were both dressed warmly. Maia wore only a longish, bulky sweater over her clothing. She crossed her arms and gave a little shake.

Frannie said, "I'm sorry. I didn't mean to interrupt."

"Not at all. Were you looking for me?"

"I wanted to ask about a painting."

"Lovely! But first I want to introduce you to my friend, Juli." She nodded toward the woman. "And this is her darling, beautiful son, Danny."

Juli held out her hand. "Are you new around here?"

"Yes. I'm staying at my uncle's house, in Emerald Isle."

"We live there, too, on the sound side. I hope you like our town. It's a quiet time of year. Not typical beach weather, but I like it."

Frannie looked down at the infant. "He's precious. How old is he?"

"Nine months."

"Almost ten months," Maia corrected. She added, "He's a sweetheart."

Danny was watching them, his eyes moving from his mama to Maia to her, a stranger, but with that semi-vacant, slightly unfocused look that signaled he was on the edge of sleep. His mama smiled, but there was something in her expression Frannie couldn't decipher. Different emotions, including something like confusion, played across her features. It kept Frannie from feeling comfortable. She was well trained at taking cues, but she couldn't read anything with certainty in Juli's face.

"It's nice to meet you. Please don't let me interrupt. I'll wait in the gallery."

Maia touched her arm. "Juli is the artist who painted the beachscapes your uncle commissioned."

"Really?" She extended her hand. "I'm pleased to meet you."

A man walked past and up the steps. Maia said. "A customer." She turned to Frannie. "I'm freezing anyway. Come on in when you're done chatting. Juli, I'll see you soon."

Maia dashed up the steps and into the gallery.

Frannie tried to refocus. "I don't want to keep you, but I'm glad to have the opportunity to tell you the paintings are beautiful, and I know exactly where I'm going to hang them, that is, as soon as Brian paints the dining area."

Juli appeared to be listening politely, but when Frannie expected her to say, 'I'm glad you like them," instead, she said, "Brian is painting? Brian Donovan?"

"Yes." What did Juli have against Brian? "He's doing a beautiful job. Very…reliable."

After a pause, Juli answered, "I'm sure he is very reliable." She shrugged, laughing a bit, and added, "It's a pleasure to meet you. Your uncle is a very nice man. I met him a few times. He makes an impression. I suppose being career Navy doesn't go away with retirement." The baby whimpered. "My alarm clock is going off. Danny never lets me down."

Juli headed toward the parking lot and Frannie went into the gallery. The man passed her on his way out.

Frannie said, "I'm sorry I interrupted you and your friend."

"Nonsense." Her voice was stern. "Don't apologize. You didn't interrupt."

She stutter-stepped, then caught sight of Maia's face. It was mock anger. Teasing. She drew in a deep breath and tried to reset her expression.

Maia gave her a funny look. "Would you like a cup of coffee? I have hot chocolate, too."

She shook her head. "No thanks. I'm fine."

"Seriously. Do you have to be anywhere? Can't you stay for a bit? It can be so lonely around here this time of year."

"I guess so."

"Good. Then take off your coat and let's take a break. What's your preference? Coffee or hot cocoa?"

Maia was so brisk and business-like that Frannie found herself obeying. Between the bell over the front door and a clear view of the sales floor from the break room door, there was no risk of missing a customer arriving. Inside the break room was a sink and counter and a narrow stove.

"You can hang your coat on the hook over there. Cocoa?" Maia turned on the fire under a shiny kettle.

Suddenly uncomfortable, Frannie shoved her hands in her coat pockets and pulled it closer. "I'm fine."

"You won't be for long, and you won't feel it when you leave if you don't take it off while you're inside. That's what my mother says." She pointed to hooks on the wall. "Hang it over there and have a seat." Maia she pulled a couple of ceramic mugs from the cupboard.

Frannie did as she was instructed. She watched Maia rip open the envelopes and shake them into the cups. As the water heated, Maia removed her sweater and draped it over the back of a chair.

The kettle wailed and Maia poured the hot water into a cup. She stirred it briskly as she set it on the table.

"Here you go."

She went back to the counter and did the same with her own. Frannie swirled the spoon, enjoying the steam rich with the aroma of cocoa.

"It has little marshmallows."

Maia laughed and her dimples deepened. "Is there any other kind?" She sat opposite Frannie and the metal chair squeaked on the floor as she moved closer to the table.

"Tell me what you had in mind."

Guilt bloomed. For what? Because she'd been jealous of the easy friendship she witnessed between the two women? But Maia wouldn't know that. For heaven's sake, Maia was a store clerk. They barely knew each other.

She asked carefully, "What do you mean?"

"The painting? You said you wanted to ask about a painting." She reached across and patted her hand. "Is the cocoa too hot? Did you burn yourself?"

"No," she sputtered.

"Then what? What's wrong?"

"Nothing. Really." She shook her head.

"I can tell you're a thinker. A deep thinker. I can be pushy. I hope you aren't offended."

"No." She pressed her fingers against the mug. She was a bit off-kilter. She wasn't used to shopkeepers inviting her in for hot chocolate. If this was a new sales technique, she thought it might prove effective.

"Good. You look more comfortable now." Maia sipped her cocoa. "So, tell me, what sort of paintings are you interested in?"

"I want to dress up my uncle's house. A little extra color, you know? I want a local feel."

"You're at the right place."

"I liked some of the paintings I saw when I came before.

One, in particular."

"What caught your attention? I'm a great believer in first impressions." Maia had an extra twinkle in her eye.

"Those sunrises and sunsets by Anna Barbour were very nice, but since Uncle Will bought that other set, we have enough of that." She smiled. "There was one other I particularly liked. It's hanging next to those sunrise-sunset paintings. Sand and dune grass. With sand and grass actually mixed in?"

Maia leaned forward, grasping her cup as if she might upset it in her joy. "Small world, right? Not only did Juli paint the set your uncle bought, but that's her painting, too."

"Really?" Something about that unsettled her again.

"Funny, too, because you two remind me of each other."

"How so? We don't look alike or anything."

"Well, not to argue the point, but you both have brown hair and blue eyes."

Frannie laughed. "True, but it looks different on her. It looks good on her."

"Listen to you. All I know is that you're both slender, and I have more than my share of curves."

She knew Maia was teasing. She didn't mean any harm. Frannie changed the subject.

"That was a precious little boy. His name is Danny?"

Maia's eyes lit up. "He is. Such a sweetie. I babysit for him whenever they let me."

"Do you have children?"

"Me?" She shook her head. "No. You?"

"No."

Maia looked a little wistful. "I'm good on my own." She sighed. "I'm tired of hoping to meet the right guy and being disappointed. And of enjoying only other people's children." She gave a mock shiver. "Ouch. That sounds awful, doesn't it?"

Frannie's heart did a little crunch. She understood. "I know what you mean. I guess I've stopped looking."

Maia nodded. "I'm too picky. I bet you are, too."

It wasn't a bad thing to be picky, right? It could be a lonely thing. She said, "Better to be alone than chained to the wrong guy."

Suddenly, Maia's mood picked up again. She giggled. "I've heard that said before, but not with the word, chained. Gives it a little more resonance." She shook her head. "I know what you mean. I've been friends with some truly excellent men, but love? Their hearts went to other women. Is that good or bad? I don't know. If they'd fallen for me, maybe our friendship wouldn't have survived a closer relationship." She shrugged. "Who knows?"

Maia stared through the door, into the empty gallery, then said, "Do you think he'll be able to come back home?"

"Uncle Will?"

"Yes. You said you're fixing the house up, right? Brian said he fixed some loose lattice the other day." She trailed off, again looking sad.

"Brian? You've been talking to Brian?" She hadn't thought about being the subject of a human information pipeline.

"Oh, goodness yes. Didn't he tell you? He's my brother."

"No."

"Well, not much to mention these days, I'm sorry to say."

Frannie refused to ask what that meant. She had enough of her own trouble. And, unreasonable though it might be, she felt deceived. Brother and sister? No wonder Maia thought she knew Frannie so well, but she was only getting the slice of Frannie that Brian saw and that was probably a good thing.

Maia stood and placed her cup in the sink. "Why don't we go take a look at that painting?"

Frannie set her mug next to Maia's. She took her coat from the hook and her purse, too, and followed Maia out to the sales floor. She went directly to the painting.

"This is the one. It's structured, yet unstructured at the same time. I like the texture, too, and the color should go well with the paint Brian chose."

Maia was staring at her.

"What's wrong?"

"Brian chose a color?"

"Yes. For the living room."

Maia continued to stare.

Floundering a bit, Frannie added, "I chose the color for the bedroom, although Brian hasn't seen it yet, so I don't know if he'll like it." She meant that as a joke, but Maia's expression stayed grave.

Maia reached out and touched her arm. "I'm sorry. Truly. Brian doesn't tell me much these days. He's painting your living room?"

"No, he finished the living room. He's painting one of the bedrooms now. You didn't know?"

"No."

Frannie saw something changing in Maia's expression as it morphed from sad to speculative. She said abruptly, "I'll take the painting."

Maia smiled. "I'll wrap it up." She lifted it from the hooks and carried it over to the counter.

"Juli's going to be over the moon that her painting sold. You wouldn't believe how hard I worked to convince her to offer it for sale in the first place. She's got a couple of others I'm trying to get my hands on." Maia drew the brown paper around it and secured it with a piece of sealing tape. "It made all the difference in the world to her when Will commissioned those little beach paintings. And now you'll have this one to go with it. I'll admit, this is a particular favorite of mine. We don't have anything else like it in the gallery." She picked up the wrapped canvas. "This should do it. It's not going far, right?"

"Right."

"She hasn't had a lot of time to paint, what with Danny, plus her husband's been traveling a lot lately. Maybe this will encourage her to get back to her easel."

****

When Frannie returned to Captain's Walk, she carried the groceries up the stairs, a bag in each arm, and over one forearm hung the handles of a fancier bag from a department store that contained sheets with a much better thread count, along with a few other creature comforts. She put the bags on the counter and then headed back down again for the painting. Brian's bike was parked to the side. She could've asked him to help with carrying the purchases, but he'd signed on to paint the house. Anything else would be a favor, and she didn't like to ask for those.

She propped the painting against the dining room wall. Still no sight or sound of Brian.

He was in the smallest bedroom. Will had used it for storage. Brian stood on the stepladder removing a ceiling fixture.

"Hello, how's it going?"

He gave her a brief glance and grunted something that sounded like 'okay'.

"I didn't realize Maia was your sister." She said the words in a level voice. Non-judgmental, non-committal.

Brian didn't turn around. "Yeah."

She walked closer to where he was perched and accepted the screwdriver he handed her. "I mean, it would seem a natural thing for you to have mentioned."

"Why?" He removed the last bolt and then eased the glass fixture down. "It's dusty."

He said it like an indictment—it's dusty—as he handed it to her. He stepped down, but then paused on the last rung.

"Is something bothering you?"

"Well, no. It's just that there's no reason to hide the relationship." She kept her eyes fixed on the dirty glass and held it away from her clothing. "Is there?"

Brian came close. She didn't think to move. She did stop breathing.

He paused a couple of feet away. Softly, he said, "Did Maia say something to upset you?"

"No." She shook her head briskly. "I thought she looked a little sad at times."

"Sad? Maybe. I can't help that." Without moving, still looking at her, he added, "If you're worried about me talking about your business, you can forget it. I wouldn't anyway, but the truth is, Maia and I don't talk much anymore."

He folded the ladder and carried it out of the room.

Frannie followed. "I met a friend of Maia's. I bought her painting." She was still holding the fixture and looking for a safe place to set it down.

Brian took it from her hands and laid it in the kitchen sink.

She continued, "I bought it, but not because I met her. I was already intending to purchase the painting."

"Is that it? Propped against the wall?"

"Yes."

He nodded. "Tell me where and I'll hang it."

"Brian." Funny, she felt a little tingly saying his name out loud. "I want to thank you for all that you're doing here."

"Not a big deal." He gave her a look. "Anyway, it's a job. A paying job," he added.

"Please send the bill whenever it's ready."

"Sure." He continued to look at her, as if waiting.

"I know you have obligations in the afternoon. I hope this job hasn't interfered."

"Personal obligations." He smiled as he said it, but the smile didn't reach his eyes. He walked away.

She followed him back to the small bedroom. She hadn't meant to pry. Or maybe she had. But she knew when to back off, so she dropped the subject.

He turned abruptly. "Did you choose the color for the room?"

"As a matter of fact, yes."

"Do you have the paint chip?"

A few boxes were stored in this room. The vacuum and unused curtain rods were against the far wall. Brian picked up a box testing the weight.

"I'll move these out of here."

"I'll give you a hand." She picked up a box. No. She tried

again. The box was too heavy. She couldn't budge it. "Books. Maybe I'll leave these for you to move."

The difference in their biceps was obvious. His look made her feel foolish.

"I'll move them tomorrow." He held out his hand. "The paint chip?"

"Oh, sure." She went up the short hall to the kitchen. She pushed through her bag. "Here it is." She spun back around, intending to return to the bedroom, and nearly crashed into him. At a loss, she pushed the paint chip into his hand.

He raised an eyebrow. "Do you have picture hanging hardware?"

"You mean a hammer and a nail?"

"This painting needs stronger hardware. I'll pick it up when I get the paint."

"Make sure you include that along with the cost of the paint in the invoice."

He hadn't moved away. He stood so close she could see a pulse beating in a vein in his neck. Her eyes fastened upon it. For a long, strained moment, they were silent.

"Fran. Can I ask you a question?"

It was on the tip of her tongue to correct him, the automatic It's Frannie, not Frances. Not Fran. But she didn't. Frannie would sound odd somehow coming from his lips. His lips. Now her eyes were trapped again. She closed them.

"Fran?"

When Brian called her 'Fran,' it sounded right.

"Okay, what?"

"Where do you want me to hang the painting?"

Her eyes flew open. The words didn't match his posture, his position.

"Where do you think would be best?" Breathless.

Still, he didn't move. There was this unnatural suspension, this narrow vortex they occupied, with the tension torqueing. He should leave. He must not leave.

"Why don't you let me know when I come back

tomorrow?"

She nodded, unable to find words, overwhelmed by the charged air surrounding them, grateful that she appeared to be the only one aware of it.

She was scared to realize she wasn't afraid. Not even of that potential third strike.

Chapter Seven

What was he thinking? He couldn't resist teasing her, testing her, but something had changed. He stepped back. What was this in his hand? A piece of trash? No, the color chip.

"What color is this?"

"It's called Misty Celery. It's a lovely soft shade of green. I think it complements the green you chose for the living room."

"Soft shade? It's white."

"No, see the name at the bottom?" She pointed at the chip. "See? It says Misty Celery."

"It's white." He waved his hand. "Well, if you want white, then white it is."

"It is what I want. Exactly what I want. And it's not white."

"Fine. I aim to please."

She crossed her arms. "No need to be sarcastic."

"I wasn't."

"You were."

He opened his mouth to retort back and then remembered he wasn't five. Not even fifteen. A little more than twice that, in fact. Too old for games like this. He waved the chip. "I'll get the paint."

He could see it churning in her expression. She was all set to contradict him again. Brian looked at her more closely, then quickly away. That's exactly what she was doing. She was gearing up for the next strike. Deliberately contradicting him to start a fight. He tried not to grin. Hard not to like a woman with spirit and gumption and who carried herself with a certain kind of flair.

"Whatever you want." He kept his back turned, certain his amused expression would give away that he was on to her game.

"Want me to hang up those drapes?"

"What?"

He pointed to the windows and the sliding door. "Need help hanging those back up?"

"No. I like the windows uncovered."

He agreed with her, but he hated to spoil the fun by saying that, so he grunted.

"Well, if you disagree, please tell me."

Brian shrugged to hide his smile. She could find an argument in a turnip.

He said, "We should take down the hardware then. No need to have it hanging out and looking like we left something undone."

"Take the hardware down, by all means. Could you pick up some vertical blinds?"

She tossed her head and put her hands on her hips. He figured she was annoyed again, but he noticed how her hair looked when it brushed her shoulders. Silky hair. It picked up the sunlight.

"Nothing high-end, though. Something that will work until the house is sold."

Sold. That stung. Subdued, he answered, "Whatever you say. Any other orders?"

Fran went into the kitchen and started slamming through the cupboards. He was no longer in the mood to harass her, but she was still worked up and he couldn't resist a last jab.

"Don't break those cabinet doors."

She stopped mid-movement and looked over at him. She said coolly, "You never answered my question. What about those strips of paper with verses? I found a couple more. Why does my uncle hide them around the house?"

"Ask him."

Astonished, she said, "That's insensitive."

"I didn't say when to ask. You might have to wait awhile."

She was still holding on to the cabinet door handle, and staring fire at him. She spoke in a civil, but icy tone. "Thank you for the clarification, Mr. Donovan. Would you care for a cup of tea?"

"No, ma'am. I'm not a tea guy unless you're talking a tall glass of iced tea. What is it with you and tea?"

"What is it? Lots of people drink tea, even the hot kind in cups."

"Sure they do." He picked up his shirt and took his time sliding his arms in and buttoning it. He couldn't help himself. "I hear it's supposed to be calming. You know, that means it calms people down."

"Sure." Her eyes narrowed. "Tea can be very calming depending on the blend, and whether anyone needs calming."

"Chamomile. Is that it?" He grinned, surprised he'd remembered the name. He saw instantly that she'd taken his grin to mean something else entirely which amused him all the more.

"Chamomile? Yes, I'm familiar with the properties of Chamomile tea. I happen to be drinking Samurai Chai."

"Samurai?"

She kept her eyes fastened upon his face as she slowly, deliberately eased the cabinet door closed. "Maybe one of these days I'll give you a lesson in the art of tea."

Her voice sounded different. He didn't know how to describe it, but her body had changed. Even as she gave the appearance of imminent eruption—that was it, her voice had a smoldering quality—she stood taller, straighter, ready to take on anything, anyone. He suspected he was about to meet the real Fran.

Chapter Eight

It was fun sparring with Brian. It didn't come naturally to her. She preferred peace. Obviously, petty bickering was Brian's preferred pastime.

After he'd left she ran through their conversation in her head. She usually thought of snappy comebacks when it was too late, but she was proud of the Samurai line she'd delivered. His baby blue eyes had seemed to take on a whole new focus. Even now, it made her smile.

Then, well, she'd realized what was happening. The swagger that had suddenly come over her, that caused her to broaden her shoulders, to lift her arm, to shift her hips, to all but pose between cabinet and counter, practically preening—that was a cliff she didn't want to go over. She reined it all back in. Brian left soon after. She felt deflated.

She'd do better to take care of business, the real business she was here for. Like going through Will's papers. Reluctant to read his truly personal papers, she'd put it off, but there might be creditors she didn't know about or maybe a storage unit that held treasured items he'd lose if she didn't pay the rent.

Frannie sat at the roll top desk and began searching through the drawers.

There were several packets of letters. Judging by the yellowing of the envelopes, some were much older than others. She picked up the first bundle and the thick rubber band disintegrated. The letters cascaded to the floor and scattered. She knelt to pick them up, and with each one, her curiosity grew. Letters from home? Faded ink. Aged postmarks. She couldn't help herself.

A letter dated 1959 began, My Dearest Son. This will reach

you at sea. It was a newsy letter, but she didn't know the people involved.

In the act of re-folding the pages, she stopped herself.

She should've known these people, or at least, she should know about them. They were her people, too, whether she'd met them or not.

Uncle Will's mother would've been her father's grandmother. Her own great-grandmother. Frannie did some quick math. If her dad was still alive, he'd be in his mid-fifties. Uncle Will was about thirty when her dad was born.

Except for a handful of tales, her dad hadn't said much about his family. Her mother certainly never had. There might be distant cousins she didn't know about, but not all families stayed close. Her family was proof.

She flipped through Uncle Will's stash of letters. Clearly he hadn't saved every letter he'd ever received, still there were quite a few and she was beginning to see a pattern. All of these were from his mother and each contained some special news among the usual chatter. In 1960, Millie wrote Will that he was now an uncle to his newly-born nephew, Edward. Her dad. A year later, Will's sister, Penny, got married.

The part about her Dad's birth felt really special.

She hadn't known her great-grandmother, Millie, but these letters did mean something to her. She gathered them up and found a fresh rubber band in a kitchen drawer.

****

Frannie curled up that night with Millie's letters. The penmanship was strong and clear. What did they call it? Cursive? She didn't think they taught that in school now.

In 1982 the big news was that her dad had eloped, and the subject was worthy of the entire letter. Per Millie, in his last year of college, Edward had met a woman. Millie didn't call her a young lady, but a woman. The reference seemed to be that she was questionable in some way, but he married her. His parents threatened to stop paying for college and he said fine, he'd drop out. They backed down. Millie seemed to approve of that outcome.

Her grandparents. Marshall and Anne. Her middle name was Anne for her grandmother. She had a vague memory of them. They died when she was six or seven, but this letter was from 1982 and grief wouldn't arrive on the scene for several years.

So, her mom and dad had caused a scandal. They'd never shared that with her. What else didn't she know about their young-and-in-love days together?

Feeling a little sneaky, and hoping for some juicy tidbits, she snuggled down to finish the letter. It ended too soon. She fumbled for the next one, which was dated a month later. When she pulled the folded pages from the envelope, a small faded photo fell out.

You asked for a photograph of Edward and his bride, and it took some doing, but here it is. She's a pretty enough thing. Anne hints that she's wild, yet won't explain. Can't blame her for worrying. A mom's a mom no matter how old her children get. Same goes for a grandmother—no surprise I'm worried, too. When I have the opportunity for a private chat with Marshall, I'll ferret out the details about Edward and his wife.

She picked up the photo and saw a much younger, very handsome version of the father she remembered, but the woman next to him, no matter how hard she stared, she couldn't make her look like Mother. She turned it over. Someone had scrawled in pencil, January 26, 1982. Edward and Frances.

Frances. Could Laurel have had a nickname?

Not likely. Her middle name was Marie. Maiden name was Parker.

Frances.

A first marriage, then? Prior to Laurel?

At first, she refused to consider the implications, but though she tried to keep reading, her brain wouldn't allow her to move on. She was Frannie. Specifically, Frances Anne Denman. Who would name their baby after a former wife? Laurel wasn't generous or understanding by nature. Not at all.

She shivered. She folded the letter carefully and put it back into the envelope. She added the photo, too, and slid it into the bundle and placed the bundle into the nightstand drawer. Drawer closed. Everything was tucked away, safely out of sight.

The thermostat indicated the heat was working fine. She pushed the sheet over the sliding doors aside to get a glimpse of the night. Must be windy because she was shaking as the cold worked its way in through all of the cracks and crevices. Frannie put water on to heat. She measured out the rooibos. The fruity fragrance of the dry tea leaves gave immense comfort. She thought of Brian. After all of his teasing, Brian and tea would be linked in her mind for a while. Better to think about him than about other things.

Foolishly, ridiculously, she wished he was here. She could talk to him. He might make fun of her, but he would listen.

But this. How could she discuss this with anyone?

She poured the tea in her cup and stood with her face over it, letting the steam waft up. She closed her eyes and breathed deeply, holding it in for as long as she could, and then released it slowly.

Frances.

The chill, damp fingers of a winter night were skipping down her spine.

She knew it was truth as surely as she knew anything. She picked up the cup and attempted to sip, but her lower lip trembled and maybe her hand did, too. Tea dripped down the front of her nightgown. With both hands she sat the cup gently down on the counter.

Undeniably true.

She pressed her fingers to her temples. She needed to reason this through. She'd seen her birth certificate. For school, for her driver's license. What else? A birth certificate was the kind of thing you looked at once, then hardly ever thereafter. Most people probably didn't know where their birth certificate was, unless they kept papers like that in a safe deposit box or something. She presumed Laurel still had hers.

How could this have happened?

She went to the nightstand and reclaimed the letters. Back at the counter, and with careful deliberation, she removed the rubber band. She reread the letter about her father's marriage. His first marriage.

The next letter was postmarked 1983 during her birth month. In it, Millie announced Frannie's birth to Will who was now a great-uncle.

She thumbed through the remaining letters. There were big gaps between them. Most had news about people she didn't know and mundane news at that.

The next letter was early 1986. It announced the marriage of Edward to Laurel and referred cryptically to things in the past being best left in the past.

What had happened to Frances?

She sat on the stool reading all of the letters and then re-read them. Suspend thought. Suspend emotion. She was good at holding it in no matter how fiercely it burned inside of her. She'd had lots of practice.

Frannie spent the last hours before sunrise curled up on the sofa. She opened the window blinds wide wanting to see the day, wanting the night to be done. As soon as the sky began to lighten, she yanked down the sheet.

She needed to talk to Uncle Will. If only Uncle Will were able to converse. Blink once for yes and twice for no? She didn't know what questions to ask, except one: why hadn't anyone told her Laurel wasn't her birth mother?

That left Mother. Laurel. In Raleigh.

And she had a lot of explaining to do.

****

Frannie had hoped the sight of the rising sun would soothe her, inspire her, anything except keep this hard anger knotted up inside her.

Somewhere out there in the winter cold, a woman named Frances might still be alive. Might be a mile away, maybe a thousand miles.

She stood in the hot shower, feeling the tension ease in her neck and back, but nothing could erase the dark smudges from under her eyes.

Brian arrived early. She opened the door and stood aside without a word. He entered carrying a long box. He stopped and eyed her warily.

"Something wrong?"

She sighed heavily. "No. Yes. It doesn't matter." She turned away running her fingers through her hair. Was Frances out there? Or with another family? Why did she care? Was she so desperate to put Laurel out of her life that she was ready to replace her with a total stranger?

Father had loved Laurel. She should at least respect her for his sake.

Father. He'd never mentioned Frances either.

"Fran?"

She said, "I have to go to Raleigh."

"Do you want me to skip painting today?"

His movement was awkward when he knelt to set the paint cans in the hallway.

"You're limping. I noticed you doing that before."

"Old injury. The cold tightens it up." Suddenly, he stopped. He was looking at Will's desk. She'd left it open.

She stammered, feeling an irrational need to justify the intrusion. "I put it off as long as I could, but it's time."

He turned his back to fetch the ladder. When he faced her again, his expression was clear. "When will you be back?"

Out of nowhere, she blurted, "I'm exhausted. I was up all night." She sat heavily down upon the couch.

After a pause, he asked, "Do you have to go?"

She nodded.

"Not safe to drive if you're that tired."

"True."

"You sure it's not something you can take care of over the phone?"

She smiled but there was no happiness in it. "No, this is something that has to be discussed face to face."

"Then put if off a day or two. Does the timing matter that much?" When she didn't answer, he added, "Make yourself a cup of that fancy tea you like and then go do what you girls like to do when you're down."

She frowned. Doubtful, she asked, "What's that?"

"Manicure and pedicure, right? That's what Maia does."

It tickled her somewhere deep inside. She was worried about a mother who wasn't hers, and a missing Frances. The suggestion of a manicure, coming from Brian, was almost too much.

"Thanks for the advice, but I'll pass."

"Then a movie with a big bucket of buttered popcorn."

She slumped, leaning her head against the back of the sofa. "I haven't seen a movie in… I don't know how long."

"Well, then?"

Her spirits rose. Over the prospect of a movie? Sort of.

Brian added, "Get Maia to go with you."

Not an invitation to go with him. She covered up her brief confusion by saying, "Nice of you to offer her up. It's not like she's busy or anything. Seriously, your sister is sweet, but I don't think I know her well enough. We're not really friends. She sold me a painting. I don't think that's an invitation to hang out."

He sat in the chair. "Maia told me how much she likes you." He waved his hand. "No worries. I don't discuss other people. Privacy. I demand my own and respect that of others." He shrugged. "I only mention it because you don't seem to know many people around here."

"Well, that's true. Only Uncle Will."

"It's a pretty lonely place in the winter."

"I like quiet. No problem there." She sighed. "Maybe you're right. Maybe I'm not up to the drive today. Too far and I'm too tired. I could use some fresh air, though. Maybe I'll go pay my uncle a visit."

She noticed the long box Brian had brought with him was on the floor near the sliding doors.

"What's that?"

"Your new vertical blinds."

She didn't want to seem ungrateful. She tried to show some interest. "Need some help hanging them?"

"No. I've got it handled. Want to approve them first?"

She shook her head.

"Yeah. You're too tired. You'd better stay local."

****

It was a bit of a drive to Morehead City and the mainland, but distance was relative and the off-season road belonged to her. She rolled down her window for a few miles to allow the cold air to blow through.

She'd been all caught up, racked up, overwrought, too much so to think clearly. She owed Brian a thank you although he didn't fully understand the favor he'd done her. It wouldn't hurt anyone for her to slow down. She'd take another look at those letters tonight. Now that she was more familiar with them, the information wouldn't be such a shock. She might notice details she'd missed last night. She'd do it cozied up with a blanket on the sofa, or maybe business-like at her uncle's desk. Until then, she'd try to put it out of her head.

****

He was sitting in his room in a wheelchair, situated such that with little effort he could see out through the window or into the hallway. He wasn't looking at either, but stared straight ahead, his head tilted to the side and his face expressionless. He could've been asleep except that his eyes were open. His hands were half-fisted, fingers curled, lying empty on the armrests.

His face might be expressionless, but an aura of gloom and despair surrounded him. If she stepped into that energy field—a minefield of negative energy—every happy thought, every dream would be sucked right into it, like a void. A black hole. What was she doing here? She couldn't help him out of his dreadful state. She had nothing to offer.

She coughed and said, "Uncle Will?"

He blinked, but otherwise didn't move.

Frannie moved to stand in front of him. He was wearing pajamas with a robe.

"Hi. How are you doing?"

Still nothing. Perhaps his eyes shifted, but that might have been imagined or a reflex.

She looked around, "Where's Janet?"

No answer. She dragged a chair over. That ugly pink vinyl-covered chair. She sat so that their eyes were at the same level. "I'm here to give you a painting update."

This was going to be another one-sided conversation. She forced animation into her delivery.

"So, remember I told you I was giving the inside of your house a fresh coat of paint? Well, I am and it's looking good. Remember Brian? Not only did he do house repairs for you, but he's a painter, too, and doing a beautiful job."

Yes, now his eyes were definitely turned her way.

"The shade is neutral, but with a little color. I was going to keep it off-white, but Brian convinced me to try it and I have to admit it's gorgeous." A little over the top, maybe, but anything for a reaction. "If you don't like it, we'll put it back to off-white, but I hope you'll reserve judgment until you've had the chance to see it."

This time his attention focused on her, unmistakably. She saw his lips move and thought he might be trying to smile, but he wasn't.

"Home." His head bobbed forward as he said it and his hands shook.

"Home," she echoed softly. "Soon, I hope." She felt like a liar. She reached over and touched his hand and then withdrew hers quickly, surprised she'd done that.

"Hello, Ms. Denman."

Janet stood in the doorway with a tray. She entered and placed the tray on an adjustable table, which she positioned in front of Will. "He didn't like what they served for lunch." She pulled up her own chair. "You're getting real particular these days, aren't you, Mr. Will?"

Uncle Will shook his finger at Janet, but didn't speak.

"What about your van, Uncle Will? Do you want me to sell it?"

Where had that question come from? To make him care, or to express that he cared about something, other than going home? She couldn't ask the question uppermost on her mind. When they'd met a year ago, why hadn't he said anything about Frances?

Because he assumed she knew?

The old man with the sunken cheeks glared at her. The spoon Janet held hovered nearby, ignored.

"No."

Hardly a syllable and raspy, but he left no doubt. No.

"So I shouldn't sell the van?"

Janet was glaring, too.

"No. Van."

She shrugged slowly, casually. "Up to you. But if you plan on driving it again, then you'd better eat and get your strength back. Why don't I ask Brian to drive it every so often? How's the physical therapy going?"

"Every day, he does therapy. Plus we do exercises."

"Good. Keep it up." She was suddenly out of steam. "Can I bring you anything the next time I come to visit?"

His watery hazel eyes fixed upon her again. A speck of pudding marred his chin. His jaw tensed. He pointed at her and clearly said, "Sister."

She'd had in mind some special food or personal item, not a person. She started to correct him, to remind him that he didn't have a sister, but caught herself.

"You mean Penny?" Wasn't she deceased?

He shook his head 'no' then 'yes'.

"Mr. Will, you need to eat your dinner."

"I'll be on my way."

Janet followed her out, saying, "I'll be right back."

She confronted Frannie in the hallway. "What's going on?"

"Nothing. Well, that is, he looked so sad when I arrived. I thought he could use a bit of stimulation."

Janet stared. "That's not necessarily a bad idea, but don't overdo it."

She nodded. "Yes, ma'am."

Frannie went out the front door and climbed into her car.

What now? Had she secretly hoped to get answers from Will? If so, she knew now there was no help coming from him. Not at this time. Maybe never.

She sat in the car in the rehab parking lot and watched the traffic go past. The sky was a steel gray blanket of clouds and the late winter trees were drab.

Was there some tiny memory of Frances buried deep in her brain? Did she remember a time before Laurel? No. And there was no one else to ask.

****

Frannie expected Brian to still be painting the bedroom, especially since his bike was parked next to her car. She didn't expect to see a child sitting on her porch.

She'd entered by the side door, so her first view of the child was of her back through the window fronting on the ocean. She opened the door and looked outside. The girl was bundled up in a coat and knitted cap. A purple scarf was around her neck and her hands were stuffed in her pockets.

"Hello?"

The girl turned to look at Frannie. She pouted, or glowered, and without a word, she looked back toward the ocean.

The wind was kicking up and the gusts were icy. In between, it was actually nice. The sun was like a gift that kept trying to warm the day. The clouds had cleared away, at least here on the edge of the ocean.

"Fran?"

Brian was in the living room. She closed the front door.

"Is she yours?"

He was holding a paintbrush. "Yes. Megan. Her mother dropped her off unexpectedly."

She hadn't had any idea that Brian was married. Not that it mattered, but still, she felt a twinge of disappointment. More than a twinge. She looked toward the porch, then back again.

"Why is she outside?"

He shrugged. "What she wanted. I guess she's mad."

"Mad? Are you going to leave her sulking on the porch? The wind is cold." She left it implied that as her father, it was his responsibility to make her do what was best for her regardless of her mood.

"Give it a shot. Maybe she'll listen to you."

"Fine, then." She stuck her head out of the door again. "Inside. Now."

She stood there, holding the door ajar, until the girl rose and did as she was told.

"Hang your coat over there. I'm fixing tea. Who wants some?"

"I'll get back to painting."

She fixed her eyes on Brian. "We'll all have some. How about that?"

He stared at the brush he was holding. "Do you have a plastic bag? Like a sandwich bag?"

"I think so." She opened the drawer next to the fridge. "In here."

Brian wrapped the bag around his paintbrush and put it into the fridge. He saw her questioning look and answered, "It'll keep fresh until I'm ready to get back to work."

She found three mugs and pulled down the chocolate chip cookies. One thing she knew about was sweets and tea. Creature comforts for human creatures. This little girl had an aura that cried for comfort.

The child's hair was stringy and mussed, probably the result of that knit cap—pressure combined with static electricity—but the sad eyes stole her heart.

"My name is Frannie Denman. This is my uncle's house,

but he's away right now. You're Megan?"

She pulled her lower lip in and said softly, "Yes."

Brian spoke, "She's ten."

Frannie heated the water and then poured it over the tea to steep.

"Here you go." She placed the plate of cookies within everyone's reach, then went back to pour the tea into the mugs.

Brian's features had softened. Not exactly smiling, but he looked less grim. Megan looked about the same. She touched the warm ceramic.

"Careful not to burn your mouth."

"Megan's mom had some kind of last minute thing so she brought her. I'll finish up here and we'll get out of your way."

"She isn't in my way. She can watch TV. Or do you have homework to do?"

Megan muttered, "Oh, great," and rolled her eyes.

"That's rude," her father said. "It's not Ms. Denman you're mad at so don't take it out on her. It's unfair."

"People are always telling me life is unfair."

"Life may be unfair. That's why it's important to do what we can to keep it civil and as fair as we can make it."

"Okay." She said it with the second syllable drawing out and ending with a huff. She looked at Frannie. "Sorry."

"You are welcome to visit any time, Megan. When will you mom be back?" She said it with a polite smile, but the tension was tangible between Brian and his daughter. She felt like she'd stepped into something potentially combustible.

"Later. Not sure when." Brian said the words and kept his eyes on Megan. "I'll get back to work."

"Me, too. Get to work, I mean." She touched her laptop lying nearby.

Brian looked surprised. "You work?"

"I'm making an inventory of Uncle Will's property and expenses."

He rubbed his jaw and kept his mouth shut. He turned and left the room. Frannie noticed he'd barely touched his tea.

Talk about rude. Like father, like daughter?

Megan distracted her. "Is your name really Frannie?"

She looked up from the computer. Her workspace was the kitchen counter. Megan was across the room on the sofa.

"Yes, it's short for Frances. I'm Frances Anne."

"Megan Lee."

"Pleased to meet you, Megan Lee."

She giggled. "No one calls me that."

"Same here. Mostly just Frannie." She giggled a bit at the memory. "When I was little, my dad called me Frannie Annie."

"Really? Like…."

"Like what?"

"Well, like everywhere? In front of people? Weren't you embarrassed?"

"Oh, gosh no. I adored my father."

Megan looked doubtful. That lower lip had eased out and pushed up. Frannie closed the lid of the laptop and walked over to sit on the sofa.

"Your dad is a good house painter. Does your mom work?"

"No. She did, but she lost her job. She's looking for a new one." Megan arranged the sofa throw around her legs. "What about your mom?"

That startled her. "My mom? What do you mean?"

"Did she call you Frannie Annie, too?"

"No, always Frannie." Suddenly tongue-tied, she'd almost tacked 'my stepmother' onto the end, as if it were fact.

Megan must have sensed the withdrawing because her little face became closed again.

"I guess I should get back to work."

Megan nodded, already focusing on the television.

She'd barely settled back at the laptop, when Brian reappeared.

"That room is done. When I come back tomorrow, we'll move the stuff back in."

"Sounds good."

"Question for you. Do you mind if Megan stays here while

I take my bike home and come back with the car?"

"It's fine, yes, but I have a better idea."

"Which is?"

"Will's van. It needs driving."

Brian chewed on his lower lip, considering. "If it starts. It's been sitting there awhile. Salt air is corrosive to the soft engine parts."

She pulled out her key ring and worked to detach the van's key. "Give it a try."

She walked outside with Brian while Megan watched TV. The engine turned over and purred, first try.

He smiled at her. "Sounds good to me."

She looked aside, avoiding his blue eyes and his smile, and saw papers scattered on the center console and across the passenger seat. An old paper coffee cup was on the floor. General disorder.

She frowned. "It's kind of a mess."

Brian shrugged. "Not so much. I'll bag the papers and anything that looks worth keeping and bring them back to you. Maybe put Megan to work."

"Thanks." She nodded.

"It's a great idea. This van needs to stay usable, ready for Will when he comes home. I'll get someone to bring me by later to pick up the bike."

"Seriously, Brian. Do you think he'll ever be able to drive it again?"

"Drive? Probably not, but it means more to him than that. Drive or not drive, it means independence to him."

"Sure." She shrugged and walked away, feeling stung. Independence. Everyone wanted it, but it was harder to hold onto than people admitted. She knew that, for sure.

****

The crepe myrtles were flourishing. The lawn was still immaculate. Glimpses of the Denman home through the trees were attractive and impressive.

Nothing had changed here.

Frannie sat in the parked car and held the letter to her heart like a talisman—a talisman more than thirty years old and fragile. She slid it into her purse. Better safe than sorry. She exited the car half-expecting the front door to open and Mother to pop out, ready to rule, fully prepared to subdue anyone or anything inclined to be unruly. When Frannie pushed the car door closed, it gave a thud. All the way to the house, she watched for the front door to swing inward and Laurel to appear on the threshold.

She was thirty and afraid of her mother. No more excuses about wishing she could be dutiful and loving. Today she admitted she was a coward who needed a secret charm to carry with her into battle. Or, perhaps more appropriately, an ace in the hole, to be revealed if Laurel tried to continue the... Myth was the kindest word she could think of.

What was Laurel to her anyway? Her mother? Stepmother? At the very least, she was the woman, the mother, who'd raised her. She was also a last link to her father.

Frannie unlocked the front door and let herself in.

No Laurel in the foyer. Not in the living room, not in the kitchen. She went down the long hallway to the garage. No car. No maid. No Laurel.

Perhaps a reprieve? She kicked off her shoes and went upstairs. As long as she was here, she could grab a few things to take back with her to Captain's Walk.

Her room was as tidy as ever. The bed was made and the bureau was dust-free.

She opened the closet door and flipped on the light. The closet was almost as large as Uncle Will's smallest bedroom, and incredibly neat—small thanks to her. She pulled out her roller suitcase, tossed it on the bed and unzipped it, throwing it open. She went through the drawers, gathering an item here, a shirt there. Shoes. What shoes did she need? She wouldn't mind having those fur-lined booties. Winter wasn't over yet. She headed back to the closet.

Custom shelving ran from floor to ceiling. The safe was

secured on a lower shelf. She'd brought her sapphires with her, still in the sock and tucked in her coat pocket. But maybe she wouldn't put them back into the safe. Not yet.

She pushed aside a couple of purses and caught sight of an old cigar box tucked into the shadows of a dark corner. The box. She hadn't thought about it in a long time. It held only a handful of small treasures and it was stashed in that dark place because Laurel was all about organization. In the same way that the carefully planned closet sections organized and controlled the shoes and clothing, Laurel had solutions for every potential untamed action. Frannie climbed onto the bed and sat cross-legged with the old box balanced on her knees.

So little here. A letter her father had written her at camp was on top. Had she been ten? About Megan's age. Below that was an old bar of hotel soap, still in its wrapper, from a trip they'd taken once upon a time. In the bottom lay a tarnished silver bracelet. She cherished it because of the engraving. To Frances with all my love.

Her heart shivered.

To Frances, not Frannie. Was 'with all my love' a strange thing to say to your young daughter, especially when there was a wife, Laurel, on the scene?

She tried to remember when her father had given it to her. She hadn't thought about the 'Frances' part back then. It was her proper name, after all.

The sounds of movement downstairs got her up and moving. She added the cigar box and a few more items to the suitcase and then zipped it shut.

"I saw your car." Laurel stood in the open doorway. "If you'd called ahead, I would've had lunch waiting for you." She made a point of staring at the suitcase. "You're going back so soon?"

"I am."

"Not right away, surely."

"That depends."

"Come down to the kitchen. Martha made some fresh

scones." She treated Frannie to her almost-laugh. "Cranberry. Terrible on the waistline."

She couldn't help herself. She had to respond in the way she always had in that special code language that families have, responses that said all was well, or wasn't. "But so good on the way down."

Mother smiled and took that as an invitation to move further into the room.

Frannie asked, "When did it go so wrong between us? Was it always this way and I don't remember?"

"What do you mean?"

"Adversarial. That's our relationship and has been for a long time. Even when we were doing the mom and daughter things."

She touched Frannie's shoulder. "We can't help being who we are, but that doesn't mean we don't care."

Another cue, one with which they were both familiar, and she almost gave the expected response, but instead, she said, "Was my father married before he married you?"

Laurel paled except for a bright splotch high on each cheek that grew redder. She stepped back.

"What? Why do you ask that?"

Frannie persisted. "Was my father married before he married you?" She watched Laurel's face and after a long silent moment, she added, "I'll take that as a 'yes'."

Laurel strode across the room and back again, agitated.

"We never told you. Why would we? It was brief, a disaster of a marriage."

"Who was she?"

"I never knew her."

"You know her name."

"I refuse to discuss this. If your father had wanted you to know, he would've told you. You've never respected me or my feelings, but I hope you still have some respect for your father's wishes." She turned away and marched out of the room.

"Wait." She couldn't allow Laurel to walk away, taking

her knowledge with her, knowledge Frannie had more right to than anyone. She followed her down the hall and across the open area that overlooked the foyer. The master suite was on the far end. She heard the door close as she reached the corner.

She started to call out 'Mother' but couldn't say the word. She leaned against the door, fighting the desire to beat her fists upon it. Uncertain, she called out, "We need to talk." She took a deep breath. "Please, I need to know about Frances." She whispered against the door, "Please."

Laurel opened it slowly, saying, "Understand, it was your father's wish. He thought that moving here to the city after we married was like a fresh start. He wanted to save you a lifetime of explanations. Questions. Fretting over a woman who didn't want you." She shook her head. "I'm sorry. That sounds hurtful. I don't mean it that way. It is simply fact." She added, "I never knew her."

Laurel was pale. Tiny beads of perspiration showed around the edges of her hair.

"But you knew about her."

"Of course, I did. After all, there was you."

Chapter Nine

Laurel opened the door wider.

Frannie entered. The flowered chairs were a cozy invitation and the lace panels that cascaded from ceiling to floor softened the light that filtered in. She tried to be patient, tried to hide the pain. Her lungs were on fire and her heart was in her throat, choking her, but she'd had lots of practice at hiding her feelings and she'd do it this time, too, because if she pushed too hard, Laurel might refuse to talk. So, she sat, but Laurel didn't. She paced back and forth between the fireplace and the chairs.

"Why did the two of you let me believe that you were my mother?"

Laurel flushed a bright red. "Excuse me, I am your mother. Who raised you? Who cared for you when you were sick, comforted you when you were unhappy?"

Laurel had never been a fount of comfort, but Frannie figured she'd done the best she could, so she didn't object, and instead, moved on, "You know what I mean."

"It was your father's decision. I abided by it." She smoothed the front of her sweater and arranged a cuff. "You were so young. Barely three when your father and I married. You'd been with sitters a lot before that. You accepted me, and before long it was as if I'd always been there, at least as far as you were concerned."

"You weren't worried that she might show up one day?"

Laurel shook her head and Frannie gasped.

"Is she dead?"

"Yes."

Disappointment. Silly ridiculous disappointment. She tried to shake it off. This was her chance to ask questions.

"So you adopted me."

"Yes. Then we moved here. No one really knew us. Everyone just assumed."

"Tell me what you know about her."

Laurel stared at Frannie as if trying to read her mind. "Are you sure you want to know?"

"Yes. Why not?"

"Things, once told, can't be untold. Your father never made a decision about you that wasn't wrapped in love. Shouldn't you respect his wishes? He isn't here to defend himself, or his choices."

"If father was still alive, he'd tell me the truth now."

Laurel shrugged. "So be it, then." She sank into the chair and focused on the large windows that overlooked the woodlands out back. "I never met Frances. She and your father met in college and married in haste with lots of time for regret later. You were born shortly before their first anniversary. Your grandparents didn't approve and cut off his allowance. He told me it was a hard time when you were born. Not because of you, but because Frances was never right after."

"Not right? Don't stop there."

"Unstable emotionally."

"Like postpartum depression?"

"I don't know. There were some drug issues, too, as I understood it. At least, the mental issues, regardless of cause, never went away. She'd get better, then bad again. It was terrible for your father. He didn't like to talk about it." She looked down at her hands and rubbed them together as if they were cold. "As I understand it, you weren't even a year old the first time she ran away."

"Why? Where did she go?"

"I don't know. She took you with her. Your father searched high and low. She came back briefly, but then it happened all over again. They would reconcile, things would settle down, and then all of a sudden, she'd take off again. The last time, she was missing for almost a year. On and off, she wanted a divorce, but your father wouldn't agree. Finally, he had to, for your sake if for no other reason. He agreed to give her a divorce if she gave up her rights to you."

"And then?"

"She left and he never saw her again. A few years ago I heard she'd died."

"A few years ago. Only a few years ago and I never knew? Never had the chance to know her. How could you keep this from me?"

Laurel's eyes narrowed and her face flushed. "You ungrateful girl. No different than you've ever been so why should I be surprised?" She hit the arm of her chair with her fist. "Don't you understand? Your father didn't want you to know about her condition. To protect you, and when we began to see certain traits and behaviors, he feared you'd inherited her instability, and he didn't want you to know."

She was speechless, as if Laurel had reached her fingers into her mouth and snatched the words away.

Laurel stood and pointed her index finger at Frannie. "You see? I told you. What good did it do for you to know this?" She directed her finger back toward her own chest. "It hurts me. I feel like I've lost a daughter today. I did my best to provide structure for you, support, everything I could to keep you from her fate." She gave a sigh, a heavy breath that was almost a groan. "It was Frances who signed you away. It was Frances who left you. I was the one who helped your father pick up the pieces. I helped him make a better life for all of us." She jumped up and headed toward the bedroom door.

"When did she die? Where?"

Laurel paused at the open door, her hand on the knob. "I don't recall. Somewhere up north. That's all I know. Now, I need to rest."

"This isn't finished. I have to know it all."

"Then you'll have to wait."

Reluctantly, Frannie stepped out into the hallway. Laurel closed the door and the lock clicked.

She leaned back against the wall, certain she would collapse without its support. A few feet away, on the other side of the wall, Laurel was surely going through her version of heartbreak. Maybe even regret.

Up north? Years ago. Under what name? Frances Denman? And where?

She pushed away from the wall and walked slowly, light-headed, touching the wall as she made her way back to her own room. Fragments of information and more questions chased each other in her brain and nausea threatened.

There were too many questions. She didn't know where to begin. She suspected a good private detective could figure it all out relatively quickly. After all, the details were a matter of record somewhere. But a private detective? Who really hired those? Aside from in movies, that is. She had no idea how to go about it and was too overwhelmed to figure it out.

She fell back across the bed and closed her eyes. She wanted to know, but maybe not yet. She had a lot to digest as it was. She needed to think it through.

Exactly what 'odd things' was Laurel talking about? Moods. Didn't everyone have moods?

True, certain things made her nervous. She was shy and withdrawn, a little awkward around people. Lots of people were. Sometimes her imagination carried her away.

That wasn't instability.

She pushed upright. The anxiety, the rush of learning a chunk of her personal history, something as personal as her parentage, had left her weary and her stomach was irritable. She wished she had a glass of water handy to take her medicine, but she didn't and she refused to get up. She breathed deeply to ease it, and rolled over onto her side. But she couldn't sleep. Couldn't even doze. After a few minutes, she gave up. She unzipped the suitcase and pulled the cigar box out. She flipped the lid and took out the photo of her and her dad. She was an infant wrapped in a blanket and her father held her. It was a close up shot, but only the tip of her nose and the curve of one small cheek were visible. And maybe a tiny fist. Her father was holding her and smiling at the camera.

Who was holding the camera? Frances?

****

She fell asleep, but in a light, fitful doze. The old dream came back. The baby was crying. Sometimes loud and demanding, sometimes with soft whimpers. She lay there, half in and half out of consciousness and decided the symbolism was beginning to make sense now. The baby was crying for her mother who'd gone away. The baby was Frannie.

Laurel had said Frances went away for good when she was little. Before she was three, anyway. Sometime after she turned three, her dad had married Laurel.

She knew Mother wasn't telling it all. Mother. Laurel. Laurel never did. She managed information like she managed her social life and her house—with a steel fist.

The mental instability. Had Laurel used that as a distraction? Maybe, maybe not, but she thought it likely. It was her mother's...Laurel's style. But Frannie had the gist of it now, and she was done dancing to Laurel's tune.

The clock on her nightstand read 7:48 p.m. She'd actually slept several hours.

She went downstairs to lie in wait for Laurel. She needed to squeeze a little more info out of the woman who'd raised her.

****

Laurel hadn't been a great mom, but she'd kept her alive and well and had been there for her when her life had fallen apart. Frannie's hands trembled and she clasped them to still them. Intimidation? Laurel wasn't in the room, but years of conditioning set the pattern. Every time she thought she had control of herself, that she had found some confidence, ultimately it failed her. Yet again, she was about to give in to the past as she told herself she had all the information she needed or would get.

The kitchen tile was smooth and cool beneath her feet. The lights below the cabinets had been left glowing, so there was plenty of low light to move about in. She put the kettle on to heat and pulled the tea canisters down from the shelf. Something calming. Soothing. She rubbed her tummy. For her, and it might mellow Laurel, too. They'd both missed supper unless Laurel had left while she was sleeping. She took a quick peek in the garage. The car was still there, so Laurel was still here, too.

She opened a package of Lemon Danish cookies. Laurel's favorites. She arranged them on a decorative china plate with a couple of the scones. A dainty, yet elegant arrangement, the way Laurel preferred. As the tea steeped, she set out the fragile cups Laurel favored. She counted on the aroma to waft up through the stairway, perhaps up through the ductwork. Rituals were important. Tea and cookies in the evening after a major blowup was tradition. The equivalent of their shared peace pipe. Maybe a negotiation.

With the pot of steeped tea on the kitchen island and the soft lighting, Laurel appeared on cue. Her eyes were swollen and red-rimmed. Her nose was rosy.

Frannie poured the tea, first in Laurel's cup and then in her own.

"I smell citrus and lavender." She closed her eyes and breathed in slowly. "My favorite."

"One of your favorites."

Laurel opened her eyes and smiled. Her voice was sad. "Yes. One of my favorites. You're correct."

"I am, and you know that I need better answers." She dropped her voice and spoke to the plate of cookies and scones. "The more info I have, the easier it will be for me to find out more, and thus less distress for everyone else."

"You are determined."

"I am."

"Wasn't I mother enough? Was I so terrible?"

The forlorn voice, the red eyes, it tugged at her conscience.

"It's not about you. I want to know about…Frances." She'd almost said 'mother'. How cruel would that have been?

"I need to know. You said she died a few years ago somewhere up north. How did you find out? Who told you?"

"It was so long ago." She shook her head.

"Not that long ago. Something like that, your husband's first wife, would stick with you. I'm sure you recall exactly when and what you were doing when you heard." She picked up a cookie and examined it, as if its form mattered. "I might have grandparents out there. I've never had any, none that I knew of. I might have cousins."

"I should have known I wouldn't be enough. No matter what I did or how hard I tried."

Another diversion.

"It's not about you. Love is inclusive, right? It doesn't divide, it multiplies. I'd like more family. You can understand that."

"I'm hearing platitudes and I don't see how any good can come of this."

Frannie sensed her pulling away and building up the barrier again. She laid it out as clearly as she could. "I'm going to pull this thread until the whole garment unravels. If you want to have anything good left to show for the past thirty years, you'd do well to help me."

Laurel's expression turned stony, as cold and remote as a sculpture.

Frannie picked up the china plate and held it out.

"Cookie?"

"You can't imagine how hurt I am. You think I have no feelings."

Civil. Keep it civil.

"I think you're going to tell me what I need to know."

Laurel closed her swollen eyes and drew in a ragged breath.

Diva.

"I met her once."

"You met her? You said you never knew her."

Laurel nodded toward the front of the house. "She showed

up here one day. One meeting doesn't constitute 'knowing' in my opinion."

"She was looking for me?" Breathless.

She shook her head. "No. She wanted Edward."

"And?"

"He was out of town. Actually, overseas on business. In Germany."

"Wait. I remember that. I was in second grade. He brought me back that nutcracker soldier, and I took it to school for show and tell."

"Yes, about then. She looked awful. I don't know if it was illness, physical or mental. Maybe drugs, but whatever, she was terribly thin and not very clean. I was so grateful you were in school. I couldn't begin to imagine how I'd explain her to you."

Frannie's head spun. She didn't know what to think. She tried to listen, but the mental image of a gaunt, frail Frances on the doorstep asking for her ex, for Frannie's father, while their daughter was in school, was almost too much for her to process. Perhaps Laurel realized this because her pace picked up and she rushed through the next part.

"She asked to see your father. I told her he wasn't home. I said I'd tell him that she wanted to speak with him, but she wouldn't say anything other than that she had something for him, or maybe it was that she wanted to say something to him. I think she was looking for some kind of favor. Probably money. Regardless, that's what happened and then she left. I told your father when he returned home and he made the decision to leave the past in the past. That's it."

"Hold on." Frannie waved her hands. "There had to be more. How did she expect Dad to contact her? Did she leave a phone number? An address?"

"I don't remember. It was more than twenty years ago. Twenty-three? A phone number, I think. Does it matter? No, it doesn't. In the end, your father chose not to respond and I agreed with him. It was the best decision for everyone."

Her head was still spinning, now she was also speechless.

What else? She had to ask Laurel now while she was talking.

"You said she died. When? Where?"

"Please, Frannie. Dearest. Sweetheart. I don't remember."

"Someone must have told you, right? Or did you read it somewhere? A newspaper, maybe?"

Laurel leaned forward. She put her hands on her face and then rested her forehead in her hands, her elbows on the table, a posture of exhaustion. "I don't think I can take much more."

"Did someone tell you?"

"Someone told me? Or was it in a letter? Some distant relative of your father who happened upon the information. Not someone I knew. Maybe that's why I can't recall who."

"When?"

"Truly, I do not remember. It was a few years after she'd been here."

"You said she went up north somewhere and died?"

"I'll give it some thought and try to remember. I can't do anymore tonight. Please, Frannie, please tell me you know I've tried. I've been honest with you. You believe that, right?"

She nodded. Reluctantly, she said, "Yes. Thank you."

"I'm exhausted now. I hope you're not leaving right away."

Frannie looked at the clock. It was almost nine p.m. "No, I'll go back tomorrow."

"After lunch, then? Let's have ourselves a nice lunch. You choose the restaurant." Laurel gave a weary smile.

"Maybe brunch." Inwardly, she groaned. She wanted to head straight back to the beach house, but there was a carrot dangling in front of her—maybe Laurel would remember more by morning.

****

It was past noon when she pulled into the driveway and parked under Captain's Walk. As soon as she exited the car, she realized the air had changed. What had happened? It wasn't only milder inland, but also here. Seventies. Blue sky. She left her suitcase and bag on the porch and walked straight out onto the dunes crossover. She stood at the end, overlooking the beach. A light wind, gusty, but warm, teased her hair. No chill.

She lifted her face and closed her eyes. The waves sounded gently forceful and rhythmic, and from somewhere nearby, a child's laughter filtered in. Her jacket was too warm. She pulled it off, draped it over the back of the bench and leaned forward against the railing.

A few couples walked by in the sand. They waved and she waved back. A child chased a dog. A spaniel, maybe.

A man was holding tight to a kite string and far above his head, the kite danced in the more powerful winds aloft. The kite swooped low and Frannie thought he might lose it, but he made some sort of adjustment and it sailed high again.

She'd hadn't stayed long with Laurel this morning. Laurel hadn't recalled anything else, and, in fact, her good mood seemed to have fully recovered. Since Laurel wasn't inclined to resume the discussion about Frances, Frannie wasn't inclined to hang around, even for brunch.

"Hi."

She jumped and spun around. "Brian? Where'd you come from?"

Chapter Ten

Brian pointed a short distance down the beach. Megan was near the water's edge staring at the ground.

"Is she looking for shells?"

"Yeah. We were taking a walk on the beach." He laughed and rubbed his thigh. "Or, she wanted to take the walk and dragged me along."

Frannie leaned back against the railing. "From coats and scarves to spring. I can't believe I brought my boots back with me."

"No worries. It isn't spring yet. There may be more winter yet to come."

"Is your leg bothering you? Before, you mentioned an old injury. What happened? If this is too personal, please forget I asked."

His mood clouded, but only briefly and he shook it off.

"About a year ago. A bike accident." He brushed a hand over his thigh. "It's recovered pretty well, but gives me trouble from time to time."

He shook his leg as if to prove it and then felt stupid.

She smiled, "Good to hear."

"You seem a little happier today." In fact, he noticed those vertical lines between her brows were almost gone. Remembering how he'd thought of smoothing out those lines with his thumb, he made a fist, perhaps afraid he might, after all, be tempted to help her get rid of the remaining trace.

She shrugged. "I went to see my mother. I'm glad I'm back in time to enjoy a bit of this gorgeous weather."

"It's supposed to be nice for the next few days. You should take advantage of it. Spend some time out here instead of hidden away in the house."

"I'm here to take care of business—Uncle Will's business. It's off-season now, so there's time, but I'd like to have it all done and the house ready to go on the market at whatever point it's necessary."

There was a long silence. It drew out and she turned toward him. "What?"

"What's the rush? You don't know what's going to happen. He could recover."

"You're protective of him. That's nice, but when it comes down to it, I'm his protector, at least of his property. I don't want to be the disposer of his property. I want to believe he'll be able to come back home."

"He'll come home."

She stared down at the railing. "Do you really think so? I've spoken to his doctor. He hopes for more improvement, but how much?" She pushed her hair behind her ear and watched him from the corner of her eye. "Do you have reason to believe differently?"

His shoulders moved in a funny kind of hitch and shrug. "No, but anything's possible."

She turned to face him fully. "Well, I hope you're right. I'd like nothing better than to welcome him home."

He liked the words and the way she stood and returned his look without blinking. Seemed like he should say something to her, but he didn't know what. He focused beyond her, searching for the missing thought, and his attention shifted when he saw the empty beach.

"Where's Megan?"

Frannie turned quickly and scanned the beach. "I think that might be her up that way, near those other children."

"I told her to stay nearby. She's in trouble." He raised a hand, but she wasn't looking this way. "Interested in a walk?"

"To catch up to Megan?"

"That too."

He watched her face. Her expression seemed to brighten,

but there were shadows under those eyes. "It will do you good and it's a crime not to appreciate a day like this."

"Thanks, but I came straight out here." She waved toward the porch. "I dumped my stuff by the door and there's more in the car."

"It's not going anywhere."

She looked doubtful.

"When we're ready to leave, I'll carry your stuff up."

She smiled broadly. "It's a deal."

She started down the stairs. He gestured at her to stop.

"Leave your shoes there. You don't need them."

Dubious, she frowned, but stepped back up and slid her shoes off.

From his vantage point a few steps down, he said, "You're wearing hose or nylons or something. Get rid of them."

She raised her eyebrows, but cooperated, hiking up her pants legs. She slid off the trouser-socks.

"Those aren't allowed at the beach at any time."

"Beachcombers are now determining what's acceptable to wear? I don't think so."

He couldn't tell if she was serious or just wanting to start another one of those word jousts. "When in Rome...."

"Touché."

"Roll up the pants legs."

She was making a mess of it, so he stepped up and reached over. She stood passively while he folded the fabric up to below her knees. "There."

Stiffly, formally, with her hands on her hips, she asked, "Am I now acceptably dressed for a walk on the beach?"

"No, but don't worry, we'll work on it." He extended his hand. "Come with me."

Chapter Eleven

He had a lot of nerve putting her through all that 'dressing right for the beach walk' stuff, and then fretting over how she rolled up her pants legs. Nonsense.

Rolling up her pants legs hadn't mattered anyway. When she stopped to look at a shell embedded in the wet sand, and didn't move fast enough, those pants got soaked to above her knees. And what did he do? He laughed. She did, too. It was a lovely antidote to the hours spent with Laurel.

Frannie rubbed her arms. "It's getting late. Sun sets early this time of year and takes the warmth with it."

Brian called his daughter and she came willingly enough which was a testament to the chill that was setting in. Watching Megan running through the sand toward them, Frannie suddenly realized how odd this would seem to Megan's mom, and Brian's wife, if Megan mentioned their walk on the beach.

She struggled to find something to say that would be friendly, yet helpful in forestalling misperceptions.

She smiled at Megan and said, "How's your mom? Maybe when the weather's nicer you can bring her, too, and we can all have a picnic."

Why did the child's smile crumple? In her eyes, and in Brian's, too, Frannie saw such pain. What had she done?

Brian spoke softly, "Megan's mom and I are divorced."

Megan huffed and scrambled down the outside stairs. Her dad yelled, "Megan!"

She threw back, "I'll wait by the road."

Her voice was so short, so terse, like quick little knife slices. Brian flinched.

"I'm sorry. I didn't realize."

He shook his head. "Not your fault. It's hard on her. She blames me." He added, "She'll get over it. I'd better catch her before she takes off on her own—which she'd do if she could reach the gas pedal from the seat." He actually laughed a bit and shook his head. "Give me your keys and I'll get your gear."

"No, forget it. Go take care of your daughter."

"I take care of my daughter."

She'd done it again.

He added, "I also keep my promises."

"Bringing in my 'gear' wasn't exactly what I call a promise. I can manage."

"Keys please." He extended his palm. "I have my reasons."

Reasons? She pulled the key ring from her pocket. It was damp and sandy.

Brian accepted the keys and brushed the sand off. "Proper beach attire is essential."

"Wait. I forgot that the door is locked."

"At your command." He paused to unlock the front door and then disappeared down the steps.

She went in through the front door, out the side door, and down the steps to help. Brian had her suitcase. Megan was behind him. She was staring at her feet and holding a grocery bag.

"Carry it inside." He nodded at Megan.

"I can get it." She reached forward and Brian said, "Nope. Megan's got it. Get up the stairs, Meg." He nodded at Frannie. "After you."

She preceded him up the stairs because she didn't know what else to do. At the top, Megan scooted past her without meeting her eyes. As soon as she and Brian stepped inside, Frannie started to apologize again.

"No. Hold it right there. You've done nothing wrong." He put her suitcase on the floor and put her keys on the counter.

"This exercise was for Megan. Let's call it a small attitude adjustment." He added a yellow plastic bag to the mix. "These are Will's papers from the van."

He pulled the door closed behind him.

An attitude adjustment.

She was such a klutz. Never an athlete, but maybe a contortionist because she could put her foot in her mouth just fine. When it came to words, the simple act of opening her mouth and allowing verbalizations to emerge often wrought havoc. Why?

You could change your clothes, but you couldn't change your nature. That person, the true you, was still inside. Always saying the wrong things.

Then again, screwing up wasn't the same as instability.

Take that, Laurel.

She sank down on the sofa. Her delight at the beauty of the weather and the beach had evaporated. It was winter again and even the fresh color on the walls faded as the night came on.

****

She was in that dark place. Her own high tower in a castle under an evil spell. Maybe she should call that the 'Frances' place now. What was the truth about her mother?

Her dad should've told her while he could. She should've heard about Frances from someone who'd loved the poor woman, if only briefly.

She stayed in that dark place, all motivation gone, through Saturday morning. Saturday afternoon, she forced herself back to Will's desk. There was still work to do there. Top side drawer, office stuff. Pencil, pens, staples. Middle drawer, neatly ordered envelopes containing bills and receipts. She stacked those on the counter to compare against the spreadsheet ledger she was already keeping.

The bottom drawer was more of a jumble. She sorted through an assortment of flyers and coupons. Nothing seemed important. There were a few odds and ends she wasn't sure about and she set those aside.

The shelves in the hutch held books and dust. There were a few stale novels from the dollar bin at the local grocery store and some books about the mechanics and history of sailing. The

Bible. Next to it was Uncle Will's book about the USS North Carolina. That slip of paper peeked out above the top.

Jonah. Belly of hell, hadn't it said? She knew a little about that herself.

She picked up the church bulletin. She'd found it, along with his Sunday school book in his desk. Not unlike what she was used to in her own church. She looked through the church bulletin. The date was shortly before Uncle Will had his stroke.

The church was on the island. The line drawing on the front depicted a small building with steeples. There was a prayer list inside and the hours of services.

The pastor was named Heron. Sounded like the seabird. Or was that a fresh water bird? Whichever, it sounded friendly.

Frannie reached out and touched the Book, then brushed the edge of that paper with her fingers.

Tomorrow she was going to scrape herself up off the floor of this black depression. In fact, she was already feeling better. She got up and turned on the television. She channel surfed looking for one of those soft, sweet movies, or an oldie, but goodie. She settled on one and then went to check in the fridge for a likely meal.

She left the front blinds up. The stars were so bright over the ocean. She curled up on the couch with her steaming microwave fettuccine, with the blanket over her legs, and watched her movie in the near dark lit only by the television and by starlight.

****

What to do? Her improved mood threatened to crumble again. It was that dream. She wished she were a jogger. A good run to clear her head would be excellent medicine. Oh, wait. Not this time of year. Unless today was going to be another beauty.

It might be. The thought perked her mood back up a little until she looked outside. The day was overcast and thick with a mist that looked like it had sunk its claws in and was here to stay.

She brewed her tea.

The fact was that her uncle, a retired sailor, kept his items in good order. Brian was handling the painting. Until she knew whether to move forward with clearing the house or putting it on the market, or not, she was suspended in limbo land. She could go visit her uncle again. Her gaze shifted around the room and landed on the church bulletin.

She looked at the clock. Had she actually planned to go? Yes, there was time. And after, she'd go by a restaurant. Take herself out for lunch. Not really for companionship, but to be in the midst of people for a little while.

****

The sanctuary was smallish and simple. She chose an open pew about halfway up and removed her coat and laid it on the cushioned bench beside her. The sanctuary was about half full. The first few pews were occupied and then folks had chosen more sparse spacing. She met the eyes with a woman seated nearby and exchanged a polite smile and nod.

After the opening prayer, as everyone stood, their hymnals open, a small group near the front caught her eye. The woman turned briefly to the man next to her and spoke a few words. Maia's friend. Had to be. The man was tall and slim. Tanned. She watched them as she sang along with a hymn she knew well. Judging solely from the partial side view, he was good looking. Maybe distinguished looking. No doubt he would be. A woman like Juli had everything. She was probably really nice, too. She'd been pleasant that day in Beaufort. She wouldn't know that Frannie had purchased her painting unless Maia had told her.

She tried to listen to the pastor's sermon, but thoughts and images kept intruding. His sermon was about forgiveness, but it kept mixing in with remembering, and inevitably took her back to Raleigh and the perfect lawn and crepe myrtles.

It hadn't been her father's house for fifteen years.

It belonged to her. Her father had left her the house, but he'd known she and Laurel would live there.

She'd moved away when she graduated from college. First apartment. Living on her own. All that. The man she'd fallen in love with and to whom she'd been engaged changed his mind and went away. She never understood why, but it nearly killed her because it was too much like what had happened with her first love in college. That relationship had been good until it wasn't and then it was over and she was left wondering what she'd done or hadn't done. Then things really got crazy. Strange things happened. She hadn't been able to sleep. Couldn't rest. Finally, she lost her job.

Suffice it to say, she'd ended back up in Laurel's house.

The pastor's sermon was based on Ecclesiastes. These were some of her favorite verses, and her father's. The words fell on her ears like sweet, familiar music. They lifted her. Held her. And she felt steadied.

One thing she'd learned in the last few years was that some things just were. There were no answers; there was only getting along.

She stood with the others for the closing prayer and then walked out to the vestibule. She paused to shake hands with the pastor.

"I'm Will Denman's niece. I believe he's a member of your congregation?"

He clasped her hand in both of his. "Indeed. I was so very sorry about the stroke. We've had him on our prayer list."

"I'm here to help with his business affairs while he's recovering."

"I'm so glad you joined us this morning. I hope you'll come back. How is your uncle doing?"

She shrugged and pulled her hand back. "He's at the Harris Rehabilitation home in Morehead City. You're welcome to visit him. I'm sure he'd like that."

He released her hand and touched her shoulder. "I have. We prayed and I hope, as he does, for a recovery." He cleared his throat and said, "If you need anything, any help, please let me know."

She started her car, but sat. She'd been petty. She'd assumed, hadn't she? Jumped to the conclusion that he had neglected Will.

A small group exiting the church caught her eye. Juli with the man and her baby. The man held the baby on his hip while Juli shuffled a diaper bag and purse.

Frannie turned off the engine and reached to open the door. As she paused, Juli looked up and laughed and the man looked down and said something, then turned to the baby and, smiling, said more words.

She laid her head back and let out a long sigh. She gripped the steering wheel.

A sweet, tender family moment. Had it ever been like that for her dad and Frances? Had she been that treasured child balanced on her daddy's hip? Had Frances shared gentle touches and hugs, and smiled on her little family with love?

Did it matter? How much? She dabbed at a tear and laughed at herself. It worked both ways, didn't it? She had information now about something that was totally unknown to her a short time ago, including the information that her father had turned his back on Frances when she'd needed him.

****

Monday meant another call with her uncle's primary care doctor. Small progress, he said. He was still hopeful. Then she received a call from Maia inviting her to lunch. No telling what Maia wanted, but Frannie was looking forward to it. In the meantime, she tackled the closets and boxes that served as Will's storage. She'd expected Brian to show up, but he didn't.

Hadn't he said he'd be back on Monday? She was a little sheepish anyway after her foot-in-mouth moment down by the beach. How was she supposed to know his marital state? He'd never mentioned it. She'd assumed he was single until she met Megan.

A quick glance at the clock. It was time to get herself together. She was hungry.

****

"Thanks for driving over here to Beaufort."

"Happy to."

"Can't travel too far on my lunch hour." Maia smiled. "Plus this place is one of my favorites. It has the best sweet tea in the world."

"In the world?" Sweet tea. Big deal.

"In my world."

Frannie knew she'd sounded critical. She hadn't intended to. She added, "I think this place is charming. The view of the marina and water is wonderful." She looked down to read the menu. "What's good here?"

"Everything."

The waitress asked, "Do you know what you want? Need a few minutes?"

Both of them shook their heads. Maia clearly had her favorite dish and Frannie played it safe with a salad.

"All right, ladies. I'll be right back with your drinks." And she was. Sweet tea for Maia. Water for Frannie.

She settled back and said, "Thanks for suggesting this."

Maia said, "I'm glad you could come. By the way, Brian told me Juli's painting looks fabulous in the dining room."

Fabulous. She couldn't imagine that word making it past Brian's lips.

"It does. In fact, it may be hanging on the wall of my uncle's house, but I'm not leaving it behind when I leave."

"How is Mr. Denman?"

She shrugged. "I don't know. The doctor thinks he'll keep improving, but no way of knowing how much. According to his doctor, he's responding well to physical therapy. I haven't seen that myself, but he did speak a little the last time I visited." She sat back while the waitress refilled her tea glass. "Thank you." The waitress moved on and she turned back to Maia. "Only time will tell."

Maia picked up her glass and napkin. The condensation had built up on the outside of the glass. Maia put the napkin under the base and then folded the rest of the napkin up the sides. Instantly, it was damp and Maia gave it a bit of a twist effectively securing the napkin to the glass.

"You didn't know him when you were growing up? You didn't live that far apart."

"Different kinds of distance, I guess. I met him only about a year ago when he contacted me." The words sounded odd. She tried to explain. "He and Dad were in touch, at least by phone and letter." She shrugged. "I recall my dad mentioning him, but he never came to our house that I know of."

"Wow." Maia went silent for a minute as she stirred her soup. "Maybe he didn't get along with your mom. Oops. I shouldn't have said that. I'm sorry."

Frannie let it go unanswered. "Your family is close?"

"Very. That doesn't mean we don't have our differences and sometimes we argue or get angry, but we keep trying."

"You have a large family?"

"Yeah. There's more than a few of us." She laughed.

"Not so many of us. I always wanted siblings, lots of cousins and aunts and uncles. But it was just us two. Me and Laurel. Then Uncle Will."

"That makes it all the sadder that you didn't have your uncle in your life earlier. Family is special, something to treasure." She shook her head. "Were you young when your father died?"

"A teenager."

"How sad."

"My father and I were very close. When he died, my mother and I were—" Was she really going to take this next step? It felt like a giant leap. "She's actually my adoptive mother. When he died, Laurel and I were left with only each other. We've always had a difficult relationship."

"I'm sorry. I can see I've forced you to relive sad memories."

She shrugged. "I have good memories mixed in. Not everyone can say that."

Maia looked embarrassed. "I seem nosey, I know."

"You can ask anything you want." She almost added, and it's nice to have someone friendly to share a meal and conversation with. Instead, she said, "Talking about family and relationships, you and Brian seem so different. You are upbeat and cheerful. He's so grumpy. You are so petite and friendly while he's tall and well, just plain grumpy. Is that how he usually is? Or is it me he's grumpy with?"

Maia focused on picking up crumbs from the tablecloth. After a moment, she sighed. "No, it's not you. Brian has been through a lot in the last couple of years."

"His daughter, Megan, is sweet. I said the wrong thing the other day and upset her. I didn't know her parents were divorced."

"Megan is a doll when she's not having an attitude. I can't blame her. The breakup was difficult. That's part of Brian's sadness."

Brian's sadness. So, he hadn't wanted the breakup.

Maia continued, "When things started going downhill, it went fast and ugly. He's getting better. Better every day." She sat up straighter and smiled. "He'll be fine. Healing takes time, both the physical healing and that of the heart." She touched her chest.

"That sounds poetic, Maia."

This time her smile was sad. "No poet here."

Frannie studied her face. "But lots of family. You're lucky."

"Everything comes with both the good and not-so-good."

She laughed. "Listen to you. You won't even say the word 'bad'."

****

Why was Maia so interested in her? Frannie enjoyed her company, and Maia seemed to feel the same. Still, Maia had plenty of friends. Why seek out someone she barely knew?

As she washed her hands in the ladies room sink and checked her hair in the mirror, it struck her that maybe there was a bona fide reason for Maia's interest. After all, Brian had gone through a divorce and had some rough times and now he was working for her and they were spending time together. Maybe Maia thought they might be developing feelings for each other. Brian on a rebound? Lonely, awkward Frannie? She laughed out loud.

A woman exited the other stall. "You okay?"

"I am." She giggled some more. In the mirror, she saw a different face. A lighter face, with shiny eyes and upturned lips. She needed more laughter in her life.

Maia was sweet to worry about her brother. As she left the ladies room, she was tempted to tell her she didn't need to worry, that Brian had no romantic interest in her, not even much of a friendly interest. In fact, his interest apparently centered on his suspicions of her plans regarding Will's property.

But she didn't say it because Maia was kind and if Frannie had had a brother or sister to worry about, she might've cross-examined the new person in their life too. Now that she understood Maia's motivation, she was almost effusive as she thanked her for a fun lunch.

"I know so few people around here, this was especially nice. I'm glad you suggested it."

Maia patted her arm. "It was a good idea, wasn't it? What if Mr. Denman hadn't ordered those paintings? I'll make sure you have the chance to meet some of the other year-round residents. There's lots of folks worth knowing."

Frannie almost had to bite her lip to keep from laughing again. Maia was so transparent. She wanted to find someone else for Frannie, so her brother would be safe. Maia was so sweet she couldn't hold it against her.

Maia gave her a quick hug. "So, if you need anything at all, you let me know."

Chapter Twelve

Maia, again. He kicked the stand down, reached up and removed his helmet. Maia was upstairs in her apartment. Waiting.

What would it be this time? Your family misses you? You're not far away, but you might as well be a thousand miles distant.

Or would it be her speech about getting custody of Megan?

One topic he knew she wouldn't bring up was give Diane another chance. She says she's changed and you owe it to yourselves and your daughter to try. No, she would never go there again.

It was already getting dark and there was no shelter here on the street. The cold wind swept through like the idea of spring or summer was fiction. No point in sitting here freezing his butt off.

She was there at the door, the interior lights shining bright behind her. She opened it wide and smiled like the loving sister she was. Always ready to forgive. But he didn't necessarily feel forgiving.

"Brian." She threw her arms around him, saying, "I'm so glad to see you."

"It's cold out here."

"Come inside." She pulled him in and shut the door. She kept talking as she led him up the stairs to her flat. "Thanks for coming over. No Megan? So Diane came back?"

"This time." He dropped his jacket, gloves and helmet on a chair. He hadn't been over in a while. Maia's small flat was neat and homey, but arranged with perfection. An offshoot of her gallery touch.

"Hungry? I'll make you a sandwich." She was already halfway to the kitchen.

"No. I can't stay."

"Meatloaf. Cold meatloaf. I made it the way you like it, with onions and garlic. A meatloaf sandwich. On sourdough bread. Your favorite." A hint of a smile, her dark eyes earnest.

"Sure."

She pulled out the kitchen chair and gently pushed him down, sister-style.

"I'll have it ready in a minute." She leaned into the fridge and emerged with mayonnaise, mustard and a jar of dill pickles. "Coffee or soda?"

"Maia, I can't stay."

"Then stay as long as you can." She said it without turning around, as if keeping her back turned would force him to stay. "Don't say anything. Please listen. I've apologized before and I will again, if it will make any difference. I admit I should've minded my own business. I should've trusted your judgment regarding Diane and your own life." She turned to face him, knife in hand. She pointed it at him. "And I'll say it as many times as I need to."

"It's done. It's over. Let it go."

She whispered, "When you do." As she placed the plate on the table she said, "Guess who I had lunch with today."

"Just tell me."

Her tone dropped. "You know how rude that sounds, right?"

He ran his fingers through his hair in frustration. Not only frustration with her, but also with himself. It wouldn't cost him anything to be civil.

"Yes. Sorry."

"Is your leg hurting?"

He almost bit back at her again, but took a deep breath instead. After a moment, he replied, "Cold weather."

"Have you talked to the doctor? I'm sure there are options."

"Physical therapy and drugs. I've done PT and I don't want the drugs."

"Maybe you shouldn't ride that bike."

"I'll decide what I can manage."

She nodded and spoke in a very level voice. "I can't help being concerned."

It was Brian's turn to nod.

"So, lunch. I wanted to tell you about it. And you needn't worry that I'm messing in your life despite having lunch with your client."

The change of subject was almost a relief. "Client?"

"Yes, your painting client. Frannie Denman."

"Fran Denman? Why did you have lunch with her?"

"A number of reasons, and you can relax. The reasons have nothing to do with you."

"Okay."

"She's a client of the gallery. Not only as Mr. Denman's niece and representative, but on her own accord. She purchased a painting."

"I know."

"It's one of Juli's."

He watched his sister's face. He knew she wanted to tell him something despite his unwillingness to hear it. Gossip, interfering in other people's lives, it all did damage. He knew that personally. For Maia, though, it was different. She wasn't given to malicious gossip. But once she'd taken you into her 'fold' she felt very proprietorial, even protective, and did what was necessary—necessary as she saw it. He almost felt pity for her. It was a wonder she hadn't been hurt by them more often than she had. She needed a better life of her own so she could leave other people to tend to their own business.

"Okay."

"Did you know Juli was abandoned by her mother when she was young?"

"No. Yes. She was a foster kid, right?"

"Has Frannie talked about her family? She was adopted,

you know."

Brian hit the table, but softly. "Really, Maia? Is that why you took her out to lunch? To satisfy your curiosity?" He started to rise.

She reached out and touched his arm. "No. I told you. She's new and doesn't know anyone." Maia rushed into the next words as Brian turned away. "She and Juli have a lot in common. I was thinking they should get to know each other... Please don't go yet. I'll drop the subject. Can we start over and talk about something else?"

"Sure." But he was angry, too angry and he regretted the words before the last one left his lips. "Let's talk about why you have no love life of your own because you're so busy butting into everyone else's."

Wounded, that was the only word he could think of when he looked at her face. The words might be true, but that didn't mean he should say it to her like that, and it wasn't totally true. Not the way he'd made it sound.

"Not fair, Brian."

Her face had screwed up into that crying look. Even the trembling lips couldn't dampen her dimples. The top of her head came only to his shoulders and he felt like a bully. True words or not. Meant or not.

He put his arms around her. "I'm sorry. I shouldn't have said that."

She whispered, "And what about you, Brian?"

He shook his head. "Different situation. I tried and it didn't work for me. I'm done with this thing you women call love."

****

Brian stepped back as Diane left his apartment, pulling the door closed behind her. He grabbed the doorknob and fought the urge to chase after her in the winter rain. It had started that morning and was on and off, but the air was damp and bitter. Instead, turned to look at his daughter who was seated on the couch. As he watched, she scooted back, pulled her legs up beneath her and clutched her backpack tightly.

"Where's she going? What did she mean when she said a few days?"

Megan shook her head. She didn't speak and pulled at the strings of her backpack.

Only a backpack on her lap. He looked past her at his apartment. Two small rooms. And Megan was still sitting there, and now she was staring at him.

"A backpack. Is that all you brought with you?"

"My suitcase, too."

"Where is it?"

"It was in the car." She shrugged. "I guess I left it there."

Brian went outside. His daughter's child-size pink roller bag lay in the gravel, half in a puddle. He picked it up and brushed it off, but that didn't help where the water had already soaked through. Back inside, he set the suitcase on the living room floor.

"Get the wet things out and hang them in the bathroom."

She didn't acknowledge him, but did take the suitcase by its handle and roll it into the next room.

Now what?

He wasn't set up to take care of her. On the days when he had her, he picked her up and they went places and did stuff and then he took her back home. When she was on vacation, she spent time at his parent's home, but that wouldn't work this time because it was the middle of the school week and his parents lived north of Beaufort. Different county, different school district.

Diane wasn't his idea of a good mother, but the courts were okay with her, so he had to be.

He stood at the window and stared across the yard. In truth, he had options. They didn't have to stay in this cramped apartment. It was enough for him but cramped when a ten-year-old girl was added.

Megan could make do with the couch. It would only be a few days.

Meeting her at the bus stop wouldn't be a problem. If he

wanted to paint longer, Fran wouldn't mind if Megan came along. But what about today? He'd been about to leave when Diane changed his day.

Fran answered her phone right away.

He kept his back turned toward the bedroom and spoke in a low voice. "Megan's with me for a few days. No school today. Do you mind if she comes along?"

"She's always welcome."

"Thanks. Sorry for the inconvenience."

When he turned around, there she was. If her eyes had blades, he would've been headless.

"What?"

"I don't need a babysitter. I'm ten. I'm old enough to stay by myself."

"It's not about having a babysitter. It's about courtesy, and having the courtesy to ask instead of barging in."

"I wish Mom was here."

He almost responded, so do I, and then caught himself. "Life is what you make of it. You can spend your time wishing for what isn't, or find the good in what you have." He tried not to see the small, sparsely furnished apartment and tried not to imagine how long Diane might be gone this time.

****

Done for the day, he was putting the lid back on the can when Fran spoke from behind him.

"Does she do this often?"

Her voice was low. Megan was in the living room with the TV on.

"Diane, you mean?"

"Yes. Does she leave Megan without making arrangements with you in advance?"

"Nah. She might drop her off because she's got an appointment or a date, but that's only for a few hours and she usually gives me notice. Lately, it's been getting erratic."

Fran stayed by the doorway and peeked up the hallway. Reassured, she said, "It's not my business, but have you considered whether that home environment might not be the best for your daughter? Maybe your ex-wife has problems that she needs to take care of before she can concentrate on being a mom?"

"My place is small. A day here or there is fine, but I'm not set up for the practical side of fulltime fatherhood."

She breathed. "Aren't you already? A fulltime father?"

He was embarrassed. "I wasn't welcome. Diane didn't like me coming around, but I did. I'm always there when it's my day." He stacked the cans on the side of the room with the folded up plastic sheeting. "Look. I'm not claiming to be perfect. My situation isn't unique. I'll work it out."

"I don't doubt you will. I'm happy to help in the meantime."

Chapter Thirteen

The day before, Maia called and said, "Come as my friend."

"I don't know anyone. A party and strangers…."

The invitation was to a get-together at Juli and Luke's house. Nothing fancy, Maia said. Not dressy. Jeans were fine. A few friends….

A last minute invitation. A late addition. She didn't want to be that person.

Maia added, "Think about it. Don't say no yet."

Minutes after they disconnected, the phone rang again.

Joel said, "Frannie, how are you? Would you like to go out to dinner tomorrow evening?"

She scrambled for a polite excuse. "Sorry, Joel, but I already have plans." To make it sound true, she added, "A small get-together at a friend's house."

"Oh." He sounded disappointed. "Well, I'll be in the area anyway, so maybe we can find a few minutes to meet up."

"I'm sorry, but I'll be in and out. I don't want to waste your time."

"I understand."

And now, this afternoon, thinking about it, she knew he hadn't understood, not really, and her excuses hadn't kept his feelings from being hurt. She should've been blunt. Hurt was hurt.

She sat at the counter with her laptop and brought Will's household financial record up to date. Expenses, receipts, yikes. She wasn't an accountant and didn't want to be.

Someone knocked on the side door. She went through the kitchen to open it.

"Joel?" He stood right there on her doorstep despite her telling him not to come.

"Hi, Frannie!" He held out a small bag, brown with little handles. "I brought you a little something. A small gift." The smile stubbornly stayed on his face. "I hope I didn't come at a bad time."

"Yes. No. I thought we'd decided...."

"I hope you aren't angry."

She leaned against the door, puzzling. "I'm not angry. Come on in." She opened the door wide.

"Thanks. I'd love to." He stepped inside. "Your uncle has a nice place here."

His words were no more than a courtesy; this place was tiny compared to his family's homes, and simple. However, she'd grown fond of simplicity.

"Uncle Will loves it here."

"Easy to see why."

All the right, polite responses. He was so pleasant that it was an irritation, like that speck of something that gets into your shoe. You tried to get along with it, until finally, you had to stop and shake it out. But she couldn't do that to Joel.

"Would you like a cup of tea?"

"Whatever you're having." He placed the small brown bag on the coffee table.

"Have a seat." She gestured toward the dining table. "What brings you here? Emerald Isle is out of your way, isn't it?"

He shrugged, but his expression remained sunny. "I was in Hatteras and the weather was nice. I decided to swing by here on the way back."

"This is not a 'swing by' by any means."

"I had to come over to look at a couple of properties for my father, but that's on tomorrow's schedule. I took a chance on catching you in."

She added the steeped tea to the cups and placed them on the table.

"Do you still have plans for that party tonight?"

"Yes. It was kind of them to include me. It's small gathering. Nothing fancy." What a liar she was, and she was embarrassed about it, but only a little because she meant well, right? To save Joel's feelings?

His face lit up. "If I wouldn't be crashing, I'd be happy to go along with you. At least, you know me, right? A familiar face?" He grinned. "BYOF. Bring your own friend."

Frannie was stunned. This was totally unexpected. Joel inviting himself along? "I don't think it would be appropriate for me to bring someone."

The phone rang. Frannie grabbed it like a lifeline.

"You're coming to the party, right?" It was Maia.

"Um. I'm not sure."

"Oh, please come. You know you aren't a stranger now."

Glad that Joel could only hear her end of the conversation, she answered, "Well, actually I have an old friend visiting."

"Bring him or her. The more, the merrier."

It was on the tip of her tongue to ask why it mattered to Maia, but she stopped herself. Joel could go along and then Joel could go home. Maia would be happy she showed up and Joel would be her excuse for leaving early. It worked for everyone.

****

The Winters' house was on the sound side of the island. It was situated on the crest of a hill and the moonlight and bright exterior lights lit the landscape and house. A one-story house made of brick; it looked low and wide. Several cars were parked along the side of a curving asphalt driveway. Joel pulled in behind the last parked car.

Joel unsnapped his seatbelt. "It's peaceful out here. There's only a couple of lights on in the windows. If it weren't for the cars parked out here, I'd be wondering if we'd come to the right house."

"With that cloud cover, it's very dark out here." She

laughed. "Thank goodness for GPS."

They knocked on the door and a man answered. He was tall and slim with amazing cheekbones. Juli's husband.

He extended his hand. "Welcome. I'm Luke."

He had a beautiful smile. Odd thing to think about a man, but it was true.

"May I take your coat?"

Between Joel and Luke, the coat was slipped from her arms and someone else whisked it away. The men started speaking to each other, but the view ahead snared her attention and she walked toward it.

She glimpsed a kitchen on the left. Ahead of her the foyer opened into a wide area. There was a railing and there appeared to be a gap between it and a wall of windows. She leaned over the railing and looked down. A sitting area was below, but the windows in front of her stretched from the floor below to the ceiling above her head. The moon looked lonely in the black night while its reflection danced on the surface of Bogue Sound as the water moved in rhythm to currents she could only guess at.

A hand touched her shoulder. Joel spoke softly, "Frannie? Are you all right?"

"Quite a view, isn't it?"

"It is."

"Who knew all of this was hiding behind that demure brick front?" Wood and leather and stone, and a two story view of the sound.

"Oh, I'm so glad you made it!" Maia rushed up and hugged her.

"Thanks." She pointed to Joel. "This is my friend Joel. I hope you meant it, about bringing him, I mean."

"Oh, absolutely. The more, the merrier." She extended her hand. "Welcome Joel."

He shook her hand. "Thank you. I'm pleased to be here. Is this your house?"

She giggled. "Oh, goodness no. This is my boss's home.

125

Luke Winters. He owns the Front Street Gallery in Beaufort. Are you familiar with it?"

"Actually, I am. I've been there, though it's been a while. I love Beaufort. I'm overdue for a visit."

"Well, I hope you'll step in and say hey next time you come to town."

Joel smiled his usual, genial smile and said, "I will. It's a pleasure to meet you, Maia."

"Frannie?"

"Brian? I didn't know you were coming."

"Maia called."

She half-smiled. "Yeah, she called me, too."

"And a good thing I did. You can thank me later." She touched Brian's arm. "Joel, this is my brother, Brian. Brian, this is Frannie's friend."

Brian nodded. He extended his hand, saying, "Nice to meet you."

"You said it was a small get-together. There's a lot of people here."

Maia shrugged. "It's Emerald Isle. It's a small town at heart and everyone, especially in the year-round crowd, knows everyone. We're a friendly bunch." She took her arm. "Come along. Let me introduce you to some folks."

Frannie didn't know these people, but the nervousness she usually felt in a one-to-one situation wouldn't trouble her here. The armor that Laurel had fitted her for, slid over her, along with the right degree of smile. This Frannie occasionally said the odd, awkward thing, but she owned it like she meant it. No apologies. Like going onstage. Costume straight, yes. Makeup right? Check.

Maia took her arm and pulled her into the mix.

****

She talked to people. They were pleasant, and she congratulated herself on being appropriately sociable. Even Laurel would approve. Then she noticed a woman, distinctive in appearance. Tall, slender and with long salt and pepper gray hair. The woman looked up and they caught eyes. The woman moved toward her, a smile growing on her face.

"You are Frannie Denman."

She said it matter-of-factly and held out her hand. Frannie shook her hand, noting the firmness of her grip despite the woman's age.

"I'm Anna Barbour."

"Yes, I know your name. I saw it on a card at the Front Street Gallery, next to some paintings."

"That's me. I teach art locally and do a bit of my own." She waved off any further conversation about herself. "I know your uncle. I'm sorry for his illness."

"Did I see you at the rehabilitation home? On your way out, maybe?"

"You might have. I've visited Will a couple of times."

Frannie couldn't suppress her interest. "You're friends?"

"Yes." Anna nodded. "Although I haven't known him long, really."

Not a long acquaintance, but still a friend. "How did you meet?"

Anna set her empty glass down on a nearby table.

"No more iced tea for me or I'll be awake all night." She laughed and shrugged. "Goes with the age, I think. Your uncle came to my house to pick up a friend, one of my art students, Bill Dodge. A dear man, Bill was. They knew each other in the service."

"Bill Dodge. You said 'were'."

"He died recently. A heart attack in his sleep."

"I'm sorry."

"Well, we all get old…or we don't and that's another story. Bill had his health and was active right up until the time he went to bed that night." Her eyes grew bright and teary. "Sorry for that. So, I met your uncle and found him to be delightful."

Delightful. Frannie thought she, herself, might like to be thought of as delightful.

"I'm glad we had the chance to chat. Please tell Will I said hello when you see him next." She pressed her hand gently on Frannie's arm. "I need to find Juli and Luke and tell them good night. If you stay in town, I hope you'll drop by and visit."

Frannie resisted the impulse to follow her. There was a special glow about Anna that she couldn't quite make out. Maybe it was the aura of someone who knew who she was and was happy with it. Suddenly alone, Frannie looked around for Joel and saw him across the room speaking with a man she didn't know. Satisfied, she was turning away when someone tapped her shoulder.

"Having a nice time?" Brian asked.

"A lovely time. Everyone is very nice." She smiled in a breezy, relaxed way.

"You sound different. Not like yourself."

"Really? I don't know what you mean." But she did. She was wearing her party manners. He meant she sounded better. Better than her real self. She felt her lips tighten. She forced herself to speak in a friendly tone. "Where's Megan tonight? Back with her mom?"

"No. Diane's still away. Megan's with Danny. Juli asked her to babysit Danny this evening. She was ecstatic."

"She's only a child herself. Is it safe?"

"Oh, sure. Juli and Luke, not to mention Maia, are checking in on them every few minutes. They're down the hall." He added, "You didn't mention a boyfriend. Joel seems okay."

"Joel? He's not my boyfriend. He's a friend. I've known him for years. He showed up unexpectedly this afternoon."

"I see. Well, I'm glad you came even if it took Joel to get you here."

A man came up and slapped Brian on the back. He said something to Brian, and when Brian turned toward him, she took the opportunity to slip away. She wanted a quiet place in which to decompress for a moment or two.

In the hallway, she heard the soft whimper of a baby crying. Was she awake? It sounded so much like her dream that she almost pinched herself. She moved a few feet down the hall and put her ear to the door.

Perhaps Megan didn't know what to do? Or had fallen asleep? Children could sleep heavily. The cry wasn't frantic, but fretful.

She eased the door open.

A softly lit scene, a day bed was against the wall on one side and the white crib was on the other. Megan was standing beside the crib, her arm between the side slats and her hand patting the infant's back. She glanced up as Frannie walked over to her.

"He's crying on and off. Should I get Miss Juli?"

Frannie reached down and touched his small back. He was dressed in a soft, flannel one piece, blue with teddy bears on it. "I don't know. I can stay with him while you go find her."

"Would you? Thanks. I'll be right back."

Juli arrived within moments.

"Hi," she said softly as she came into the room. "Is he okay?"

She touched his dark hair and he didn't stir. "He's restless, I guess. He probably picked up on the craziness around here with us getting ready for the party."

Frannie nodded. "Thank you for inviting me, and I hope you truly didn't mind me bringing Joel."

"Not at all. I'm so glad you came and Joel seems very nice." Juli's hand stilled, but rested lightly on Danny's back in reassurance. "I understand you purchased my painting."

"Oh, yes. It's beautiful."

"That's not why I invited you."

"No?"

"Maia has so many good things to say about you. Brian, too." She turned her attention back to her son and tidied his blanket. "I hope you don't mind me telling you that. You don't know many people around here, right? It's always good to have friends. One never knows when one might need them. That's my personal experience, anyway."

"You three make a lovely family. I saw you and your husband and son at church."

"I'm sorry I missed you. I usually notice new faces."

"I've only been once."

"I hope you'll come again. Did you have enough to eat tonight? I told Megan to grab a snack before coming back. She's a sweetie."

A touchy sweetie, maybe. "She's clearly fond of Danny."

"She's good with him, but not really old enough to babysit. I told Brian to come and bring Megan with him. I told him she could hang out with Danny. I really expected her, and Danny, to be sound asleep by now." She walked over to the bed.

Something was peeking out from under the cover and she pulled it out. "Ah, a book." She flipped it over to read the cover then put it back under the blanket. "I'm glad to see she's a reader."

Danny stirred again and this time his cry was sharper. Juli leaned into the crib and gathered him up.

"I think he's teething."

Frannie watched her gather up the babe and lay him against her chest, his face snuggling into her neck. She touched the fragile head gently, cradling his small body. She looked over and said quietly, "Won't you have a seat and keep me company while I rock him for a few minutes?"

Jealously curdled in Frannie's belly. She sat because her legs felt weak. Perfect family. Attractive, loving parents, a cherished baby. Everything she didn't have and didn't expect to ever have because money couldn't buy it. She was grateful the dim light concealed her inner ugliness.

Juli's humming turned to soft words, "How do you like Emerald Isle?"

Frannie tried to match her tone, low and even. "I'm sure

it's more inviting in the summer."

"Spring. It's almost spring. That's my favorite time of year. Everything starts coming alive after being wrapped up in winter. I met Danny's father in the spring, and Danny was born in the spring."

"You grew up here?"

"No. Here and there." Her hand stilled on Danny's back. "I live in Raleigh."

"Beautiful city. They have the most amazing crepe myrtles."

Crepe myrtles. Silly, but that tiny connection reassured her, as if it meant she wasn't as far removed from this lucky woman and her perfect life as she'd felt in those dark moments.

"Your family moved around a lot?"

"Sort of. I grew up in foster homes."

Not so perfect, then. "Good ones, I hope. You seem to have come out very well."

Juli laughed very softly. Surely, Danny felt that comforting warmth coming from his mother.

"Not so much, but I managed. I didn't really get lucky until I met my husband, Danny's father."

"Luke. I hope you don't mind me saying that he's a very handsome man, and clearly devoted to you."

"Oh, he is, indeed, but he isn't Danny's father. That was Ben Bradshaw. He and Luke were cousins. No, Ben was the person who gave me the greatest gift and changed the course of my life."

Frannie wanted to ask why they'd divorced if Ben was such a great guy, but no amount of curiosity would entice her to cross that line.

Juli's soft brown hair fell across her cheek as she eased Danny from her shoulder and into her arm. She brushed his soft cheek, rosy from where his face had pressed against her blouse.

"Is he asleep?"

"Yes, but sometimes I just like to hold him. To give him a little extra loving to tide him over while we're apart. I try not to spoil him, but...oh, well."

"Giving him what you didn't get in the foster homes?" She shocked herself, asking such a personal question, but Juli didn't change expression at all. She continued smiling down at her Danny.

"Perhaps. I hadn't really thought of it, but it makes sense." Juli looked up at Frannie. "Who really understands the human heart?"

Frannie shook her head. "Not me."

"Did Anna find you? She wanted to speak with you before she left."

"She did. She told me how she happened to meet my uncle. She gives art lessons?"

"Yes, indeed. I've studied with Anna myself. I was there, you know. That day when he came by? That's how I met him. He was very sweet. Very gentlemanly."

"When was that?"

"Well, let me think. I was expecting Danny. About a year ago."

Juli gently repositioned Danny in her arms and stood. She laid him in the crib and wrapped the blanket more tightly around him. She touched his cheek and he stayed silent.

She motioned toward the door and the two women slipped quietly out into the hallway. Juli eased the door closed.

"I hope you're having a good time."

"I am."

They paused as they reached the large open area. The people she didn't know were moving around or standing in small groups chatting, but those she did—Brian, Maia, Joel and Megan—were huddled together at the end of the dining room table. Plates of food were being enjoyed and the conversation seemed lively.

Megan looked up as they approached. "Is Danny okay?"

Juli paused and leaned over to put an arm around

Megan's shoulders. "He's fine. Back in bed and sound asleep."

"I'm sorry I didn't know what to do."

"You did exactly the right thing." She placed a light kiss on Megan's forehead.

Megan glowed.

Brian looked pleased and proud.

Joel said, "Hey, Frannie. Brian has promised to show me some prime fishing spots."

"You fish?"

"Not in a long time." Joel jumped up and pulled another chair up close. "Have a seat."

Frannie put her hands on the back of the chair. Both Brian and Joel were watching her.

"I'll be back. I'll get a plate of food first."

"Have a seat and I'll fetch whatever you want."

"I'll take care of it. I'm not sure what I want."

Maia said, "I'll go with you, Fran. I need to check out the dessert table." She looked at Juli. "You've outdone yourself."

"I couldn't do it without Luke." She laughed as Luke joined her. "And neither of us could do it without Esther."

Frannie asked Maia as they walked away, "Who's Esther?"

"She's the housekeeper, but more importantly, she's the keeper of the recipes. Wait until you try her fudge."

"You are a chocolate fiend, aren't you?"

"Guilty." She handed Frannie a dessert plate. "I like your Joel."

"My Joel? He's a friend. I've known him most of my life."

"Sometimes those relationships lead to more."

"Not for Joel and me."

"What about Brian?"

Frannie fumbled her plate. It fell to the floor and the food scattered.

"Oh, no. Look what I've done."

"It's not a big deal." Maia helped retrieve the bits of fudge from the floor.

"I'm sorry. So sorry." She trembled inside. She'd lost her armor or maybe it had been knocked askew. Either way, she panicked.

"Frannie." She touched her shoulder. "It's nothing. Really. I mean it."

The rush of tension had nearly swamped her. She drew a deep breath. The words came out on their own.

"I always screw stuff up."

"What?" Maia looked incredulous.

And so, yes, she'd done it again. Her face grew hot and she felt queasy.

"Hang in there." Maia dug her fingers into Frannie's upper arm. "Come with me."

She led her out to the deck. The cold air hit her like a life preserver.

"Is this better? You turned so red. For what? For nothing. A piece of dropped fudge? You scared me."

"It was warm in there. It kind of hit me wrong."

"Okay, take another deep breath. I apologize for asking personal questions. I confess I have an ulterior motive."

Ulterior motive? She knew about those. Laurel had taught her well. She simply looked at Maia and didn't answer.

Maia leaned against the deck rail. The thick clouds had parted, and behind her the moon was fully round and surreal. It was impossible to look at Maia and miss that moon and the stars spreading out, filling the dark skies.

"About Brian, I mean."

"Brian?"

"He and I have been on the outs recently. I think I told you."

"You mentioned something." Not about her, then.

"He's angry with me, and not without reason." Maia hugged her arms. "I interfered between him and his ex, Diane. I convinced him to try again for Megan's sake. It was a mistake. I should've stayed out of it."

"Probably. But you're his sister. You did what you thought was best, right?"

"Good intentions. What's the saying?"

"The road to hell is paved with good intentions."

"Yikes. Well, I don't think I'm on that road." She touched Frannie's arm. "I want to thank you, though. You and Joel. I think Brian's warming up to me. He's been more himself this evening." She dabbed at her eyes.

"Don't cry out here, you'll have icicles hanging from your lashes."

Maia giggled. "It is pretty cold out here. I guess we'd better get back inside."

As they reached the door, Frannie said, "Thank you."

"For what?"

"For being a friend."

****

Shortly after Brian ushered a sleepy Megan out the door, Frannie told Joel it was time to go. She thanked Juli and Luke for a lovely time. Joel helped her on with her coat, and Maia told them goodnight. When they pulled into the driveway at Captain's Walk, Joel spoke.

"Can we talk for a moment?"

"Sure." Now what?

"The party was nice. I enjoyed meeting your friends."

"Friends? Maybe. Certainly, they are friendly. I had a good time, too."

"I need to ask you something. It's awkward, but it's important."

She couldn't say no, so she nodded and waited.

"How do you feel about me?"

"What do you mean?"

"How do you feel about me? You're always kind and friendly. A friend. Is there more or is that all?"

Awkward, but in true Joel fashion, he was dignified and gentle.

"You are a friend." Frannie shook her head. "I'm sorry if I gave the impression there was more. I don't play with people's feelings."

Joel stared straight ahead for a full minute before answering. "I see. Your mother suggested you felt more. She encouraged me to contact you. She said, well, that doesn't matter. Maybe she had it in her head that we'd make a nice couple." He met her eyes. "I think so, too, but that's only good if it goes both ways." He took her hand and kissed the back of it. "Thank you for being honest with me."

"Joel, thank you for being you." Her eyes felt misty. "I'm sorry."

"Don't be. I'll walk you to the door."

"No need. Take care, Joel." She slid from the car.

Joel sat with the headlights on while she climbed the stairs and unlocked the door. She paused and waved. His car didn't move right away, so she went inside.

Laurel. She should've realized Laurel wouldn't be content to stay out of it. What had she said to him? What mischief had she attempted?

Joel's gift was sitting on the coffee table. Oh. A twinge of guilt. She went over and picked it up, opening the bag gingerly.

Tea. One of her favorite blends. Plus a box of the little bags for making one's own teabags.

She sagged back against the sofa, dissatisfied. It wasn't that she didn't appreciate the thought, plus it was nice that people were aware she enjoyed tea—as if they could miss it. But if gift-givers didn't know what else to get her, then maybe she was hiding herself too well.

****

She picked out a couple of items, a framed photo and a tiny ship in a bottle, to take to the rehab. It would be a little piece of home for Uncle Will.

She went straight to his room. He wasn't there. She situated the frame and ship on the windowsill, which was more eye level than the top of the bureau. The small room seemed so empty, so anonymous, without him. Too restless to sit and wait, she wandered down the hallway in the direction of the dining room and the physical therapy room. She was bound to find him in one place or the other. Both were down the hall and to the left.

As she reached the corner, she almost crashed into a couple of people—or they nearly rolled into her.

Seeing the wheelchair, she tried to reverse direction too fast and stumbled, catching herself against the wall.

Was he laughing? One frail hand was raised as if he might've attempted to catch her if she'd fallen in his direction, but the grin was broad, and yes, the noises coming from him sounded a lot like laughter. Uncle Will. And pushing the chair? Brian.

Brian flew around from behind the wheelchair and grabbed her arm. "Steady now?"

Frannie looked back and forth between them and then settled on Brian.

"What are you doing here?"

"Visiting?" He released her.

"Uncle Will, were you laughing?" She asked in mock horror, now that her heart had slowed. "You two were hot-rodding it down the hallway and nearly ran over me."

He pointed at her. "Fran." A breath. "Okay?"

"Uncle Will!" Her eyes stung. "Yes, I'm fine."

"Will was doing his PT."

"On Saturday? Isn't that during the week?"

"Yeah, but we do a little low-level workout on the weekend."

"Really? How do you know what to do?"

"No worries. I've worked it out with the therapist."

"I wasn't worried, but...oh, here's lunch."

"We'd better get back."

Brian wheeled him into the room and then positioned the adjustable table over his legs.

"Where's Janet?" Frannie asked.

"Running an errand. I told her I'd handle lunch."

"But he has trouble eating."

"We'll take it slow and easy. Is that right, Will?"

She let Brian take the vinyl-covered chair and she perched on the foot of the bed. Brian spoon-fed her uncle, but without any of the cutesy or condescending stuff. Man to man. If Will tried to say something. Brian would ask him to wait or slow down. He was so patient. Such patience wasn't in her. She knew it wasn't.

"Well, hello, there! I see I missed lunch." Janet came walking in, unbuttoning her coat at the same time.

"Hello, Will. Hi, there, Brian. And Fran. Looks like a small party is happening here. Are y'all having fun without me?" She hung her coat in the narrow closet. "How'd the workout go?"

Uncle Will raised one hand and wagged his index finger up and down.

"Very funny. I hope you got more done than that."

****

"How is it that you haven't mentioned these visits?"

"Was I supposed to?"

"I get the feeling that this is a regular thing."

"I try to be here every weekend. Sometimes Saturday. Sometimes Sunday. We do simple movements. Goof around some."

"I had no idea."

"What is it, Fran? Was I supposed to clear it with you?"

"No. Not at all." She was stunned by his reaction. "I wasn't being critical. I was impressed." She thought about it. "Was, that is, until you decided to be mean." She turned to walk away.

He grabbed her arm. "Just a minute. Impressed? Why?"

"Your patience. With Will, at least."

"You didn't look impressed. You looked like you were cross-examining me."

"Honestly, what's up with you? Why are you so cranky?"

He dropped his hand. "I'm sorry. I guess I was remembering when I was here for my own therapy. I wasn't the best patient. Not a patient patient."

"So this is where you got your training?"

He stared at her as if she'd grown a third eyeball right in the middle of her forehead.

"What's wrong?" She whispered, made uneasy by the intensity of his gaze.

He reached over and she waited, mesmerized, as he touched that space between her eyebrows, softly, gently. What was going on? She didn't know, but she held still, hardly breathing. His fingers slid down, tracing her jaw line and stopped on her throat. Before she had to make a decision regarding his behavior or her response, he pulled away. She didn't move.

"Join me for coffee? Maybe a bite to eat?"

She exhaled and found her voice. "Is this a date?"

"I don't know. I guess we'll figure that out."

She nodded.

Frannie followed him down Arendell Street. He rode his motorcycle. His bike was faded and dented. Reminded her of his manners. But then who was she to critique anyone's interpersonal skills? She was pretty sure she'd presented a calm façade during the…moment. She reached up and touched that spot between her eyes. She felt the two furrows and wished she could make them go away, and maybe erase a couple of years while she was at it. Maybe she should see a plastic surgeon.

Dinner with Brian. The idea made her stomach flip around a little. Play it cool. It's dinner, not a commitment.

They passed restaurants as they drove until finally, he turned into the parking lot of a small restaurant.

Irrationally, now that they had finally arrived, she was tempted to press her foot down on the accelerator and keep on going.

Chapter Fourteen

He was already off his bike and waiting, helmet in his arm, as she pulled up in the parking space next to his and got out of her car.

She asked, "I know the weather's been milder, but it's not really bike weather, is it?"

"Depends on the rider."

He held the diner's door open for her and when she headed toward the tables off to the left, he steered her to a booth over by the windows. Not much real privacy, but at least the tall board between the booths gave the illusion. He helped her off with her coat, thinking it had been a long time since he'd done that. He unzipped his jacket and stripped off his gloves, dropping them next to his helmet while Fran carefully folded her coat and laid it on the seat next to her purse before she slid in.

She sat so straight. Some sort of extreme posture. He had a flash of that scene from the movie Titanic. The one where the girls were taught to sit like that. The idea of Megan in one of those lacey dresses and sitting with a board-straight back at a tea table almost choked him. Then, in a brief flash, he felt a loss, as if important things were missing in Megan's life and it was his fault. But not that. Megan would kill him if he tried to make her do that. The thought made him smile and Fran smiled back.

"Have you been here before?"

"Many times. It's not fancy, but the food's good and it's easy on the wallet. You haven't been here?"

"No."

"I thought everyone in eastern North Carolina had eaten here at one time or another."

"Cox Family Restaurant." She read from the menu.

"I forget that you're from west of I-95."

"Hah. You say that like it's a different country."

"It sorta is." He watched her focus on the menu items, running one finger down the list, moving like a speed-reader. Her finger came to a halt.

"Something look good to you?"

She tapped the menu. "Grilled cheese. I don't think I've had a grilled cheese sandwich since I was a child." She smiled. "It reminds me of my dad and autumn afternoons. Not sure why. I guess there's memories deep down inside somewhere."

"Your dad. You don't talk about him. About your mother some, though I can't say it's good. But not about your dad at all."

"My dad died when I was a teenager." She drummed her fingers on the table. A sharp drumming, then an abrupt stop.

Her eyes, her fingers, moving and fidgeting like when she was watching him paint. Always moving except for when he'd seen her with Megan.

"Laurel is my stepmother."

"Yeah? As in evil stepmother?"

"No, that sounds childish and, besides, she's actually my adoptive mother. I've only just found out and I'm still getting used to the idea. She and I have some things to work out."

"Just found out?"

She grimaced. "Long story and not good for the digestion."

She'd said it with finality and he let it go. "You're a mystery woman."

"Me? Sorry to disappoint, but there's nothing about me or my life worth being mysterious about."

"Order?"

They both jumped. He didn't recognize the waitress. He knew most of them and would've engaged this one in conversation, but didn't want to annoy Fran by making it look like he was flirting in front of her, so he jumped right into ordering.

He asked her, "Grilled cheese for you, right? Coffee or soda?"

She raised her eyebrows. He knew right away he should've let her speak for herself. Maybe her edginess was catching.

"Do you have sparkling water? With a slice of lemon?"

The waitress said, "No, ma'am. Glass of water?"

"That will be fine." She threw up her hand. "No, wait. Do you have iced tea?"

"Sweet or unsweet?"

"Sweet tea. Yes, with lemon, please."

Sweet tea. Yet she looked so pleased with herself. Almost smug. But those eyes. Was it the innocence in them, or the wariness that kept snaring him?

She caught him staring. "What about Megan? It's not a school day."

"She's with Diane."

"Her mom's back?"

He shrugged. "Yep. No idea where she went. She didn't have much to say about it." He'd asked, for all the good it did him. "She's keeping her secrets to herself."

"Secrets." Frannie sighed and put her elbow on the table and rested her cheek against her hand. "Now that I think of it, by the time a woman gets to be my age she ought to have a few secrets."

"I'd say so." He grinned. "It's not that hard to get into enough trouble to have some. I can give lots of advice on that."

"I'll let you know if I need some of that advice."

Was she flirting? Sounded like it. "You seem more relaxed now. In the beginning, you were pretty nervous."

She shrugged, but looked down at the pepper shaker as if it were fascinating. "You were a stranger. Isn't every woman uneasy around strange men?"

He tried not to laugh and it came out sounding like a snort. "Actually, no."

"Well, I am."

"Do you mind if I ask what you do for a living?"

"Do? As in a job?"

"Yes. You must have a very flexible employer if you can hang around here for several weeks without them complaining. Or maybe you took leave?"

"I tried a couple of jobs, but they didn't work out. Mostly, I do volunteer work. A little here, a little there."

"Isn't it boring, staying at someone else's house? With not much to do, I mean."

She shook her head. "It's too far to keep driving back and forth. Besides—"

"Besides what?"

"I'm enjoying the break from Laurel."

Brian found himself pushing the salt shaker back and forth between his hands. He set it aside.

"Am I getting too personal?"

"Like I said, I don't have any secrets. Other people, but not me."

"So you live at home?" He stopped short of adding still.

Sigh. "I moved back home for a while and stayed. It's only my…Laurel and me. She was lonely after father died. She asked me to live at home while I was going to college, so I did, but when I graduated, I insisted on striking out on my own and she was supportive, but, well, there were problems and I went back. I didn't intend to stay with her, but you know how that is."

"How what is?"

"Best laid plans."

"I do know how that is." He did know and he knew how painful reality could be. He smiled but thought it probably looked forced, so he dropped the attempt. He sat back abruptly as he realized the waitress had returned with his food.

"Oh, wow. This looks good." Fran picked up one half of the sandwich and blew on it lightly. "And hot."

"Now, what about you? Let's talk about you for a change. I'm willing to bet that your life has been a lot more interesting than mine." She bit into her sandwich like she was punctuating her sentence.

"Me? Okay, fair is fair. I was married. We had a daughter. We divorced. She wanted the divorce, but in the end she did me a big favor."

"She has custody?"

"Technically, we share custody."

"But she lives with her mom."

"My apartment is small. I'm not really set up for long term stays." He chewed on his burger, seeing those lines between her eyes again. Knowing she wasn't accepting or at least, not approving, his excuse.

"When did you hurt your leg?"

"After the divorce. Actually, so you know, we were in the middle of a fight over primary custody of Megan when it happened." Maia had urged him to consider reconciling because Diane had changed her attitude. "We had a fight and I had a wreck. My rehab was long. Megan ended up with her mom." After a pause, he ended with, "Since then, my life has been unsettled."

She seemed to be savoring the second half of the sandwich, not wolfing it down like the first half, yet her eyes stayed on his face as she listened. Big eyes. Eyes so dark blue, almost navy blue, almost black, yet the lights in them brought to mind the depths of the ocean when sunlight makes it through, pressing down through the deep water. Long lashes like…like he didn't know what, but they gave her big, round eyes that should've looked innocent, a serious look. Mysterious. Yet, Fran was the least mysterious brunette he'd ever met. She was a puzzle, though, full of puzzling contradictions.

"Life, huh? Nothing's ever easy. And the easier it would seem to be, the messier it gets."

"Sorry. You lost me."

"Like me." Fran pointed at herself. "I've had everything going for me my entire life, except for losing my dad, and yet I feel like I'm still waiting for it to start."

"Waiting for what to start?"

"My life. I always have the sneaking suspicion that

someone else, anyone else, would've done a better job with it."

Brian shrugged. "Maybe. But then it's really about perspective, right? I mean, it's about how you see it. Like the glass half-full, half-empty thing. Sometimes you have to find a better perspective to look at it from."

"Is that how it works for you?"

"I do the best I can."

Frannie closed her eyes and groaned. Opening them, she said, "Sorry. I'm always saying the wrong thing." She managed an embarrassed little chuckle. "Thank goodness this is just sharing food, and not a date."

Brian asked, "Not a date?"

She gave him a funny little smile and tilted her head as she asked, "Is it? Is this a—"

Chapter Fifteen

"Is this what?"

A feminine voice startled them, maybe him more than her, she thought, because Brian almost jumped to his feet before he gathered his cool and sat back down.

The woman leaned against the upright post of the booth and laughed. Petite and blonde, she wore jeans so tight that Frannie hurt for her.

"Hello, Brian." She waved her hand toward Frannie. "This is your new friend that Megan was telling me about?"

"She's my friend, yes." He looked around. "Where's Megan?"

"Ladies room. Aren't you going to introduce us?"

"Fran, this is Diane."

Frannie tried not to stare. There was something a little past pretty about Diane—like a hard way of living that was about to eat away enough of her prettiness to age her, make her look worn. She blinked and looked away, and saw Megan as she came around the corner. Megan saw her mom and then saw who was seated in the booth. She did a quick stutter-step.

Diane put her arm around Megan's shoulders and pulled her in close. "Hey, Megan, say hello. Use your manners."

Megan looked wooden. Or maybe sullen. Far from friendly.

"We're on our way to do some shopping. We've got special plans. Isn't that right, sweetie?"

Brian's face was turning dark. Frannie tried to break the tension.

"You've got a lovely daughter, Diane. And smart." She looked directly at Megan. "I hope you'll come by soon so we can visit again."

Diane ignored her. "We have to be on our way now. Nice to meet you." And they left.

Had Megan been upset to see them together? She wouldn't be the first kid to cherish the dream that her parents would get back together. She felt sad for Megan. If looks and behavior indicated anything at all, Brian was right—Diane had done him a favor by leaving him. It was sad that Megan was caught in the middle.

"Sorry," Brian said.

"About what?" She was reluctant to assume. After all, it was possible he was sorry they'd been seen together.

"Let's drop it." His good humor was gone. "Are you done?"

Apparently, the fun was spoiled all the way around. In a really sick way, she was more comfortable with that than with everything going well. She was more comfortable with the half-empty glass.

"No." He said it so loud, it startled her.

"No?"

"She won't win." He hit the table, but gently. "We won't let her spoil the day."

A small electrical charge tickled her spine. He'd found their time together good enough to be able to be spoiled. She asked, "What would you like to do?"

"Let's get out of here."

At that moment, she thought she'd follow him anywhere, but the feeling wouldn't last. That was for sure.

"If it was warmer I'd take you for a ride on my bike." He looked like he was still considering it. "Come on."

"The bike—"

"No, don't worry. Follow me. We'll drop the bike off at my place."

He signaled the waitress and handed her some bills, told her to keep the change, then helped Fran on with her coat and hustled her out. She could already feel her feet dragging with doubt.

In the car, once again following in his wake, she started thinking of excuses to duck out on him. His energy seemed reckless. It made her uneasy. But also excited.

****

They left Morehead City and crossed the bridge back to the island. In an area along Atlantic Avenue where the live oaks grew thick and were entangled in masses of green growth more effective than a man-made privacy barrier, there were few houses to be seen, but only driveways, and they turned off onto one of them. It sloped up between the tall jungle-like hedges and emerged into an open area, landscaped to wintry perfection and complementing a large house.

He'd said a small apartment, right? This place was substantial.

He continued around the side. She followed and saw Will's van parked next to a garage. A single story garage, but wide and deep. There were three wide garage doors and one of them lifted and Brian pulled his bike inside alongside a shiny, expensive looking SUV. As she drove around she saw the door and windows. His apartment was behind the garage.

She'd planned to wait for him in her car, but instead she got out. The back yard was as private as the front, surrounded by wild hedges mixed with live oaks and pines. The house was buff-colored stucco with a slate patio. On the far side of the yard was a covered pool.

The house looked and felt empty. Any outdoor furnishings were stowed away somewhere. The windows had a vacant feel.

"I live in the garage apartment and keep an eye on things."

"It's beautiful back here. Even this time of year. Absentee owners?"

"Sure."

She did a three-sixty, slow and appreciative. "Very peaceful. Secluded."

"No one bothers me here."

Sad, somehow. She looked at his light blue eyes and the

lines around them. Sad, maybe, but he didn't look unhappy.

"Would you like to come inside?"

Inside? Instantly, her defenses flew up. She stepped away. "No, thanks."

"Hey, I didn't mean anything. Relax."

She'd offended him. Maybe he hadn't meant anything. She'd overreacted. "Sorry."

He laughed. "Don't be. Wait here and I'll get my other jacket. I don't need this one if I'm not riding. It's not that cold."

She watched him go. Her feet were cold. She could've gone inside. He wasn't a monster. Not all men were. She shivered.

Frannie walked up to the patio doors. With her hands cupped around her face, she could make out the dark forms of furniture, the occasional odd shape of a vase or a lamp, shadowed in the unlit interior. Uncle Will's house might not be a match for this, but good things could also come in smaller packages. It only needed the right touch.

"Boo."

She jumped and spun and found herself in Brian's arms. Her reaction, the heart pounding and knees softening, were almost instantaneous and alarming. He tightened his arms, pulling her in close to his chest.

For one long breathless moment, they held that pose, and then he smiled and slowly eased his arms away.

"Steady?"

Steady? Was that intended to steady her? "I'm fine."

"Glad to hear it." He stepped back. "I have the key to the house. Would you like to take a look inside?"

"No thanks."

He laughed.

She was confused. And annoyed. He was playing games, toying with her.

His phone rang. He looked at the screen and said, "Excuse me." He stepped a few feet away. "Yeah?" A pause as the listened. "At the apartment."

Was she grateful or annoyed at the interruption? She waited, trying to figure it out.

Brian said, "Can't you get a tow or a mechanic?" Then, "I see. But...." He finished with, "Got it. Hold on." He put his hand over the phone speaker and asked, "Change of plans? Maia needs help. She's stuck at the gallery with a flat."

"Sure. No problem. I can get myself home."

"About twenty minutes." He spoke into the phone and then returned it to his pocket. "The problem is that this late on a Saturday she can't get anyone else."

"I understand, totally. Everyone should have someone who'll rescue them when needed."

"Come with me. You can keep Maia company while I change the tire, otherwise, she'll talk me to death." He grinned. "She could distract me. I could be injured."

She laughed. "All right. I'll drive."

She drove, but Brian ruled the car. He changed the station to country music and worked the invisible passenger side brake vigorously at every light. Her nerves were nearly fried by the time they arrived at the gallery.

Brian guided her down the back alley. Maia's car was parked close to the rear of the building. Customer parking was across the street in lots fronting the marinas. Back here there was only enough space for two, maybe three, cars.

She must've been watching for him. She came out the back door, saying, "Hi! Hey there, Frannie. How'd he talk you into coming along? Not only along, but driving him?"

She smiled and waved hello, then slid her hands in her pockets. She should've brought her gloves, but then she'd expected to be home long before this. It seemed ages had passed since she'd run into Brian at the rehab home. This felt awkward.

Maia handed over her keys. Brian popped the trunk and Maia was right there telling him how to find the jack and going on about the spare and such. Brian was complaining that the way she'd parked left little room for him to work. He added, "Take Fran inside. She's freezing."

Maia looked at him oddly. "You just want me to get out of your way. Frannie. Come on in. Let's have some hot chocolate."

As soon as the door closed, Maia said, "Well?"

"What?"

"Hah." Maia put the water kettle on to heat and pulled out the mugs and the packets of hot cocoa mix. "I sense an interesting story here."

"Like what?"

"Well, for one thing, Brian said he was at his apartment when I called him."

Her faced flamed. Maia's insinuation mingled with the suspicions she'd had of Brian's invitation to tour his apartment, and the house, like a couple of....

"Uh oh. I guess I shouldn't have asked?"

"It's nothing. We ran into each other while visiting Uncle Will."

"And?"

"And we went out for a bite after."

"That's nice." Maia's grin was aggravating and contagious. She turned her back to fix the hot chocolate and then brought the cups over to the table. She shrugged. "None of my business anyway."

"No, really. That's all there was to it." Frannie sat back. "Oh, I see. You're joking."

Maia laughed. "I am. I'm sorry. I'm almost giddy. It's so wonderful to see Brian interested in someone. And this time, it's someone nice."

"Really, it was food."

"Maybe for you, but Brian doesn't hang out with anyone whose company he doesn't enjoy, not man or woman. You've got his attention."

"I didn't ask for it."

Maia tilted her head and looked at Frannie questioningly. "Not the response I was expecting. Truly, I wasn't suggesting you were chasing him. Heaven knows, he's no catch. I mean,

I'm his sister and I love him, but he's way more trouble than he's worth if someone's only looking for a boyfriend or a good time." She sipped her hot chocolate. "He's had a rough few years." After a pause, she added, "As I told you before, some of it's my fault."

Possible replies flitted through Frannie's brain—not your fault, people are responsible for their own decisions—seemed the best, but she didn't give any of them voice. She decided to let the moment rest.

Maia sighed. "I promised Brian not to interfere again. Yet, listen to me teasing you. I like the idea that you and he are getting along. It's good for him. I hope it's good for you." She waved her hands. "And now I wash my hands of it. If I butt into your business again, you have my official permission to throw something at me."

Frannie pictured herself throwing something at Maia, maybe a pillow, and broke into giggles.

Maia eyed her suspiciously, and said, "I'm thinking you look like a girl with a secret."

She laughed. She laughed so hard, she clutched her middle and tears formed at the corner of her eyes. Maia laughed, too, and Frannie laughed at Maia laughing.

As the laughter wound down, she picked up her hot chocolate and raised the mug high, saying, "To secrets—every girl should have a few."

Chapter Sixteen

He shouldn't have let his temper get the better of him. When Diane appeared and threw her special brand of poison around, he should've kept it cool, but Fran had been a good sport. He'd been enjoying testing her defenses until Diane interrupted. He wasn't sure why he enjoyed teasing Fran. There was something about her that begged for....what?

Something in her eyes. And her kindness to Megan. And an attraction he felt for no good reason that showed how bad his judgment was. First, Diane. A disaster. Now Fran, a woman who was as screwed up he was, but at least he knew she wouldn't harm a flea. She'd be more likely to get eaten up by them and then blame herself for not wearing bug spray.

Out there at the house, he'd almost kissed her. Instinct had pulled him back. What was it about her? His instinct had told him 'not yet'. Maybe never. Two screwed up people weren't likely to equal a whole.

He pushed up to his feet. His thigh has suffered from the kneeling and the cold. Not too bad, though. Curiosity helped him move along faster. The laughter was so loud it came right through the door. Sounded like he was missing a party.

Maia had better not repay his help with interference. Not only did he not want it, but when in full form, Maia's matchmaking could be heavy-handed. It would scare off someone as skittish as Fran in a heartbeat.

Not sure why he cared. But he did.

He secured the jack in the trunk and rolled the flat around to the back of the car. He hoisted it into the trunk and then slammed the trunk closed with his elbow and headed toward the door. His hands were grimy.

As he entered he heard Maia say, "Have you thought about looking for her?"

Fran said, "I have. I don't know where to begin. I thought about hiring a private investigator but I have so little to tell him. I don't know if I should...or even if I want to."

"If you don't, won't you always be wondering if you should've?"

"Enough, Maia." He walked past, angry, and yanked the faucets to get the water running. He soaped up his hands. "Fran can handle her own business."

The silence, aside from the sound of running water, was profound. He refused to turn around and look at their faces. As he rinsed the soap from his hands, Fran spoke.

"I told her about my mother situation. I can discuss this with anyone I want. It's my choice. I want her opinion."

He dried his hands and tossed the paper towel in the trash. "Suit yourself."

Maia's face was red and her eyes were downcast.

He almost felt guilty. Almost. But he knew very personally what could happen when people interfered in other people's business.

"Fran. Ready to go?"

Fran ignored him and walked around the table to give Maia a hug. Maia was tearing up. Anything to make him feel in the wrong. That's what women did. He was sorry she was hurt, but he had to stand his ground.

She whispered, "Thank you for changing the tire."

He stopped and looked back. "It's the spare. Make sure you get that tire over to the shop tomorrow. Don't drive on it more than absolutely necessary."

"Yes, sir."

But she said it with a twist, as if there was some sort of irony in him telling her not to drive on the spare. But that was about safety. His sister's safety. Not about being bossy or intrusive. It wasn't the same thing at all.

By then, Fran was already out and at the wheel. She was

staring straight ahead with a stony expression on her face. He climbed into the passenger seat.

Icy, that's what she projected. Fine. He put his head back and closed his eyes. He could play that game.

Chapter Seventeen

Trust Brian to bring a lovely, promising day to a sour conclusion.

At least he was a better passenger when he was asleep, even if he was pretending. He didn't want to hear what she thought about his behavior, so she looked straight ahead, unwilling to make the situation worse or better. It was what it appeared to be—a standoff. Brian resented Maia for interfering between him and Diane, but this seemed more like a grudge. It was unbecoming in a grown man. And poor Maia. How could he talk to her that way? In front of her, Frannie? How humiliating for Maia and embarrassing for Frannie.

She was fortunate to see his true colors now.

The daylight was almost gone as she drove onto the estate and dropped Brian by the garage. With the loss of the sun, the air had grown cold. Winter had returned. It took everything she had to keep her lips sealed and to not say goodbye or good riddance. As soon as he shut the car door, she took off.

It was a short drive back to Will's house.

Frannie pushed her coat collar up around her neck and chin as she sat on the porch at Captain's Walk.

The dead looking weeds on the dunes moved slightly, whispering as the light breeze played through them.

Brian. Laurel. Both bullies at heart. Petty tyrants.

The house painting wasn't done. Two bedrooms, the kitchen and hallway still needed to be painted. Would he show up to finish the job?

She kind of wanted him to. Why? So they could resume their argument? Stupid.

The rocker treads squeaked to the rhythm of just as well,

just as well. It was a sad refrain. She couldn't continue to use this as a hiding place indefinitely. At some point, she'd have to declare this job done and move on. On the other hand, she couldn't declare anything done until she knew what Uncle Will's final recovery would look like.

What was so wrong with a good hiding place? She laughed out loud. The sound startled her, seeming brash as it broke the silence. It reminded her again that she was alone. There was no one here to laugh with. Was there ever? No matter where she was, she was alone.

There were lights far out on the horizon. Passing ships. The beach was empty. The water was deadly cold. Depressing. She wished for a change of heart. Star light, star bright, grant the wish I wish tonight. Like maybe a heart that would see this as peaceful, not desolate. As an opportunity to relax and play, not as a place to hide away from things she wanted to avoid.

But that was up to her. No one could work that magic for her.

She remembered the verse that had fallen on the floor when Brian was moving stuff around.

Wherefore if any man is in Christ, he is a new creature: the old things are passed away; behold, they are become new.

A new creature. A new person. The words suggested a change of heart was required, but if she hadn't managed to fix herself in thirty-one years, it wasn't likely to happen now.

****

On Sunday, she returned to Uncle Will's church. Juli's church. She and Juli and Luke might not be real friends yet, but they were friendly acquaintances and she could feel comfortable approaching them. They had it all. Looks, contentment, each other, and a successful business and gorgeous home. Aside from that moment in the nursery, she wasn't jealous. They seemed like a rare species—a happy couple and loving family. She wished she knew how to emulate their success.

This time, Juli saw her and waved. They spoke briefly

after the service. The pastor made a point of finding her after the service and speaking with her. She'd made some mental notes thinking all of this could contribute to her conversational monologue on the next visit to Will.

A week had passed since she'd run into Brian at the rehab. They'd had a delightful day, until his sharp words to his sister ruined it. She hadn't seen him since. Not even a telephone call. The top of the paint cans had accumulated a thin layer of dust.

She'd stood by those cans and considered popping the tops herself and wielding a paintbrush.

Nope. Before she did that, she'd hire another painter. But it wasn't time for that yet.

Her Sunday afternoon visit with Will was brief. He wasn't there. Janet wasn't around either. Frannie sat for a while, waiting and counting ceiling tiles. She noticed the framed photos she'd brought were turned toward his bed so that he could see them with his head on the pillow. A little glow warmed her at having thought to bring them. That had been a good thing to do. Finally, she gathered up her bag and coat. She found an aide and asked about her uncle. The woman said Janet had taken him out for the afternoon.

That sounded positive. She wished she'd known. She might have liked to go along.

She went back to Captain's Walk and packed her duffel bag.

****

The next morning, Monday, Frannie headed back to Raleigh.

Laurel had called during the past week. She was going to Savannah to spend a few days with an old friend. The timing was close to perfect from Frannie's perspective. She could stay at the house and not have to deal with Laurel. She intended to search the house in case any clues remained, however unlikely, but first she had a date at the official records office.

She submitted the paperwork and paid her fee and then sat to wait.

"Ma'am?"

Frannie walked up and held out her hand. She felt like she was crossing a threshold. This was becoming an important year in her life, maybe the most important, and this was likely to be one of the pivotal moments that formed a part of it.

"Thank you."

It wasn't pivotal. This certificate had the same details as the one she'd seen, so it hadn't been doctored. It left her feeling bereft. Irrationally bereft because it only meant that there was another explanation, and she would find it.

She looked up, aware that others were waiting, but she had to ask. "Would I be able to tell if this document wasn't the original? I mean, for instance, if the certificate was reissued as a result of an adoption?"

"Those records are sealed."

"But it's about me? How can they be sealed?" She knew that's how it was done, but from her perspective it seemed unfair and required some kind of protest. When the clerk gave her printed information and suggested she should consult an attorney, she thought of Andrew Lloyd.

Frannie drove to the house. When she arrived, she hit the garage door opener. It was empty. Good. She pulled in. She hadn't used the garage in ages. There was room for two cars, but she left the space to Laurel. It was understood the garage was Laurel's territory.

It truth it was Frannie's territory. All hers.

Her dad had left a lot of money to Laurel, but most of his estate was left in trust to her and the trust had ended when she turned twenty-five, By then she was back home, living with Laurel. Those brief years on her own, after she'd graduated from college, had been grim. She'd had a bad breakup with her fiancé—to put it mildly—and lost her job in the resulting emotional chaos.

Even after several years of therapy, some baggage was

difficult to excise. Her excess baggage had kept her tied to home and Laurel in a way that was unhealthy, even aside from any fault on Laurel's part. Just as Brian's came between him and his sister.

She went straight to the tea cabinet, pulled out the canister of her favorite evening tea and turned the water on to heat. The water was the right temp, one hundred and ninety-five degrees, in less than a minute. Five minutes to steep and voila, she held her face over the steaming cup and absorbed only good feelings. A brief meditation. Something to focus on when you didn't want to think about anything else.

She pulled the cookie tin down and slipped a few shortbread cookies onto a small plate. Since Laurel wasn't home, she'd take her tea and cookies in the TV room. The comfy room—the one with Dad's saggy sofa and the TV.

The old sofa was gone, along with the scarred TV cabinet. The television, a huge, flat-screen flashy looking piece of electronics, was now situated in a mahogany cabinet that stretched nearly the length of one wall.

Furniture. Just furniture. And yet, in the same way that the garage was considered Laurel's territory, this had been hers.

The saggy, shaggy sofa was now a sleek black leather couch with armrests all along it like individual seats. It curved. Had Laurel created a media/entertainment room? The coffee table was gone. Where was she supposed to set her cookie plate and tea?

The big picture window at the end of the room had new drapes—black ones. No doubt they were for blocking the daylight. They'd also block the view of the crepe myrtles and Carolina pines, the best feature of this room.

Frannie sat on the floor, on the new white carpet. She tried to recapture the mood, but anger kept surging in like a tide. She wrapped her arms around her legs and hugged her knees, rocking back and forth. The tea spilled. It soaked into the nap of the rug, staining it light brown. She threw the cookie plate. It hit the cabinet, but landed unhurt, bouncing on the thick, ugly carpet. Anger, raw, burned her eyes. It was anger so deep she wished Laurel were there and was equally glad she wasn't because some actions you couldn't come back from, no matter how well-deserved.

Finally, she left the teacup, plate and cookies where they lay. There was no solution for this trespass. Everything that mattered was gone.

Her dad and she had spent a lot of time on what they called the saggy, shaggy sofa. They'd turn on movies or football, but it was more a backdrop as they talked about stuff, life, and more stuff, whatever. Up until she was sixteen.

She carried her bag up the stairs.

Fifteen years gone. She'd let a lot of things ride longer than she should have.

It was time to see her attorney. She had corrections to make in her future. And Laurel wasn't going to be happy about it. Not one bit.

****

He asked, "Have you thought this through?"

She answered, "Dad trusted you. Can I?"

Mr. Lloyd leaned back in his chair. "I'm glad to see you, too."

"Maybe that's rude, but I want to be sure you represent me and not my...mother. Laurel. You were my father's attorney, so I presume you represented Laurel, too."

"Your mother isn't my client. I haven't had any contact with her since the trust reverted to you. How long ago? Almost six years? Is there a problem?"

"I need advice about separating my business affairs from Laurel's."

"Laurel? Your mother?"

"Adoptive mother."

A nearly imperceptible pause. He said, "Are you at odds?"

"I should be leading a separate, independent life. My

father's house was left to me. We, Laurel and I, continued to reside there after he died, but now, years later, she still lives there. Legally, how would I go about getting her out of the house?"

He frowned and rubbed his forehead. "But you aren't at odds?" When she didn't respond, he asked, "Have you spoken to her about this?"

"No, I want to find out how best to proceed before giving her warning. I know she won't like it and will try to talk me out of it, or fight me."

"Pardon me if I ask again. Are you at odds? After so many years, I imagine Mrs. Denman considers herself at home." He sat back and his face cleared. "Are you thinking of selling the house?"

She was aghast. "My father's house? Not a chance."

His manner became business-like. "If you have specific issues regarding her living there, you should discuss those with her. If you simply want her out, and don't have any concerns regarding the future of the relationship, then give her notice. If she resists, it will require additional legal actions. Consider this—if nothing has changed since you reached twenty-five, you are the sole owner, but this would still be thought of as the family home, and you and she have lived there as mother and daughter for three decades or thereabouts. It might not be seen as unreasonable that she would expect to continue residing there."

"She changed things." She blurted it out.

He waited.

"I've never interfered with her and the decisions she made about the management of the house, even though I have carried the financial obligations for it, but there were some mutual understandings. She knew there were things I didn't want changed, and she is now changing them." She stopped short of blurting out that the evil Laurel had replaced an old sofa and TV stand.

It sounded petty. She sounded petty in front of this grave,

thoughtful man who'd been her father's friend and advisor.

Her father's friend.

"You knew she wasn't my natural mother. You've known all along."

He nodded so barely, the movement was nearly imperceptible.

"What can you tell me about my father's first wife, Frances?"

He breathed softly, evenly. "I can't think of any reason not to discuss this with you. Your father made no prohibitions regarding it, neither to me as his friend or as his attorney. He believed it would be easier for Laurel, and you, to leave Frances out of it. She was gone and unlikely to return. You were so young, he felt it would be best for all. They lived in the eastern part of the state at that time. He moved here for a fresh start, that's what he told me." He leaned back in his chair.

"I met Edward about the time he and Frances began having trouble. I never met her. You may not know that Frances ran away more than once, and took you with her. Edward was frantic. He came to me as a friend and asked about options for obtaining sole custody of you. I referred him to a friend from law school whose specialty was in family law, but then all that was put on hold when Edward and Frances reconciled."

"Reconciled?"

"Briefly. I don't know how sincere it was on the part of Frances. I suspected she was attempting to forestall the custody battle. After a few weeks she left again, but this time she was gone for many months, and disappeared more successfully. Edward hired someone to find her and when he did, he took you home with him. He and Frances divorced and he never saw her again."

"But she came back."

"Not to my knowledge."

"Laurel said she came to the house when I was about six

or seven, asking for my father. Laurel turned her away, saying she would give Dad the message to contact her, but she never did. I'm sure of it. Laurel never told him."

He grimaced but it passed quickly and he shrugged. "Did Laurel do the right thing? Maybe not, but then again her motives might not have been ill-intentioned, and they were understandable. She might have been trying to protect you and your family from hurt."

"I want to find out what happened to Frances. I want to know who she was, or is, and who her, my, people are. My birth certificate doesn't help."

He nodded. "Because of the adoption." He leaned back in his chair. "We can go the legal route to unseal the records, but that's the hard way with no guarantee of success. Ask Laurel. She's bound to have information."

"I did."

"Ask her again. I wish I had her last name, but I don't. If I knew it, I don't recall, but it wouldn't be that difficult to find the marriage record. If your mother won't help, and you aren't sure about doing it yourself, hire a private detective." He leaned forward with his elbows on the desk. "Regarding the other issue—putting Laurel out of the house. If you are determined, then I urge you to discuss it with her. It may take longer to move her out, but the other way would likely end any hope of a relationship between you two and be very costly. It would also be public and neither of you need that."

Frannie sighed. No good options. She asked, "Can you recommend a good private investigator? Someone I can trust?"

"I can do that."

****

The house was still empty when she returned. She felt pointless and fruitless, angry over disrespected memories, yet who was she to hurt someone over a sofa?

So no eviction notice. No grand gesture like changing the locks. There would have to be another conversation with

Laurel. Something along the lines of 'Laurel, our lives are too entwined and it isn't healthy for either of us. I understand you feel like this house is yours, is your home, but I own it. Please find somewhere else to live. And, by the way, before you leave, tell me more about Frances.'

Could she do that?

Lost in disappointment, she barely noticed the drive back to the beach. Suddenly, she was in Morehead City, had totally missed the first bridge over to Emerald Isle, and was driving down Arendell Street in the direction of the rehab. From the corner of her eye, she caught a glimpse of the red neon lettering in the window of Lynette's Two.

She'd seen that bright red lettering before. She turned around at the next opportunity and drove back.

Shopping? Impulsive. Distracting. She wanted to be distracted.

She entered and saw several women, sales clerks and customers, clearly occupied. One called out a welcome, promising to be with her shortly.

A table near the front displayed tops in sheer fabrics and muted colors. The soft shades of grayed blue and browns drew Frannie. She touched the light, silky fabrics and admired the necklaces displayed with them.

"Can I help you?"

Free from her customer, the woman offered assistance, and in that moment Frannie realized she didn't need help with any of this, not at this table and not with these colors and styles. She owned a closet full of this. Beyond the woman's shoulder, Frannie saw the colorful scarves, slacks and jeans in exotic colors…well, exotic to her. She'd never considered wearing shades of apricot and turquoise and puce.

"Uhmm." She tried again. "Do you have capris pants? Not shorts."

"Sure. Right over here."

****

She laid the bag on the passenger seat wondering if she'd

really wear these garments. She'd stood in front of the mirror and liked the bright colors and then turned her back to the mirror and looked over her shoulder. She liked the way the pants fit—they were flattering, but they were tight, tighter than the slacks she usually wore. The clerk assured her the fit was right.

Clothing might look fabulous or even daring in the dressing room mirror, but in the real world they looked like what one already owned. People gravitated to what they knew. To what felt safe. But these colors were different.

She pulled into the rehab parking lot, into a space about halfway back.

The sun was shining like a crazy, blazing orb and she wanted to feel blessed to part of this day, but she couldn't shake the down mood that had stalked her since she left Captain's Walk for Raleigh. She looked around the lot. There was no sign of her uncle's old van, but on a nice day like this, Brian would surely ride his bike, if he was going to be here.

Even if she saw his bike, she was going in to visit her uncle anyway because she didn't schedule her life around where Brian might or might not be.

Still no sign of him.

She locked the car and went inside.

Will was seated in the pink vinyl chair. He wore a robe over his pajamas and a white cotton blanket was spread across his knees. One hand rested in his lap, with his fingers loosely curled around a red rubber ball.

"Well, hello, Uncle Will."

His blue eyes were lively and his face was more animated than before. It pleased her.

"You look good today." She walked into the room and dropped her jacket on the windowsill and perched herself on the end of the bed. "I stopped by yesterday, but you were out on the town."

The hand in his lap lifted, and he waved. "Hi."

Not perfect, but easily understood. Impulsively, she

grasped his hand, but ever so gently. The flesh looked fragile and papery, barely covering the bones and knuckles. It was only a quick, gentle pressure, but he returned it. As she watched, she noticed the sun streaming through the window and casting bright light on their hands. Like a blessing? She released his hand slowly.

"It's beautiful outside today."

Janet spoke from the doorway. "He can go into the courtyard for a few minutes. We can put a blanket around his shoulders. It's very mild outside."

Frannie said to Will, "Janet says it's warm enough, so let's go for it."

She helped Janet move him into the wheelchair. He didn't protest, but allowed them to move him as they needed and she was surprised to feel the strength in him as he stood with their help. Janet wrapped the blanket around his shoulders.

Taking Uncle Will for a ride beat being trapped in a room making one-sided conversation. For this moment anyway, pushing his chair, she felt useful and they were doing something other than her talking and him staring.

She parked him in a sheltered corner of the courtyard. There wasn't a breath of breeze, but only glorious sunshine. She sat in a wrought iron chair next to him.

"I just returned from Raleigh. A quick, overnight trip. I got my birth certificate."

He turned his face more fully toward her. Listening.

"It wasn't what I was hoping for. It wasn't the original certificate. This is the one with Laurel as my mother. I found out about my dad's first marriage to Frances a few days ago." Deep breath.

His eyes didn't waver, but he nodded. Encouraged, she continued.

"I found the letters from your mother and I read them. Was that wrong? They are your letters and personal. I hope you don't mind. Did you realize I didn't know about Frances?" She paused. She didn't want to seem to be putting any blame on him. "Did you know Frances?"

He shook his head 'no' but pointed his finger as if about to make a statement, but no words were uttered. She wasn't surprised, but also, she was a bit pleased. Clearly, he knew what she was talking about even if he didn't have the power to confirm it verbally here and now.

She touched his still hand and arm, the one that continued to rest without movement on the arm of the wheelchair. "I'm so glad we can have more of a conversation now. You need to get better quickly." She checked to make sure his blanket hadn't dipped too low such that it might get run over or caught up in the wheels. "I think we should go back inside now. I don't want you to get chilled."

He nodded. "Read," he said. "Letters."

The expression in his eyes was animated. Frannie paused. That was the most he'd said to her since the stroke.

Encouraged, she added, "They named me after her. I never knew."

He nodded again.

"I don't even know her last name."

Will raised his hand again and his lips moved, but his face turned red and she was worried she'd overdone it.

"Sorry, Uncle Will. I'll take you back in now."

That hand waved more strongly and he said, clearly, "No."

"What?"

He wanted to speak. He knew what he wanted to say, but the mechanics fell apart as he became agitated. She leaned toward him and again rested her hand on his arm.

"Please don't worry. We'll talk some more next time."

He spoke one last word, but she wasn't sure what he was trying to convey. It sounded like cool or cook. He was cool. Chilly.

"I'll get you back inside." She maneuvered the wheelchair through the door and then down the hall back to his room.

"Hi, Janet, we're back. Do you need assistance getting him back to his chair?"

"No, ma'am. He's due for therapy in a few minutes."

Frannie knelt in front of Will's chair. "I'll be back on Sunday afternoon. Maybe sooner."

He spoke two clear words among words she couldn't understand. "Van. Paper." His brows furrowed in frustration.

"Don't worry about your van. I asked Brian to drive it to keep it in running shape."

"Papers."

She nodded. Was he worried that it had been a little messy? She patted his hand and then remembered she'd forgotten the small scrap of paper in her pocket.

"That reminds me…I found this in a coffee mug in the kitchen cabinet." Frannie pulled out the slip of paper and with a quick smile, she read aloud, I will lift up mine eyes unto the mountains: From whence shall my help come? My help cometh from God, Who made heaven and earth. Psalm 121.

She placed the paper in his palm. "I believe this belongs to you?"

His eyes lit with an inner glow she hadn't seen before. What did these papers mean to him? Why hide them around the house? It didn't matter. They were important to him, and that was enough to know.

As she left, her eyes welled with tears. This visit had been less of a duty, and more of an intelligent exchange with her uncle, and it felt like a small blessing. It struck her, stopping her in her tracks… maybe he would recover enough to return home.

He couldn't live at Captain's Walk without help. Live-in help, maybe. It was time to chat with his doctor again, and she should price things like wheelchair ramps and the cost of refitting the house with some wider doors, etc. Brian might know. Then she remembered that she and Brian were no longer speaking and her mood took a dive again. The sunlight was bright outside and she paused as she left the building to allow her eyes to adjust.

Motorcycle. A blue dented machine. She took a quick scan of the parking lot. Brian wasn't in sight. While the coast was clear, she took off across the lot, heading straight to her car.

"Fran."

She stumbled. "Brian. Hi."

He stood by the building, near the wider entrance. He must have been going in one door as she was exiting the other.

She waved. It was a deliberately acquaintance-friendly gesture intended to soften the effect of her turning her back and getting into her car, which she did without wasting a moment. As she fastened the seat belt, she was facing the building and expected to see him still standing there, but he was gone.

No, he wasn't. Her passenger side door opened. She nearly screamed. She knew it was Brian, but her heart pounded. Adrenaline. Invasion of her personal space. Fear morphed to anger. He couldn't bother to call, but he could invade her car.

"Calm down," he said.

The nerve of him. "Me? Calm down? What about you?" She slapped the steering wheel. "I'm not the one who spoiled a lovely day by holding a grudge against my sister and embarrassing her in front of a friend."

His mouth gaped. He closed it. Her bag from Lynette's Two was on his lap. At least he hadn't sat on it.

"Then you go MIA for a week. Pouting like a sulky child."

His lips curved in a lazy smile. "You missed me."

"Me? Miss you? Hah. Not likely. Disappointed in you, that's all. Disappointed in your behavior." Her indignation was rapidly losing its punch. She stared at the windshield, trying to hold the anger close, to keep it for protection, but it was already diminishing to regret. She sighed. "Maybe that was unfair. You don't owe me anything. I don't lose my temper very often and I don't have enough practice to do it well."

"You should do it more often."

The tone in his voice was aligning with his smile, softer with a hint of something warmer.

"What?"

"Sorry for the cliché, but sometimes truth is truth. You're beautiful when you're angry."

She realized her mouth was hanging open and she closed it. He needed to leave. Now.

"Get out."

"Are you angry again?" He sounded hopeful. Or baiting.

Her eyes burned. "Please go."

The moment drew out. Finally, he said, "Whatever you want, Fran." He reached for the door handle.

"Are you here to see my uncle?"

"Of course."

"He seemed good today."

"Glad to hear it."

It was a weirdly courteous conversation, but Brian's hand came away from the door handle and he settled back in his seat.

She nodded. "I have questions I must ask him." She tapped the steering wheel. "And I was thinking about changes that might be needed at the house if he's able to come home."

"What?"

"Well, this might be getting too far ahead, but if he's improving, then he can afford live-in help. An LPA or someone like that who can handle the lifting part. But wheelchairs need more space. Like wider doorways."

"You have been thinking about this." He stared at her. "Does this mean you're backing off of the idea of selling Captain's Walk?"

"No, not necessarily. All along I've tried to do only those things that worked for both keeping or selling."

"You talked about selling it like it was the plan."

"Did I? I think all possibilities should be considered, especially when one is responsible for someone else's life, rather, I mean their property." She gripped the steering wheel lightly. "You shouldn't have spoken to Maia like that."

He looked surprised. "Maybe. But I meant what I said."

"That's not the point." Steady, girl. "What you have to say to each other is between you, but you shouldn't have spoken to her like that, in that humiliating way, in front of me."

"You're right."

She nodded. "Yes, I am. Maybe we can talk about things we, rather I, can do to make the house more accessible for Uncle Will. Just talk for now."

"Sure. We can do that. I'd better get on inside."

Then he was gone. The bag was back on the seat as if the exchange with Brian had only been an inconsequential blip on her day. Maybe it was nothing more than the adrenaline surge, but the sky looked bluer and her mood was brighter.

****

She was dreaming again of the soft crying in the night. Half awake, her arms hugging a pillow, she heard the wind wrapping around the house. It was as if the house itself was sighing and it must've fit into her dream. She peeked at the clock. Two a.m. She flipped the pillow to the cool side, closed her eyes and prepared to drift back into sleep when a thud came from the front of the house. Even over the whine of the wind, and the ocean hitting the shore, something had hit, maybe kicked, the house. Hard.

Bolt upright, her heart pounding, she threw the covers aside. She grabbed her cell phone and raced to the front door, her fingers ready to punch in 9-1-1 if anyone or anything scary was in sight.

The house was quiet aside from the natural outdoor sounds. She peered around the blinds at each window. Nothing seemed to be out of place. She hadn't imagined that thud. She'd been awake when it happened.

She checked the side door and the sliding door. Everything seemed secure, but by now her nerves were on edge and each wind gust or house creak felt like a threat. She sat on the sofa. She was stiff and uncomfortable, wanting to curl back up in her bed and knowing that wasn't going to happen. She wrapped the sofa blanket around her body and tucked her feet inside.

She did doze off toward dawn, but it was that heavy sleep that left her feeling hung over. Now that it was daylight, she could go back to bed. She would recover from the night by sleeping away the morning.

Frannie got up from the sofa. Dawn was peeking in around the closed blinds and she stopped to push them aside and look out. Nothing unusual. Nothing out of place. Normal. She opened the sliding door.

It lay on the porch beside the door. She wanted to slam the door shut, but she couldn't leave it there. Nausea hit her and she pushed the door closed anyway. Through the glass, from this angle, she could see only a few white feathers, tinged with red, scattered on the wood.

It must have hit the house during the windstorm.

She put one hand over her stomach and the other over her mouth. She had to calm the churning. A dead sea bird, lying battered on her porch, was distressing, but the roaring in her ears and the curdling in her stomach tied into memories and were far more distressing as it rebounded upon itself, growing.

She closed her eyes and focused on regulating her breathing. This was a gull who'd been blown by a super gust of wind. This wasn't like before. It wasn't like when she'd lived on her own and things had happened and she'd felt so helpless to stop it or fix it.

She slid down to the floor and hugged her knees, hiding her face against them.

Breathe. Breathe.

Finally, she stood and made it to the kitchen. She pulled out the canister of tea. The plastic lid liner was a tight fit and she worked it off with careful deliberation and then put her face directly over the open tin, inhaling slowly, deeply. Citrus. The fragrance pulled her out of herself. Like a meditation. Or medication.

Meditation medication. She felt a little smile inside and knew she was recovering.

She put the water on to heat and measured the tea into the steeper.

She turned the TV on and found a rerun, amusing and inconsequential. By then her tea was ready and she settled at the table to enjoy tea and toast.

Her hair was wild from the crazy night she'd spent. She ran her fingers through it and decided to take care of the business on the porch before heading to the shower. She found an ad circular. It would serve the purpose.

She opened the door gingerly while holding the paper like a shovel.

The bird was gone.

Had some creature run off with it? A dog with a prize? Some animal's breakfast?

What was that called? The food chain? Law of nature? The law of survival?

If not for the few, small red spots on the porch, already fading, she could almost pretend nothing had been there.

She stood on the porch, hugging her arms. It was early and chilly. No one up one way, or down the other. She was alone. Not even a dog was in sight.

****

After a pounding hot shower to clear her head, she invited herself out to breakfast. She put on a favorite blouse and her navy slacks. She grabbed a book from Will's shelf because the best companion was often found inside the covers of a book.

Mike's Restaurant was open. She'd seen it from the road, but it was the first time she'd stopped here. The breakfast crowd was thinning out and she had her choice of seating. She claimed a table near the windows wanting to feel the sun on her face.

She placed her order and opened the book, then closed it again to examine the book jacket. Wrong jacket. She'd thought she was about to read a murder mystery. This was about naval weaponry. Not her taste.

She closed the book and pushed it aside, annoyed, and then Juli walked through the door.

Juli paused as she stepped inside. When she saw Frannie, she waved and came over. "Are you here for breakfast?"

"I am. You?"

She nodded. "Have you eaten yet? Mind if I join you?"

In this one on one, chance meeting, Frannie felt her shyness, her awkwardness, blooming and oozing out of her pores. "Sure. I mean, please do."

Juli touched the book. "I read that. It's excellent."

"I was looking forward to reading it, but appearances can be misleading."

"What? How so?"

Frannie slid the front of the book jacket off the book. "Uncle Will played a trick on me. Unintended, I'm sure."

"You're kidding." Juli smiled. "Those books aren't even close cousins. You know what? Maybe he was trying to hide what he was reading." She laughed.

"I've heard of people disguising light reading as more weighty subject matter, but not the reverse."

"Maybe you'll find the cover to this book on the mystery. Maybe that's what he was actually reading."

"That makes sense. Even old retired sailors might be prone to silliness, I guess."

"I'm feeling silly right now. Or a bit giddy, maybe. I'm not used to being out without Danny."

"Where is he? Mother's day out?"

"Yep. With his grandparents."

"I'll bet they're thrilled to have him for the day. Your parents or your husband's?"

"Not mine. I grew up in foster homes."

"Oh, that's right. I'm sorry."

The waitress was there with her food. She sat back and waited while the waitress took Juli's order. After the waitress left, she resumed, "I know you told me before about the foster care, but, well, I'm sorry. Not my business at all."

Juli shrugged. "It's history, long ago and far away from today. I don't mind you asking. How would you know I wasn't an orphan? One doesn't necessarily go with the other. Is that right?"

"Yes."

"I don't know whether I'm an orphan in fact, but I am in reality. Since I was five."

"I'm sorry."

"Don't be. It was a lucky day for me when the family services people took me away. My mother had problems. I don't know exactly what they were. I was too young. But I'll never forget how I spent so much time alone. I remember being cold and hungry. I'm grateful to the foster system for what they did. It was far from perfect, but better than where I'd been."

"But—"

Juli smiled. "It's really okay to ask."

"What about your mother? Did she never come back? Did you ever go looking for her?"

"No and no." She shrugged. "I found my own way in the world, and when I was running out of options, God sent me someone to love and be loved by. I'm a very fortunate person."

Frannie sipped at her orange juice and nibbled her toast.

"You're deep in thought."

"I was thinking about something. Recently, I found out I'm adopted. I'm looking for my birth mother but I have misgivings. I'm not sure why. Listening to you, I'm wondering if I should go ahead with it or forget it."

"What works for one person doesn't always work for

another. If you started looking, then clearly you want to know. How does your mother feel about it?"

She drew in a sharp breath. "She doesn't like it, but I don't really care."

"What about your father?"

"He died when I was sixteen. He was married to my birth mother. I think he would've told me eventually. Difficult for him to find the right time, I suppose."

"You know what, Frannie? You'll do the right thing, whatever it is. But you are the only one who can figure that out. There's more than one path to the same destination."

"I'm glad you happened in at the same time I was here. So, you have a free day? What do you have planned?"

"I'll spend some time sketching along the shore. I've got my camera and paper and pencils. I love it down by the ocean."

"Your house over on the sound is beautiful."

"It is. I used to live on the oceanfront, and I love the ocean, but the sound is more peaceful and I love that, too."

"I understand. Some nights the wind gusts and the house shakes and creaks. It unnerves me, especially when it's dark and I can't see what's going on outside. Last night, I heard a big thud. I didn't sleep much after that, and this morning I discovered a seagull had flown into the house. Not inside, but into the wall. It was on the porch, all...well, messy."

"After dark?"

"Yes. About two a.m."

"That's strange. I'm not a bird expert, but it sounds unusual."

"How else could it have happened?"

"Well, you do have a mystery after all."

"I'd rather read about someone else's."

"Not an adventure lover? Yet you came to stay at your uncle's house and take on his responsibilities while he's unable to. I think you have a taste for excitement, but haven't found the right adventure."

Frannie sealed her lips. She wouldn't confess that she was hiding, that being here was more about her problems than helping her uncle. And yet, they were both benefitting, right?

Juli added, "You should stick with Brian. He's always full of adventure."

His name on Juli's lips shocked her like a big electric jolt. Brian was another failure. Someone she was developing some kind of relationship with, even if it was only a friendship, who now didn't even call. Reality was, if she hadn't been at the rehab place, they still wouldn't have spoken.

She tried to respond lightly. "Maia's brother?"

Juli raised her eyebrows. "Ah, has he offended you? You have that look and you wouldn't be the first. He has a rough manner, but it covers a very tender heart."

"A tender heart? I wouldn't know about that." She pressed her lips closed again.

"What about your friend, Joel? What a nice man he is. I enjoyed meeting him and so did Luke. In fact, Luke and Joel are talking about possible plans for a new gallery."

"Really? Yes, Joel is nice. I've known him for many years. You know, the morning is speeding by. I'm enjoying this, but you really should get out there and enjoy the day." She stood, picking up her book and purse. "I enjoyed having company for brunch. Please stop by sometime if you're in the area. You know where Captain's Walk is?"

Still seated, Juli said, "I do. You have a fun day. Take this gorgeous day as a gift and use it well."

Use it well? Have fun? It was a stunner to realize she wasn't sure she knew how to have outright, undisguised, unabashed fun.

Chapter Eighteen

He saw them immediately. From across the room and with her back to him, he could see they were deep in conversation. He wanted quiet and a little peace in which to enjoy breakfast. He wasn't in the mood for arguing, not after fighting with Diane this morning, but Juli saw him and waved. He stopped. He couldn't duck back out the door, not now.

When Juli waved, Frannie turned to look. She turned her back again so abruptly she almost did a vanishing act, like the kind a two-year-old does when they cover their eyes and think on one can see them.

He walked over. "Breakfast?"

Frannie stared down at the table. He saw the red flush creeping up her throat and up the side of her face. Juli was looking back and forth between them. He couldn't read Juli's expression and suddenly he was concerned. Was something wrong with Fran?

He touched her arm thinking he might need to catch her if she toppled over. "Are you okay?"

Juli's wide-eyed expression confused him further.

He secured his grip on Fran's arm and asked Juli, "Is she sick?"

"I'm fine." Frannie tugged at the neck of her blouse. "It's hot in here. Hot like the Sahara."

Juli said, "Yes, it's quite warm in here." She smiled.

"Sorry I interrupted you ladies. I'll get out of the way."

Frannie suddenly turned, her face flushed and her dark eyes all glittery, and said, "You're not interrupting. I was leaving." She clutched her bag and book and pushed past him. She dropped her tab and the money on the cashier's counter and kept moving.

He watched her move like something with big sharp teeth was after her. As she exited, he could see her rushing toward her car.

He looked at Juli. "What? Did I do something wrong?"

Juli's hand was now over the lower part of her face. She seemed to be struggling with something.

"Are you laughing?"

She moved her hands up to her forehead and looked down at the table. He couldn't see her eyes.

"No, Brian. Frannie's fine. You surprised us." Finally, she did look up. "Is she angry with you?"

"Angry at me?" He shrugged. "Maybe. Who knows what's going on in her head?"

"Well, then." She picked up her bag. "I wouldn't worry about it. In fact, it probably wasn't you at all. She had a rough night."

Before she could get to her feet, he sat, so she settled back into her seat.

"What do you mean, a rough night?"

"Well, it's a weird thing and maybe you've heard of something like this happening."

"What?"

"About two in the morning, she heard a loud noise. Something hit the house. It alarmed her and she had trouble sleeping, but when it got light outside, she opened the door and a seagull was on the porch. A dead one. Seems he crashed into the house during the night. Have you ever heard of such a thing?"

He considered the question. "No, can't say I have. In daylight, birds will fly into windows not realizing the glass is there. But at night? At night, as far as I know, gulls roost." He shook his head. "I don't understand you women."

"What? Why? You sound disgusted."

"You're worrying over a dead seagull, but a woman alone in a house in the middle of the night hears a bang against her wall, can't see what caused it, and instead of calling for help she sits up all night?"

"I didn't say she sat up all night."

"You didn't say she called 9-1-1."

"I see your point, but things often seem different at night, in the dark. We don't like to bother someone and end up looking hysterical. That's what you guys call it. According to you guys, we either over-react or don't react as you think we should. There's no pleasing men."

She softened her words with a slight smile. "I have a date with a beach and a sketchbook." She patted his hand. "Say hello to Maia when you see her. And Frannie, too."

There was something about her eyes that reminded him of Fran. The hair, too. Highlighted by the strong light from the window, Juli's fine, brown hair seemed almost translucent around her face. Both were good-looking women, but he wished he could give Fran some of Juli's strength and confidence. He remembered what he knew of Juli's background. Her composure and dignity were hard-won, but once she'd found it, her whole world changed. He'd hardly known her back then, but Maia was always willing to chat in the name of helping someone. Maia was a fixer, a rescuer. And a gossip, too. Well-intended or not.

"Why don't I clear these dishes from the table? Did you want to order?"

The waitress startled him. He shook off his thoughts. "Sure. Coffee. Black. Two eggs scrambled, bacon and toast."

"Can do." She carried the used plates and utensils away to the kitchen.

Maia was a fixer. Juli was down-to-earth, a kind person, loyal and a fighter when needed. Diane? Diane had never fit any of those labels. Diane was all energy and fun, until she wasn't, and when she wasn't, she was self-centered and cruel.

Suddenly, he felt surrounded by women. When had his life gotten this way?

Fran. What about her? He didn't like calling her 'Frannie'.

It seemed to diminish her even more than she already was. A hider. An avoider. Yet, every so often the real gal would peek out and she was fascinating in some way he couldn't define. He'd thought she was trouble before, but now he knew better. Fran didn't fit in her own skin because she hadn't figured out who she was. She kept getting lost, overthinking everything. Like he was doing right now.

He didn't hide like Fran tried to do. Sometimes he wished he could.

One thing he could say for her was that she knew how to laugh at herself, in a good way, when she was being herself and not worrying about everything and everyone else and what they might think of her.

Too bad she was so mixed up. It made her high-maintenance. He had enough of his own troubles. Yet he kept going back, finding himself caught up in her life.

Then he felt guilty. Fran was talking about making the house wheelchair accessible. She'd gotten off the 'get it ready for sale' path, and that's what he'd wanted. He groaned. She'd make a big mess of it if left to investigate it on her own. She might call any fly-by-night contractor. Probably wouldn't even think to ask for references or bonding or insurance. She hadn't asked him for any of that when she'd haired him to paint, had she?

She needed his help and so did Will.

Chapter Nineteen

She was horrified—horrifically embarrassed—by the thoughtless timing of fate.

She'd barely extricated herself from the 'Brian' topic only to have him walk into Mike's. That curious look on Juli's face suddenly changed to welcoming. Juli had waved and there he was. And she, Frannie, had flushed like a ripe tomato, soft and red and ready to drop from the vine. She knew because her face had been on fire.

He'd touched her. If it had only been him and her, like in the car, she could've managed the encounter, might even have enjoyed seeing him depending upon his mood, but with an audience it was a different story. Like when he'd scolded Maia in front of her.

Except this time he hadn't done anything wrong. Juli shouldn't have sown those seeds in her brain, but it wasn't Juli's fault that she, Frannie, overreacted.

She parked and walked around the side of the house and up onto the front porch. She dropped her book and purse on the porch, left her shoes with the trouser socks neatly tucked inside next to them. Brian was probably right—those socks had no place on the oceanfront. She walked barefoot through the small hills of dry sand and onto the damp sand where the waves rolled up and back. The dry sand had been warm, but the wet sand was cool. She cuffed the bottoms of her slacks, folding them neatly up her legs to her knees, as Brian had done. The wet sand was cold and the water was colder as it rushed up over her toes, but the sun was warm and if a person needed a place to hide from life, this was a pretty good option.

Still, it was a wintry beach and she'd never been much of

a beach person, but she felt drawn to the water, soothed by the rhythm of the waves. She stood in place as the sand washed away from beneath her feet.

Her heels and toes sank. Each time, the waves brought more sand, but also reclaimed it. It was like a game. Nature was toying with this petty human. Or maybe it was a challenge, a standoff because she refused to move. More sand vanished from beneath her feet as other sand was deposited on top. Her feet were buried and the rolled up ends of her pants were wet and clammy.

Like a season in the midst of change, she was cold below, rather, her feet were cold, but her body, the farther it was from the water, was warmer. She closed her eyes. Suddenly, the salty sea smell blended with other fragrances she couldn't identify. Like her favorite teas. Blends that supported and enhanced each other. Relaxed, she felt almost disembodied. No stress, no decisions, only the rise and fall of the water above and around her numb, buried feet.

The next wave hit her knee-high. She looked down realizing she was in trouble. She tried to step back, but her feet weren't just buried, they were stuck, suctioned into place.

Calm down. It was ridiculous to panic so close to houses and people.

She eased one foot free and, thus encouraged, tried to step backward again. She saw the wave, a big one, racing toward her and tried to brace herself, but it hit her mid-thigh. She fell backward. A large rush of salty, sandy water slapped her face as her fingers grabbed at the sand.

Hands lifted her. Strong hands held her above the incoming waves while she steadied herself. They helped her maneuver backward, up the slope toward the dryer sand where she sat down abruptly.

"Joel."

He dropped down beside her. "Frannie. Hi. Going swimming?"

She smirked. "Funny."

She was soaked in water straight from a winter ocean. The breeze intensified the chill.

"I'm cold," she said.

"You're lucky. You don't know how cold the ocean can get. The Gulf Stream favors Emerald Isle."

"You got wet, too. I'm sorry."

He stood and offered his hand. "Let's get inside and dry off."

He lifted her to her feet and she turned toward the house. Maia and Luke stood at the end of the crossover staring at them.

She wanted to spit the sand from her mouth, but not with an audience.

"What's…?" She coughed. "What's going on, Joel?"

"Don't get angry with me. How was I to know you were taking a swim? We're going out for lunch and thought you might enjoy going with us."

Joel. Again, trying every way he could to get into her life.

"Thanks, but y'all go ahead without me."

They reached the stairs and she climbed gingerly, her bare feet were thawing and soft from the water. Every splinter bit into the flesh.

"Frannie," Maia said, "You're soaked. Don't you know to stay out of the water this time of year, unless you're wearing a wet suit?"

Luke said, "Looks pretty wet to me."

Lame. She refused to laugh.

"Not funny." Maia took her arm and hustled her up the crossover.

Her bag was still on the porch. As she dug through it for the keys, she said, "Joel said you were going out to lunch. I appreciate you thinking of me, but I'll pass." She unlocked the door. "I have to get cleaned up."

"No problem. We'll wait," Maia said.

Obviously, Joel needed to dry off his shoes and squeeze the ocean from the bottom of his slacks. She couldn't push them out.

She motioned toward the living room. "Would you like to come in?" She stepped aside as they entered. "I'll go change." She kept a straight face until Maia started giggling, but then she lost it. She put her hands to her face as she hurried down the hallway.

Maia was right behind her. "Frannie?" She whispered urgently. "Frannie?"

Maia looked at her face. "You're laughing. I thought you were crying. I thought I'd hurt your feelings."

"No, no hurt feelings, but—and I mean this—I don't want you guys to wait for me. I don't want to go out to lunch."

"No problem. We'll order in. Is barbecue okay?"

Frannie sighed, giving in. "Only if it comes with hush puppies."

"Wait, Maia." She grabbed a towel. "Can you give this to Joel? He has some cleaning up to do, too."

Frannie rushed through a quick shower, went light with the makeup, and then ran a brush through her damp hair and called it done. She pulled the apricot capris slacks from the bag on the dresser, along with the white silk top. They were perfect for the occasion.

She found Maia and Joel sitting on the sofa. Luke was in Will's favorite chair.

"Paper plates are in the cupboard. I'll get them. I'm sorry Juli isn't here."

Luke spoke up. "She's having her own fun. She doesn't often get a whole day to spend on her art. She isn't missing us." He nodded toward the dining room wall. "I like where you've hung her paintings. Your uncle was her first paying customer."

Frannie looked and smiled. "When he commissioned the beachscapes?"

He nodded. "Meant a lot to her, you know, especially since he was a stranger. Not family. You know what I mean. Plus, he took the time to seek her out and talk to her. She felt comfortable with him and with what he wanted. It made a big difference for her."

"How is your uncle, Frannie?" Joel asked.

She perched on the sofa arm near Maia. "I think he's improving, but I don't know how far that will go or if he will recover enough to come home. With live-in help, maybe."

"Are you going back to Raleigh when you leave here?"

"Probably."

Maia jumped in, "Well, you can't leave now. Spring is just around the corner. Spring is so beautiful here. Once the beach gets into your blood, you might as well give in. Don't fight it."

Maia's smile invariably brought out those dimples and her eyes looked merry. Joel looked at her and smiled, too.

He said, "I know what you mean. I spend more and more time at my place in Hatteras."

Luke was checking his cell phone. He seemed to be reading texts or emails.

Maia said, "Don't mind him. He doesn't know how to leave business behind."

"Speaking of which…aren't you all playing hooky? Did you close the gallery for the day? What about you, Joel? You're spending a lot of time down here." Hadn't Juli mentioned that Luke and Joel were talking business? Maybe she wasn't his only draw here. That made her feel better. More relaxed.

Knocks on the side door drew everyone's attention. Joel and Maia jumped up to answer it. As she opened the door, Maia said, "Took you long enough."

Brian walked in carrying bags of food.

This day kept getting better and better—not.

He put the bags of delicious smelling barbecue, hush puppies and coleslaw on the counter. Frannie went to join them in the kitchen.

"Here, let me help." She handed Maia two serving spoons.

Brian took the spoons before Maia could grab them. He placed them on the counter and said, "Maia can handle it. I need to speak with you."

Bad news? Or bad nerves? Her stomach wrapped around itself.

"Is something wrong with Uncle Will?"

He stared. She was conscious of Joel and Maia staring, too.

Brian answered, his voice smooth and even. "Nothing more than is already wrong. I want to talk to you. It's not a big deal."

Maia said, "Go ahead, Fran. We've got this handled." She looked at Brian. "Don't take too long. The food won't stay hot."

She followed him out to the porch. She felt chilled even though the air was mild.

"What's this about, Brian?"

He moved further down so that they were in front of the bedroom windows and not quite so much on display. Brian leaned against the rail.

He said, "Can I ask you something?"

What was she supposed to say? No?

"Next time you go to visit Will, be careful what you say about refitting the house for his wheelchair."

What? Did she hear him right? She kept listening, thinking she'd get on track with him because someone wasn't making sense.

"You were talking about it last time. Remember?"

"I remember. What is it, Brian?"

"I didn't want you to get his hopes up. He's been through a lot."

His tone was patronizing. She dug her nails into her palms.

"Am I alone here?" he asked.

"Rude. That's what you are. And condescending. Furthermore, I'll tell my uncle whatever I want and I won't be consulting you first." She pointed her finger at his chest. "And that goes for anyone else I want to talk to, about anything I want to talk about."

The corner of his mouth twitched. It ticked her off.

"And another thing—"

Without a hint of courtesy in his tone, he said, "Can you listen?"

He had the arrogance to sound annoyed.

She hissed, "You—"

"Megan was asking to come by and see you. I thought that maybe I could bring her with me when we take a look at possible modifications to the house."

Megan? Modifications?

"And one more thing."

She struggled to control her breathing. He was being a jerk. He was playing games with her.

He asked, "Do you and Joel have something going on?"

His blue eyes looked guileless. His lips were treacherous. Why did he care about Joel? Was it any of his business? No.

She gasped. Maybe he wanted it to be his business? Her anger receded as something softer warmed in her chest. Was her face flushing again? She touched her cheek. It felt hot. What was she supposed to say?

"Speechless? I wasn't trying to shock you."

"I wasn't expecting you to ask."

"Sure. I understand."

Was that a smile or a smirk? Surely this wasn't a smirking situation. Maybe he felt awkward? She tried to put a civil expression back on her face.

Brian looked down, a bit sheepish, and said, "I noticed that Maia seems to like Joel. He's come to the gallery a few times and I wondered if he might, you know, like her, too."

Maia. He was worried about Maia and her social life? That's all he was concerned about? Suddenly, everything turned red. Pure red. Even as she was thinking that she would be cool and walk away as if nothing he'd said had impacted her in any way whatsoever, her fists were clenching. All she could see was Brian, only Brian, and he looked exactly like a target.

Her hand was still on its upward swing when it was stopped effortlessly and held so hard in his grasp, that it stunned her. He put his free arm around her, behind her, and pulled her close.

Her defenses failed, and so quickly. She was glad to be kissing Brian. Glad. It made no sense, none of it did. When had her hands reached his shoulders? She dug her fingers into those shoulders feeling the strength in them, glad his arms were wrapped around her.

When she stopped and pulled away, she whispered, "You did that on purpose, didn't you?"

He bent over and kissed her somewhere below her ear.

"What?"

"Being a jerk to make me lose my temper."

He pulled her close again and spoke in her hair. "I don't know when I decided to do that. It was sometime after I walked in your door. Maybe even after we started talking out here." His breath was warm. "You drive me crazy. The temptation to break down those walls you put up is more than I could resist."

"Walls?"

"The wall you keep around yourself."

She pushed back. A temptation—not her, but to break through her defenses. To break her.

"The others are waiting. We'd better get back." She tried to rally her good spirits, but her glow was fast disappearing.

He kept her hand in his, stopping her forward motion. "I doubt they're waiting."

She tried to arrange a smile on her face, and to forget the feel of his lips on hers. Mistake? That kiss had been a big one.

In fact, realizing this was almost a relief. It enabled her to walk back into the house without rosy cheeks. If they noticed anything at all, she suspected they imagined an argument had occurred, that's if they were judging by the expression on her face. She didn't dare look at Brian's face.

Frannie headed toward the sofa with her plate, to the open spot between Maia and Joel. As she approached, Joel scooted over next to Maia.

"Here you go, Frannie. Have a seat," Joel said.

The empty space was now between Joel and Brian.

No problem. She wasn't going to worry about Brian. He was responsible for his behavior. It was nothing to her.

He alternated between ignoring her to giving her that smirk

that irritated her so badly. She tried to concentrate on the food and on the conversation until her cell phone rang.

At first she didn't recognize the ringing as coming from her phone, but everyone stopped and stared at her.

Maia asked, "Whose phone?" but she looked straight at Frannie.

"Excuse me." She walked to the counter. She would've ignored it while her company was there, but they were all looking at her. "Miss Denman?"

She jumped when he spoke. She'd hired him only a few days ago. This quickly, did it mean bad news or good? She wasn't even sure what would constitute good or bad news.

"This is Ron Hamilton."

"Yes, I recognized your voice. Do you already have information?"

"I do. Would you like to meet so that I can turn over my notes and documentation?"

"I would, but I'm at Emerald Isle. I don't suppose you're here?"

"No, ma'am. I'm in Raleigh."

"I don't know when I'll be back there. Can you tell me over the phone?"

"Certainly I can. I can mail or fax the documentation. Also, I'm happy to follow up with details in an email. Whatever is most convenient?"

"Yes, yes. That's great." Suddenly she remembered she had an audience. "Hold, please.

"Will you all excuse me for a moment?" She half-ran down the hall to Will's bedroom and shut the door.

"Please Mr. Hamilton, what did you find out?"

"Call me Ron."

Her nerves became steadily more brittle. There was a war going on inside her between eagerness and anxiety and fear and somehow they all felt like the same thing. She drew in a deep breath.

"Please."

"I found a birth notice in the Greensville newspaper."

"Greensville? Mine?"

"Frances Anne Denman, daughter of Edward M. and Frances C. Denman. The date of birth matches what you gave me."

The excitement and anxiety was so sudden, so mixed up, that her throat tightened, threatened to choke her. She felt light-headed. His next words broke the spell.

"I located their marriage license—for Edward Denman and Frances Cooke—and I found where Frances is buried."

Buried.

"I'm sorry. I suspect that disappoints you, but it's better to say it straight out. I hope you understand."

"Where? When?"

"New Bern. There's no marker on the grave, but the death was properly recorded. Almost twenty-five years ago."

Nearly a quarter of a century.

"I would've been about six or seven."

"Yes, ma'am. Cause of death was noted as pneumonia. Appeared to have been living with a friend or acquaintance at the time. I haven't been able to locate that person."

"I see. What about her parents or siblings?"

"She was an only child and her mother died a year ago in Richmond."

A grandmother. Her grandmother. She'd missed her by a year, and a lifetime.

"What was her name?"

"Margaret."

"Margaret." She said it aloud, testing it to feel for any kind of rightness, and found none. In the end, she was a grandmother who wasn't, apparently by choice.

He resumed. "I have the cemetery records and a plat to show where she's buried. No grave marker, but there was a small obituary. I'm guessing the friend gave the info for that. Shall I read it to you?" Again a pause. He asked, "Are you all right? It's normal to have misgivings. Believe me, I know. I've been doing this for a long time. Another thing I know is that after this much time has passed, it doesn't hurt to take it in slowly, a little at a time. It's different for everyone. But it's the living that need the consideration."

Her heart seemed to be vibrating in her chest. "Maybe you're right."

"Again, we can meet and I can hand the paperwork over and we can discuss it, or I can scan in the material and email it. I'm always available to meet, in person or by phone."

Her hand to her chest, she willed her heart to slow. She spoke in slow, measured words, "Yes, thank you. Can you scan it and send it?"

"I'll have my assistant take care of it and you'll have it later today. You can review it when you're ready. If you have any questions, or would like me to dig further, let me know."

"Thank you. I appreciate how quickly you took care of this."

"My pleasure. Now, take a few moments and relax. Remember, this is about the past. It's been in the past for a long time."

She nodded. "Thanks."

Frannie sat for a while, mindful that the others were still out there, but unable to compose her face. In the end, she decided not to worry about it. It was what it was.

They were sitting and chatting. They looked up in unison when she walked back into the room.

Brian looked at her face and then at the phone in her hand.

She shrugged. "You all know that I recently learned that I'm adopted? I hired a detective to find out what he could about my birth mother."

She sat down on the floor. The remains of her lunch littered the plate. She'd never felt less hungry. She tried to smile. "Apparently, she died many years ago. The detective is sending me the details."

"You never knew her, right?" Luke put his utensils on his now-empty plate.

She nodded.

Maia said, "Like that matters."

Luke countered, "Never said it didn't."

"Anyway, it's good information to know. You have to give yourself time to adjust to it. It's not easy when the past you thought you knew starts shifting."

Maia was right. Shifting. She'd had an earthquake and the aftershocks kept coming.

From the corner of her eye, she caught Brian giving Maia a look.

"I'm okay, Brian. Really. In fact, it's good to know the facts." It was true. It was good to know the truth.

Joel turned to Luke and said, "Give Juli my apologies. I wish I could stay longer, but I have to run." He shared his smile generally around the room. "I wish all business meetings could be this much fun." He stopped beside Frannie and gave her a hug. "Be strong."

"Thanks." She patted his hand. "You mentioned Juli?"

Maia jumped in. "She called while you were dressing. She's dropping by to pick up Luke. His car is at the gallery."

Frannie nodded. "Thank you all for this lovely lunch. Thanks for thinking of me and coming by."

"Pretty good timing, if I say so myself. Thanks for the show." Joel grinned.

Brian frowned. "What show?"

Instinctively, Frannie knew he was thinking of their private meeting on the porch because that's what popped into her mind first, too.

"I fell into the ocean. They arrived in time to save me." She cleared her throat. "Joel saved me. Maia and Luke watched as I went under." She meant it as a joke, but no one got it.

Brian scanned each face, and apparently satisfied by what he saw, he turned back to her, saying, "Wrong time of year for a swim, unless you're wearing a wet suit."

This started a round of laughter.

Clearly puzzled, he said, "I guess that was a pun of sorts,

unintended, but I don't think it was that funny."

Maia giggled.

Frannie said, "I'll explain later." And then she hushed, thinking that might seem to imply something to the others, such as Brian lingering after the others had left. Her cheeks felt warm.

No, please, not here. Not now.

She was glad of the chance to walk with Joel to the door and turn her back to the others. She needed time to cool her cheeks. She handed him his jacket.

"I'll put it on later."

"It's still officially winter. You'll need it when the sun starts going down."

He smiled and leaned forward and put a quick kiss on her forehead. "Take care of yourself, Frannie. Give yourself a little credit, and also have some fun. Otherwise, the rest isn't worth much."

She closed the door behind him, feeling like something in her life had changed, perhaps forever, maybe in a good way.

Juli arrived within minutes. Luke teased her about looking for an excuse to come inside so she could admire her painting hanging on the wall. They didn't stay long, saying they had to pick up Luke's car and then Danny.

"Did the sketching go well?"

"It did. At least, I think so."

"You're your own harshest critic." Luke put his arm around her shoulders for a quick hug. "You missed a fine lunch."

"I smell barbecue."

"Play your cards right and maybe next time we'll invite you."

They both smiled silly smiles and went out the door.

Maia said, "I'd better get going, too." She pulled on her jacket. "They're my ride." She gave Frannie a quick hug, told her brother to stay out of trouble, and then was gone.

Suddenly, it was only the two of them.

Brian asked, "Did we finish the conversation we started on the porch?"

His blue eyes were warmer than they had any right to be. She backed around to the far side of the counter.

"I think, yes, for now we're done. It's been a busy day."

He sat on the stool. "What was that about a swim?"

She shook her head. "Nothing big. I was looking out at the ocean, my feet got stuck in the sand and when I tried to back out, I stumbled."

"I see." He tapped his fingers on the counter top. "You probably don't know, but Juli's first husband died...in the ocean. It was pretty tough for everyone." He shrugged. "For a moment, it threw me."

"I had no idea."

"You couldn't. Besides, it's history. People have to put the past where it belongs and get over things."

"Easier said than done."

"Maybe, if you let it be difficult."

"And you don't?"

"No. You're talking about Diane? I'm definitely over her. Unfortunately, I have to deal with her because of Megan."

Actually, she'd been thinking about his grudge against Maia. His response about Diane surprised her. She let it drop.

"What a day. First, breakfast with Juli. Then you walk in. Then I fall in the ocean. Joel, Maia and Luke show up for an impromptu lunch. And then you walk in, yet again."

"With the food."

"Yes, that's an important detail. But then you torture me on the porch because you want to kiss me."

He smiled and moved as if getting up from the stool. "Is that what I did?"

"Seemed like it to me."

"And now what?"

She let his question hang there. She had no answer. He reached across the counter and took her hand. He stroked her fingers with his own and she might've had an answer soon, but a knock sounded on the side door.

"Someone forgot something?" She cast a quick look around as Brian reached for the door.

A woman's voice said, "Hello?"

Brian stepped back and in walked Laurel.

She was perfect from her freshly styled blond hair and fair, unmarked skin to the sweater and jacket and the slacks that fit her with a deft combination of shape and drape. She held her clutch purse delicately, her fingers poised to show her manicure and the hands that would never be allowed to wear age spots. She strode in and then paused, as if hesitant. Softly, she said, "I hope I'm not interrupting?"

As Frannie struggled to find words, Laurel turned to Brian. "I'm Laurel Denman. Frannie's mom."

She said it with the right timing, and with a tiny hitch in her voice to betray her uncertainty and hurt—the hurt inflicted by her heartless daughter.

Brian accepted her hand. "Pleased to meet you, Mrs. Denman. I'm Brian Donovan."

"Are you a friend of Frannie's?"

He sort of shrugged, but it was more like he was trying to shake something off of his back. Laurel grabbed his hand, locking it between her much smaller, softer hands. He cast a quick look at Frannie.

"Yes, ma'am," he said.

"There are so few friends of hers that I know. Frannie doesn't bring them home." She patted his hand and then released him.

He stepped back and turned toward Frannie.

She tried to keep her face blank. Did she want him out of this? No witnesses for a scene that would surely not show her at her best? Or did she want him here as a bulwark to keep either of them from going too far?

Neither. Never mind Brian, she wanted Laurel out. OUT. Any way in which she had to make it happen was fine with her.

"Call me later, okay, Brian?"

Chapter Twenty

"Call me later," she'd said. Her blue eyes had gone as dark as midnight. It gave him chills.

He thought Fran was a hider, an avoider, and maybe she was, but she was also... He couldn't think of the right word. Dangerous?

One thing he knew, he wouldn't want to be surprised by her somewhere, anywhere, with that look on her face. He knew it was due to Laurel's unannounced visit. He almost felt sorry for Mrs. Denman.

It kind of hit home, too. Was that what he'd been doing to Maia? Punishing her with his attitude?

Call me later, she'd said. The words echoed in his mind.

Mrs. Denman looked every inch a lady. Spoke that way, too. She probably had good cause to worry about Fran. And heaven knew, most any adoptive mother would worry about her daughter chasing down her 'roots'. So, given that he didn't know what the heck was going on, he knew enough to recognize there were big problems between mother and daughter. He was more than happy to scoot. Contrary to his earlier assumptions, it was obvious Fran could defend herself fine.

He could get on with his day.

But he sat in the van, letting it idle and tapping on the steering wheel. That shiny Lexus must belong to Mrs. Denman.

He could see why the two women didn't get along. One was so smooth she was scary, the other was erratic and scary in her own right, but they were both type A's. He really hadn't seen it in Fran before. Like opposing magnets, right? Or had he mixed up the allusion? It didn't matter. Matter. That was it. Matter and anti-matter. Not good to be nearby when they mixed.

Maia would be back at the gallery by now. He checked his watch. It would still be open.

He backed out and onto the street and headed for the bridges to Beaufort.

****

Maia was at the counter speaking with her assistant. She looked up when the bell jingled.

"Hi!" Maia walked away from her sales assistant, Brendan, and came over to him.

"What's up? Oh, and by the way, thanks for bringing lunch over. It was fun, wasn't it?"

She walked straight up to him with a smile and put her hands on his arms. He looked away. He resisted the impulse to ruffle her hair. They were grown. She wouldn't thank him for messing up that mop. Suddenly, he put his arms around her and hugged her.

"Brian? Was that daddy's grizzly bear hug?"

Shoot. He hadn't thought of that. He let her go. Daddy's grizzly bear hug. When they were kids, Dad's grizzly bear hug was a consolation when things went badly—when stuff was falling apart in a big way.

"Brian, you're not sick or anything, are you?" She put her hands on his cheeks. "Look at me. Let me see your eyes."

"I'm fine, sis. Fine. I owe you an apology. I'm not good at giving them."

She smiled and her dimples deepened to hold all things good and worthwhile.

"You don't owe me anything, but don't be angry with me any longer."

He nodded. "I'm sorry. Diane, and everything that happened after her, isn't your fault. I'm sorry I took it out on you."

"I understand. I really do."

He nodded. "Good, then."

"Come step outside with me." She held his arms and

199

tugged gently.

He'd forgotten about Brendan. The kid was standing there, his mouth hanging open.

"After you." He held the door.

The sun was bright on the sidewalk. It felt good on his face. Cleansing, somehow.

They stopped where the last step met the sidewalk. Maia leaned against one iron rail; Brian leaned against the other. The toes of their shoes almost touched.

"I thought you'd still be with Frannie." She shook her head in dismay. "Oh, I'm sorry, here I go again."

"You're my sister. You can ask, but don't pry."

"Got it. I think. I hope. That's a tricky boundary."

"You know the difference." He dropped the subject. Time to move on. "I was still there, might still be there, but she has a visitor."

"Joel?"

"No, not Joel."

Maia shrugged and tried to sound offhand, "Oh, well. None of my business, anyway."

"She has no romantic interest in him."

"You asked her?" Maia's eyes grew round. "Come on, Brian. You didn't, did you? What did you say? You didn't tell her that I, that I...."

"I don't remember what I said. I asked her and she told me."

She fanned her face with her hand. "I don't know what came over me." She took a deep breath. "So, then, who came? I see it's on your mind."

"Laurel Denman."

"Laurel.... You mean the wicked stepmother?"

"Maia. Not nice. And not true. At least, she doesn't look wicked. She's pretty fine looking, in fact, and she spoke nice."

"Nicely."

"Nicely."

"So she has good manners. How did Frannie respond?"

"She said I should call her later."

"Really? Well, then." She rubbed her arms and shivered. "What's the trouble?"

"She looked scary."

"Scared? Of what?"

"Not scared, but scary. I've seen her in all sorts of moods. Sometimes it hard to tell who the real Fran is, but I've never seen her like that."

"Oh. I see. I wouldn't worry. They've got a lot of history between them and Frannie has unresolved issues about their relationship from what she's told me."

Was she trying to soothe him? She was using that big sister voice. But she wasn't the big sister. He was older than her by two years. Old soul? Is that what they called it? Someone had once said to him that Maia was an old soul.

He said, "You're cold. You should get back inside."

"I'm fine. I'll go in in a minute."

He took off his jacket and put it around her shoulders. "What about you?"

"Me?" Maia asked as she pulled the jacket more tightly about her. "What about me?"

"Joel. Anyone with eyes can see you like him. A lot."

"I do. He's very polite and thoughtful."

"You like his manners."

"Sure. And he's smart and likes art. You should hear him go on about the gallery and things he'd like to do."

"No, thank you. I'll leave that to you. I hope you let him know."

"Know what?"

"That you like him."

She blushed.

"You have to tell him. If you think a guy is going to just know how you feel about him, then you aren't as smart as I thought you were. You always have advice for everyone. Take some of your own."

"Brian. Oh, Brian." Her dark eyes looked almost panicked.

"He's nice, but I barely know him. I'm tired of—"

"Of what? Being hurt? Being alone? Does it matter? Unless you've decided it's safer to be alone and sad than to risk being hurt." He shrugged. "Your choice. But you should treat yourself at least as well as you treat others. You deserve it, sis."

"You take my breath away, Brian. That's a lot of thinking going on in your hard head."

He laughed. "And it's giving me a headache. Think I'll go home and take a nap. Or maybe change the oil in Will's van."

Maia shook her head. "You came all the way over here to tell me you were sorry?"

He gave her a one-armed hug. "See ya."

"See you around, Brian." She stepped forward. "Wait."

"What?"

"Mom and Dad want to get together for their anniversary. Interested?"

"Sure. Let me know when and where. I'd rather not wear a suit. I don't think it even fits me anymore."

"I'll call you." She handed his jacket back to him.

Call me later, Fran had said. "Yeah, I'll talk to you later."

Chapter Twenty-One

"Why are you here?"

Laurel looked at the door, which was still in the act of closing as Brian exited. "I'm here to see you." She smiled.

Her pleasant expression looked planted, artificial, calculated.

"You're back from Savannah."

"I am. Obviously."

"Good trip?"

Laurel opened her arms. "What about a hug? Maybe an 'I love you' or 'I miss you'? I exist, sweetheart. You can't erase me from your life."

Frannie put her hands on the counter. "Erase. An interesting word and it suggests a lot. I was at the house a few days ago."

"Were you? All's well there, I hope. I'm heading there from here." Her eyebrows raised and her lips formed an 'Oh,' and then she grinned. "Does that mean you saw my surprise for you?"

"Surprise? You mean the new furnishings in the TV room?"

"Isn't it gorgeous? I hired a local decorator to handle it. There's all sorts of goodies for the sound and such. I don't even know what to call them. All the electronics are hidden and, well, it's so excellent, isn't it? I even...what do you call it? I put a 'rush' on it, so I could surprise you with the finished product." She was gushing like a teenager.

"I had a lot of memories invested in the old furniture." Frannie crossed her arms. "We had an agreement that the TV room was hands off."

"Did we? I don't recall that. You're the one who always says we have to live our lives and we can't do that if we cling to the past. I want you to be happy, not nursing grudges and feeling cheated by life."

Laurel moved past Will's old chair, one hand above the head rest, not coming into contact with it. She turned gracefully and sat on the sofa.

"Tell me about Brian. Is that his name? Has Joel come by?" Laurel tilted her head to the side and smiled again. "He was so excited about seeing you down here." Laurel shoved the plastic bag of papers from the van to the far side, and set her purse on the table.

Laurel, as usual, was trying to force her own reality on everyone around her.

"You are staring at me like I might bite. Can't we please have a civil conversation? Is that asking so much?"

Still standing by the counter, Frannie said, "I asked you not to come here."

"I had to. You know that. You've been down here too long, and now that I've met your friend, Brian... What was his last name?"

"Leave him out of this. I didn't invite you here and I won't discuss him with you."

Laurel stood. She moved back to the counter and slid her hands across the Formica palms up, toward Frannie.

"Sweetheart, don't you see? How this is like last time? How it happened before?" She closed her eyes as if uttering a short prayer. "Please tell me you can see it. You must know I'm right."

"Stop it. Stop bringing that up. That was long ago and it was different. Not like this. I'm taking care of my uncle's house. I've made friends. I'm happier than I've been in a long time." Suddenly, almost shocked, she realized it was true.

"It's no shame to need help, Frannie. Some people aren't meant to live independently. Stress has a negative effect on you. You can't help it. It's not your fault."

"Oh, I see. It's my heritage, is that right? Unhappiness and instability are in my genes?"

"Don't be sharp with me. Can't you see I'm trying to spare you another breakdown? This man, Brian? He looks rough to me. He's going to be another 'what's-his-name'. I won't say the name of that mistake aloud ever again."

"Stop it, Laurel."

"Mother. You used to call me mother. You needed me when it all fell apart, and I was the one who came to your rescue. I took you back home to comfort and safety." She pressed her hands to her chest. "Please remember how it was when you left before? You were spending all of your time with strangers."

"You mean my friends?"

"They filled your head with ideas. They didn't know, didn't care, what was good for you. I do, Frannie, I do. Me." Her face changed from troubled to tortured. "I'm the only woman who has ever been a mother to you."

"Save the histrionics."

The faint lines deepened, hardened around Laurel's eyes.

"Well, if anyone knows what histrionics are, it's you. You're the expert, Frannie dear. So. Fine. When this one disappoints you, and he will, I'll be waiting to help you pick up the pieces. And when you start hearing the noises in the night and can't sleep, and start falling apart, call me and I'll come running. Because, no matter what you say, I'm your mother."

At some point, Frannie put her hands over her ears. She could shut out some of Laurel's voice, but nothing could stop her heart from being torn in two. Her will was softening. She wasn't a fighter. How could she be so cruel to Laurel? She wasn't a cruel person. But she had to do it. From somewhere deep inside, she dredged up the words. They sounded breathless as she pushed them out. "I want you to move out of the house."

No one breathed. Neither of them, not even the world.

"I appreciate that you raised me. I appreciate that you even did the best you could. Let's leave it at that. Don't push me further."

"You appreciate? Like that means anything? I gave up my life for you."

"You turned her away."

"Who?"

"Frances. She came to the house asking to see father. Admit it—you lied to her—turned her away. Soon after, she was dead. She's buried in an unmarked grave."

"Is it so wrong that I wanted to protect my family?"

"From what? She and Dad were divorced. She wasn't looking to move back in, was she?"

"Sarcasm will get you nowhere."

"I believed you were trying to be honest with me before. Were you?"

"Yes, I was."

"Yet you told Joel I was interested in him."

She pursed her lips. "I might have. Sometimes a man needs encouragement. You know I like Joel."

"You think he's easy to push around. I'm not so sure he is. There's more to him than you recognize. Why should it matter to you anyway? What was it you said? That he wouldn't interfere with how I spent my money? Most of what I spend, I spend on…" It all froze for a moment, then became startlingly clear. She continued, "I spend it on house expenses and to pay the bills you run up." Truth came too close. It swerved by like an out of control car and her stomach lurched. She felt dizzy.

Frannie was trying to stop the spinning. Her stomach was churning now. Burning inside. She pressed her hand against her stomach as if to quell the fire.

"Go home, Laurel. Go home and start packing. I'm putting the house on the market."

"You wouldn't dare."

"I've already spoken with the attorney." She didn't need to tell her the exact details of the conversation. Let the implication stand on its own.

"Honesty. Is that what you said? Honesty? Truth?" Laurel's usually flawless complexion flushed a deep, ugly maroon.

She spit the words out. "You've gone behind my back taking the good things I've tried to do for you and throwing them into my face or using them against me. You think you know so much? You might as well know this, too. That day when Frances came to the house, she wasn't alone. There was someone else with her. A child."

Chapter Twenty-Two

"I'm no one's fool. I wasn't about to raise another of that woman's children. You needn't stare at me like that." She pointed her finger in Frannie's face.

"I did right by you. You were never easy. Always clinging to your father and disrespectful to me. No matter how I tried to help you develop social skills or to conduct yourself with any degree of dignity."

Frannie had stopped hearing. She was still stuck on the words about the child with Frances.

"Who was she? Or he?"

"Who? Frances?"

"The child? Who was she?"

"I presume the child belonged to her. Only heaven knows who the father was."

"Is. Is. Not was!" She couldn't stop saying it over and over. "Is." She reached up and pulled on her hair, seeking pain, anything to interrupt the rage building in her head. "That child was, at the least, my half-sister or brother. Frances died soon after. What happened to the child?"

"How would I know? I was already bringing up someone else's child. One was enough. The rest wasn't my business."

Frannie swept the items on the counter off with one rough swipe. "Get out."

Objects sailed. One hit Laurel's arm and she screamed out, "There's my proof. Everything I've said about you is right. You try to get me out of the house, and we'll see what the courts have to say about it, and about you and your competency."

Laurel was no more than a blur as she went to the door.

It was as if Frannie could see that child standing alongside the woman, a sickly woman with a child no one wanted.

She ran to the door, flung it open and chased Laurel down the stairs. "Wait. Wait! Was the child a boy or a girl? What was the child's name?"

She saw in Laurel's face that she was considering not answering.

"Tell me."

"They all look alike at that age." She got into the car and slammed the door.

It. Was. IS.

Deep night dwelled inside Frannie's head. It was a cave void of light and feeling, for good or ill. She pulled herself back up the stairs and slammed the door. She scrambled down the hall running her hands along the wall to steady herself and found her way into the bathroom.

She tried splashing cold water on her face, but ruthless spasms gripped her stomach. She held on to the sink and lowered herself to the tile floor, leaned over the toilet and lost every bit of barbecue and hush puppies still in her system, and then some. She retched long after there was nothing more to give, and her stomach, her whole body, felt twisted and battered.

When she was done, it was no longer black in her head, but the room was dark. This was a natural dark. She lay down on the floor and curled up, her face resting on the small, cotton bath mat, and she cried.

Later, dazed, seeking normalcy in simple, everyday acts, she rinsed her face and mouth, and dragged a brush through her hair. It didn't work. She did manage to successfully complete an important task, but only because he didn't answer the phone and she could leave a message.

"Mr. Hamilton? This is Frannie Denman. I've learned that Frances Cooke may have had another child. If so, it would have been born a few years after me. Not many. Maybe two to five years after. Laurel, my stepmother, saw the child with Frances when I was seven. I don't know whether it was a boy or girl, and I don't know if Frances was using Denman as her last name, or Cooke, or some other name. Sorry, that's all I the info I have. Will you look into it? Thanks."

Outside was the night. Stars hung suspended above, and darkness filled in and all around, like being in a well, a well of cold, brisk air. It washed against her face and cooled her pounding head. Anger, base anger, even if it was righteous, was a poison—if that kind of base, dirt-throwing anger could ever be righteous.

With the sofa blanket around her shoulders, she left the porch and climbed the outside stairs toward the points of light overhead. She could almost reach those beacons by standing on the deck above the house, leaning against the railing and straining, reaching heavenward. They tantalized, just beyond the tips of her fingers. A deep night beneath a vast sky, somewhere in which to hide. From others, from herself? Alone, lost in the dark belly of night, only to find she'd taken her faults with her. It was true.

She was ashamed. Per her usual style, she'd handled a delicate situation with a nuclear strike. She had no right to be so critical of Laurel when, she herself, was so far removed from common sense and objectivity, or from a reasonable response, from actions that were appropriate to the situation.

Or hypocrisy. She'd been busy re-making her uncle's home, without asking him, assuming he'd be pleased if he made it back home, and if he didn't it would be easier to sell. Talk about cold practicality.

She'd meant well. She didn't think she could say the same for Laurel.

Admitting her errors didn't change that she was right about a few things, like living on her own. The relationship between them was toxic. Time and distance might improve that. Might not. But only the attempt would answer that question.

She drew her hands back and crossed her arms, wrapping then in the blanket, holding them tightly to her body. She shivered, but her brain was regaining its better nature, so she lingered.

Starlight ruled above. Below, a few ships' lights dotted the black water. No contest. God in his universe. A touch of God. A desperate yearning that in times of anger and frustration, she would remember God. Guilt that she often forgot to turn to God when things were good.

She didn't need to be alone. She didn't need to try to manage alone.

Frannie knelt at the railing. The wood was damp and cool against her forehead. Who was up there among the stars? Her father? Frances, the mother who wasn't? Here on earth? Laurel. No wonder she, Frannie, was so screwed up. She laughed and then realized she was crying instead, huddled in her blanket on Uncle Will's cold, exposed, beach house version of a widow's walk.

No father, no mother. Who else? A sibling? A sister or brother? Whether half or whole, there was a sibling. Hopefully, one who was still earth bound. She needed more than Laurel, and even Will, to claim as family.

"Fran? You okay?"

She hadn't heard the stairs creak. She pushed her hair back out of her face with her forearm.

"Yeah. I'm good. I was out here admiring celestial bodies, Orion and such."

He knelt next to her. "You're cold."

She pulled the blanket tighter. "I was, but I think it's actually warming up out here."

"You're too cold to feel it now."

Brian stood, somehow pulling her to her feet along with him. It was a graceful act and it amazed her, as did his presence.

"Where'd you come from?"

"From down there with the rest of the mortals. Nothing celestial about me."

"I mean, why did you come back?"

"Let's call it curiosity."

"If you say so. How did you know I was up here?"

"Your front door was wide open. You weren't inside and your car was still parked out back."

He put his arm around her in a brotherly way. She didn't want to make more of it than that.

"Now I'm warmer." And she was. That tiny snide voice of Laurel's tried to weasel in. She refused to allow it. "Did I really leave the front door open?"

"Yes. I shut it. I left it unlocked."

"Good. I didn't bring a key with me."

How quickly could a person's world shift? This quickly? Could it be true? Or was she about to be slapped down again? She felt good, really good, tucked into the crook of Brian's arm.

"Did you come back tonight because you thought I might have chucked Laurel off the widow's walk?"

Brian laughed. "Observation deck, it's called. Although, there's a certain kind of symmetry to Laurel and a widow's walk." He looked up at the stars and laughed. Frannie laughed with him.

"You know what this really is?" she asked. "Feel the wind against your face. Hear the ocean. Smell the salt. It almost feels like we're moving. This is Will's deck. His ship. His Captain's Walk."

He didn't speak, but tightened his arm around her.

Encouraged, she looked up into his eyes and said, "Brian, there's something I want to tell you. Will you stay with me awhile?"

Chapter Twenty-Three

It was late and he'd found her freezing up on the observation deck, had barely figured out she was all right, and now she had 'something to tell him'? Those words had the quality of an understatement.

She added, "But first, before I step inside with you, into the light, I need to go wash my face again and maybe do a better job with the hair brush. It's been a rough afternoon and evening. I don't think my ego can survive lamplight without a little help."

"By all means, go ahead."

"You'll wait for me?"

"If you'll let me in the house where it's warmer, yes, I'll wait."

She went in ahead of him and disappeared down the hallway. The blanket swept the floor like a long cape.

He sat at the table, then half-stood when he thought he heard a loud cry. He listened intently and hearing nothing else, he settled back into the chair.

When she returned a few minutes later, she still looked tired and her eyes were faintly red, but there was a smile on her face and she moved with confidence.

She busied herself at the counter. "I'll make us some tea."

"No, thanks. A glass of water, maybe."

Two mugs and a clear glass pot of some kind were on the counter. Frannie poured the hot water over some bits of tea that looked like scraps of dried weedy stuff.

"We have to let it steep for four minutes." She laughed softly. "Don't worry about this tea. It doesn't have any caffeine in it. It won't keep you awake tonight."

He opened his mouth to say 'no' again and then closed it.

213

She placed the mugs of tea on the table.

He looked down at his, doubtful. Tea.

"I'm not much of a tea drinker. Hot, anyway."

She smiled. "I know, but please try it. This is a different blend than what you had before. You can decide whether you like it while I tell you a story." She pushed the cup around by its handle. "I like you. A lot. You were very kind to come back here to check on me. I'm glad you didn't arrive sooner, though, because I was a mess." She brushed at the blanket. "I mean worse than when you found me."

"Much later and you would've been frozen."

"Not quite. It was cold, but not that cold."

"No offense, Fran, but I think you're crazy."

It was a throwaway line. People were always calling other people crazy. So why did she get that pale, rigid expression and then slosh her precious tea onto the table?

"It's an expression. I'm sorry. I'm not a sensitive kind of guy."

She shook her head. "No, unfortunately, I think you may be right."

"There you go. That's what I like about you. Your sense of humor. Your contagious optimism."

Now she looked confused. She'd smiled before so what was the deal? She wouldn't have smiled if she thought he really meant it, literally meant it. Right?

"I'm not crazy, but I have a nervous disposition. Sometimes, in stress, that sort of translates into crazy."

"You're a woman. Don't nervous and moody come with the territory?"

This time she did giggle. It contrasted oddly with her still red eyes. "Only in the land of generalization."

"So let's talk about crazy. Let's talk about Laurel."

Fran laughed. "You're doing this on purpose, aren't you? You refuse to let me be morose or tied up in knots."

He shrugged.

"Why? You can be arrogant and rude, but also very kind.

Why are you so kind to me?"

He didn't answer. He wasn't a rescuer or a fixer. That was Maia's shtick. He tried to think of something to say, something that would change the direction of this awkward conversation. He said, "I don't think Will would mind if I told you."

Her eyes, so dark they looked almost black, stared. He forced himself to look away.

"He showed me the verse you brought him."

"Yes?"

"He was always around other people in the navy, and his family before that. When he retired, suddenly he was alone. He'd get down or gloomy. When a verse would catch his attention, he'd write it down and hide it around the house. Sometimes he'd happen upon one of those verses. It gave him something to think about, something outside of himself." He shrugged. "That's it. Not a big mystery."

Frannie opened her mouth to speak and then shut it. Finally, she shook her head and said, "We need cookies. Excuse me."

What? Well, maybe cookies would be good. He watched her limp across to the kitchen cabinet, rumpled and still clutching the blanket trailing under her feet. She returned with a tin of some kind of girlie cookies. Tea cookies? She tucked the blanket under her arm while she worked the top off the tin. No Oreos or chocolate chips here. Nope. She pushed the tin closer to him.

"Thank you for telling me about Will and the verses. I understand about getting gloomy. Tonight I was upset about Laurel. I've told you some already, but there's more wrong with us than that, always has been. You know, like chemistry? Bad chemistry. We never mixed well even when we tried. We haven't tried in a very long time."

"It was bad when your dad was alive, too?"

"Probably, but less noticeable then. I got older and more stubborn. I'm not a good daughter."

"Judging by how you looked at her when she showed up

215

this afternoon, I'm not surprised to hear you say it. What I don't get is why you two live together? Why not live your own lives? Why force yourselves on each other?"

"I agree." She sighed. "Oh, Brian. I've tried, but not hard enough."

He took a small bite out of one of the cookies. Not great, but it was okay. He popped the rest of it in his mouth and reached for another. Not exactly satisfying, but they made the tea taste better.

"No matter what, it seems like I always get drawn back to the house and Laurel. I don't blame Laurel for that. The fault for that lies with me."

"So, it's simple. Move out." He waved his arms around at Will's kitchen and living room. "Hey, you're already on your way to being gone from there. You're here."

"You think like a guy."

"I hope so." He thumped his hand on the table.

"Believe it or not, Laurel depends upon me, more, I think, than I depend on her."

"By the way, Laurel wasn't what I was expecting. Nice looking woman. Looked more like Glenda than the Wicked Witch of the West."

"Hmmm. Well, I understand what you're saying. I wish I had her smoothness, dignity. Maybe her ability to wound with a simple word and look innocent while doing it. Not that I'd want to hurt anyone, but you know what I mean?"

"How'd she get you back home before?"

"She didn't. Actually, she helped me. Allowed me to return home. I could say she almost rescued me. She certainly says it often enough." She looked at the ceiling and then across the room before she continued. "It was a bad relationship, a boyfriend who didn't work out. We had a bad breakup and then, well, he tried to intimidate me. He was a bully. Even after he was gone, my nerves got the better of me. I started imagining things, but they seemed so real, you know?"

"Like what?"

"Like noises. Outside. At the windows. I felt followed. At first, I thought it was real, it felt real, but then, after a while, as my nerves got worse and I couldn't sleep properly and all, I lost my job. Laurel persuaded me to move back in with her and everything calmed down right away. That's not a coincidence. Some people aren't good alone."

He couldn't decide how to express himself on this. He didn't want to belittle her. Her confidence sucked as it was, but honestly, this was too much.

"I don't understand women. I tell Maia the same. Why isn't a noise, a noise? Because there's nothing there, doesn't mean there wasn't something there. Well, you know what I mean. Like a logical cause." He broke a cookie in half and pushed the crumbs into a little pile. "You girls get all worked up over those things. If something is scaring you, then call the cops. If not, then move on. Get stronger locks. Cut back the bushes. You get the idea.

"Like that gull that hit your door. If you were scared enough to sit up half the night, why weren't you scared enough to call the local police?"

"Because I knew I'd look silly. I kept my phone with me. I would've called for help if anything else had happened. How did you know about that?"

"Juli told me."

"Oh."

"They don't do that."

"Do what?"

"They roost at night. At least, as far as I know. Not that I've given it much thought. Did you have a light on? Porch light?"

"No light. It flew smack into the side of the house. It made a big noise when it hit. Besides, how else would it get there?"

"You're feeling better. I can tell because you're ready to argue. You want to start a fight."

The cookie tin was more than half-empty. He hadn't been aware of eating so many, but it must have been him. He put the lid back on and looked up. She was sitting there with that stupid blanket and her arms crossed and looking like she couldn't decide whether to throw a punch or laugh.

"There's more," she said.

"Okay."

"I'm taking control of my life."

"Sure." He didn't know what else to say.

"I'm going to pursue this family thing no matter what, no matter who gets in the way or tries to stop me."

He frowned. "Who would try to stop you? Aside from Laurel, I guess."

"I don't know, but sometimes a person can be their own worst enemy. I'm going to believe in myself."

He opened his mouth to say easier said than done but stopped himself.

"I'm going to prove I can manage on my own. I don't need anyone to protect me."

"We can all use a little help sometimes." Had he started this? He hadn't meant to, not to push her to the point of…what? Putting herself at risk? She was a nervous type. He was no better than Maia, butting in and interfering in people's lives. And what about himself? He'd kissed her only a few hours ago. Not planned, sort of. She'd been pissed about it. She hadn't even mentioned it tonight, so maybe she still was. What did that mean now that she was telling him all this stuff? Did he owe her something?

He pulled at his collar. It was getting overly warm in the room. He said, "Make sure you know what you're doing, and if something scares you call the police. That's what they get paid for." He stood and the chair scraped against the floor. "Stay off the roof, will you? At least, until the weather warms up."

"I will." She stood and walked with him.

He paused before opening the door.

"Can I ask you something?" He didn't want to, but it bugged him that she hadn't mentioned it. He could feel the words happening despite himself. "Are you still angry?"

"Laurel—"

"Not at Laurel. I mean me. For earlier today, you know?"

"When you kissed me?" She put her hand on his arm. "Feels like ages ago, doesn't it? I'd all but forgotten."

She didn't sound mad. In fact, he'd just been called forgettable. Ticked him off.

"Well, I'm sorry." And he was, too.

"That you kissed me? Seriously?" Her voice ended the sentence nearly an octave higher.

The corner of his mouth twitched. He tried to pull it back into place. Maybe he wasn't so forgettable, after all.

"I'm not sorry if you don't want me to be."

She shook her head. "I think you're crazy."

Maybe he was. Hadn't he known she was trouble, right from the first? "Meaning you'd rather not talk about it tonight?"

"Crazy smart, is what you are." She smiled sweetly and then stood on tiptoe and placed a quick kiss on his cheek before stepping back. "Frankly, it's been a long day. Thank you for rescuing me tonight."

"Was that a rescue? Looked like you had it pretty much under control."

She groaned. "Just say 'you're welcome.'"

Brian touched her cheek. "You're welcome, Fran. I'm glad I could help whether you needed it or not."

"The last word." She nodded. "That's it, exactly."

"What?"

"The last word. You want it, I want it."

He opened his mouth to speak but then stopped.

She laughed.

"So tonight the last word is mine? Then let's make it 'thank you.' Thank you, Brian Donovan."

Something was happening inside his chest. He opened the door, glad to feel the cold air blow in and cool him off as he stepped outside.

She held the door, keeping it open. "I almost forgot. Did you like the tea?"

The tea? He tried to bring his brain back around to tea.

Her face lit up and she punched his arm playfully. "You did! There, you see? Aren't you glad you tried it? You never know when you'll find something special, unless you give it a chance."

****

A couple of days later, Brian walked into the restaurant and stood in the entry way for nearly a minute as his eyes adjusted to the low light of the interior. Before the hostess came from wherever she'd been hiding, he'd already spotted the woman. She looked up. She was too far away for him to actually read her eyes, but he felt them upon him.

"Sir? How many?"

He smiled at the girl. "Just me." He nodded toward her table. "I'm joining that lady over there."

Brian followed her to the table. As he pulled out his chair, he asked, "Cup of coffee?"

"Yes, sir."

What was he doing here? He stared at the woman sitting across from him. How big a mistake was he making by being here? With her?

She said, "Thank you. I appreciate you meeting me here."

"Mrs. Denman—"

"Laurel, please."

He nodded. "Laurel. What can I do for you? Why did you call me?"

Chapter Twenty-Four

"I apologize for tracking you down. I'm sure you don't need our family drama in your life, but Frannie trusts you. I don't know if there's more between you." She held up her hand. "It's not my business until Frannie wants it to be. I don't know how to say this so, I'll just do it. My daughter is different from most women. She's different in a very special way. She seems tough and capable, but she's very fragile inside and I worry about her. I mean, I really worry."

What was this supposed to mean to him? Several times, he started to interrupt, but stopped short. He'd seen Frannie in a very vulnerable state, so he couldn't honestly dispute what this woman was saying, but he wouldn't confirm it either.

Finally, he shook his head. "Why are you saying this to me?"

"You are a kind man. I believe, Mr. Donovan, you are a gentleman."

Laurel's smile was dazzling. Almost hypnotic. Her voice, her mannerisms, they all flowed together to create a whole picture—a whole creature. For a minute or two, he was mesmerized. Then he forced himself to see critically. He noted the fine lines around her eyes and lips. They couldn't all be erased with beauty treatments. Her hands, the manicure. He wasn't a guy who noticed manicures, was he? They weren't very practical. The nails seemed artificial. Which, come to think of it, they must be. Made him glad he hadn't dressed up. His concession had been a clean pair of jeans and a shirt with buttons.

He drew in a deep breath, finally feeling like the world was restored to common sense, even though this meeting with

Fran's mother made no sense at all.

"Why did you call me? How did you find me?"

Her hand flashed across the table to rest on his.

"Please. I get the feeling you're thinking about walking out of here. I promise I won't keep you long. I care about my daughter." She withdrew her hand and looked down at the table. "I fear for her."

"Why are you telling me this?"

Laurel's lips parted and then closed, but softly. She sighed. "You mean don't I feel disloyal? The answer is yes, but I'd do anything for Frannie."

Despite himself, he was impressed that she admitted it.

"I know it looks bad for me to do this, but," she shrugged. "But that's how much I care, and I'm telling you this because I hope you'll help me watch out for her." She held out her hands as if in supplication. "Call me if she needs me. Or if you sense she might be in trouble." She pushed a slip of paper across the table. "Please take this. My phone number."

He didn't reach out. He didn't pick it up.

"I'd better be on my way," he said.

"No lunch?"

He shook his head, but as he stood, she grabbed his hand. She looked at him, her eyes wide and questioning. She pressed the slip of paper into his palm and then closed his fingers over it.

"Are you going to tell her about our meeting?"

"Mrs. Denman. Laurel. I'll try to assume you mean well. I can't imagine calling you for any reason, much less about Fran. If she wants to contact you, that's her choice, her decision."

She pulled her hand back, but didn't look fazed. She gave him sort of sideways look. "I admire character and integrity, Brian. I hope I may call you Brian? I think that's very sweet."

He frowned. "What's sweet?"

"That you call her Fran."

"That's her name, Laurel. Maybe you need to get to know her better."

****

That protective feeling, it almost floored him. He'd made it out of the restaurant without losing his temper and now he sat on his bike in the parking area at Captain's Walk next to Fran's car, telling himself that this was about nothing more than helping a friend. An attractive friend. Maybe more than a friend. But whatever else Laurel was, he could see her for the bully she was. She made his skin crawl. That was his opinion and he'd been wrong before. Interference was wrong. Hadn't he told that to Maia often enough?

Should he tell Fran about the meeting with Laurel? If Laurel was well-intentioned then it would hurt their mother-daughter relationship even more. If Laurel didn't mean well then the same was true. Plus she'd ask, with every right to do so, why he'd shown up? She'd want to know why he'd agreed to meet with Laurel without telling her first.

He knocked on the side door. There was no answer, but he'd try around the ocean side.

Fran was sitting on the porch steps apparently watching the waves roll in. Not generally her style.

"Fran?" No movement. He spoke louder. "Fran?"

"Brian. I'm glad you're here."

The words were fine, but her attitude put him on guard. She didn't sound happy.

"Judging by the tone of your voice, I'm not sure I'm glad. Did I do something wrong?"

"You? Wrong?" She shook her head and looked back down at the paper she held in her hands. "Did you?"

"Not that I know of."

"Guilty conscience?" She patted the porch beside her. "Join me? I'm glad you're here."

"You said that already." He assured himself she was joking, a weak joke from a woman who looked distracted or burdened. He lowered himself down onto the porch to sit beside her.

"What's up?"

She stared at the paper she held and waved it at him. "This was among those papers from Will's van."

"The map and the parking receipts? You mean that stuff?"

"There was an envelope among that stuff. Suppose you'd thrown it away?"

He held back from responding, trying to gauge why her voice was suddenly brittle, strained. Searching, he said, "But I didn't throw it away."

"That's right." Suddenly, she lunged toward him. The edges of the paper grazed his cheek and her arms wrapped around him and she was almost in his lap, so he grabbed her, not wanting her to fall. She pressed her lips to his ear and murmured, "Thank you, Brian."

He couldn't help himself. It was as easy as a shift of his arms, and the most natural thing in the world. She was suddenly on his lap and her lips were near his and he took the next, most logical, step.

And totally forgot about Laurel Denman.

Chapter Twenty-Five

His lips touched hers, softly at first, then more roughly. For a moment, she forgot why she was grateful and was so overwhelmed by his sudden embrace that she responded.

She kissed him back. She clung to him, fighting the gravity that tried to pull her down and away. She held tightly to him, not to keep him, but to give back to him. The kiss lingered between them even as she felt the paper in her hand wrinkling.

There was a magical moment when he pulled his lips away, a breath of space, enough to make her feel the loss, and then his cheek brushed hers as his lips moved to her neck. In that moment, she realized the paper was no longer in her hands.

"Brian." She pushed him away.

"What?"

"It's gone. Where?"

"What's wrong?"

She saw the flash of white on the step below and knew that at any moment the wind would catch it and take it down the beach, maybe out to the ocean, beyond her reach. She dove for it, heedless of possible injury. As she pitched over the side of the steps, hands grabbed her and hauled her back.

"Have you lost your mind?" His face was red. His hands were rough on her arms.

"No," she yelled. "The paper."

In one fluid movement, Brian went a few steps down the side stairs then vaulted over the railing and dropped the remaining few feet to the to the sand. She winced for him, but saw no sign of pain. There was only a trace of a limp as returned up the stairs and handed her the paper.

She beamed. She held it in front of his face. He gave it a

cursory glance and then looked more closely.

"Does that say Julianne? Last name Cooke. Juli? Why would Will have Juli's birth certificate in his van?"

She whispered, "He made a trip to Richmond a month before his stroke. Remember the parking receipts in his van?"

He shook his head. "I don't get it."

"Why would Uncle Will want Juli's birth certificate?" She gripped his arm. "Why did he ask her to paint those seascapes last year? Did he seek her out because he suspected something? Or was it random? A chance meeting at Anna Barbour's house? I don't know the answers, but I'm beginning to understand."

Frannie didn't wait for a response. "Uncle Will asked me to come visit him again at about the time he got Juli's birth certificate. I intended to visit. Good intentions. I didn't mean to neglect him. I wasn't accustomed to having him in my life. And then he had the stroke." Her voice had dwindled to silence. She shook off the guilt and sat up straight.

"But this is the point. Look at the name of Juli's mother."

"Frances."

"Frances Cooke."

"No father listed."

"Frances Cooke. Same as my birth mother."

He frowned. "Fran. You're jumping to conclusions here."

"Am I?" She stared at the paper again as if it might yield more critical, life-altering information. "I was trying to calm down, to think it out, when you arrived."

She turned to him, her hope shining in her eyes. "Brian. Help me think it through. I know from my uncle's letter that my father was married to Frances first—the Frances I'm named for. I confronted Laurel and she admitted Frances was my mother. She said Frances was dead, but, Brian, Laurel also said there was a child with Frances that day...that day when she turned her away."

"Our eye color, my dad's color, is unusual. Maia said right from the start that we favored each other."

"Maia says a lot of stuff." He sounded impatient. "Don't

they say everyone has a double? What are the odds that you would actually run into your…well, your lost family?"

Lost family. It hit her that she'd been waiting most of her life. For what? For her lost family?

"I think you've got it backward, Brian."

"Wouldn't be the first time."

He was trying to lighten the mood. She touched his cheek. "I would never have come here if not for Uncle Will. I'm not a beach person."

She pressed her fingers to her temples. "If Uncle Will hadn't commissioned those paintings from Juli—this from a man who has not made a single concession, decorating-wise, to having an oceanfront house—if he hadn't, I never would have met her. That doesn't sound like an accident to me. In fact," she pointed her finger at no one in particular. "In fact, the biggest question is how did he find out, or even come to suspect, that there was a second child?"

Frannie sighed and groaned at the same time. "He must get well so he can tell me."

Brian acted as though she hadn't spoken. He touched her hair, then her ear and ran a finger along her neck.

She drew in a sharp breath. "If this is your attempt to dissuade me, don't try. You've expressed your opinion and maybe you're right, but this is it, Brian. This is my chance." She cleared her throat. "Don't I owe it to Juli to share this information with her? That Uncle Will had a special interest in her? He did all of this on purpose, Brian. Am I supposed to just walk away?"

"Fran. Listen. Do you really think you're going to find a sister you never knew about living down the road? I need you to buy me some lottery tickets, and remind me not to stand beside you in a thunderstorm."

"Not funny." She moved down a couple of steps and leaned back against the railing. "If she didn't live a short distance down the road, then I don't think it would've happened. In fact, maybe she already knows…at least about his interest." Suddenly, one little thought burst into her brain and optimism overrode doubt. Excitement spurred her words.

"Maybe she even knows there's a relationship, but won't speak unless I ask. Maybe she's waiting for me to say something."

"Calm down. You're getting ahead of yourself." Brian massaged his knuckles. "If Will knew, he would've told you. He doesn't play games with people's lives. Same with Juli."

She returned to sit beside him. Her voice went soft. "Maybe he wanted to be sure before he said something. Or he could've had the stroke while he was waiting for me to arrive, to tell me in person."

Brian leaned forward. His arms resting on his knees, he stared out at the ocean. "One thing I know, Fran, is that if you open this up, you won't be able to close it again. Somehow, I don't think Juli is going to thank you for this. There's no good way to have this conversation. Even if you knew for sure, it would be an incredibly difficult conversation." He shook his head. "You know how I feel about messing in other people's lives."

"This is my life, too."

He took her hand, wrapped his fingers around hers, and squeezed. In reassurance or in warning?

"Brian, I've spent a lot of years being controlled." She dropped her head and covered her face with her free hand. When she looked up, she added, "Controlled. I thought I was fighting it, rebelling, but I was just bad-tempered. I stayed there and accepted it and became mean and resentful. I think it became a habit. My fault. But no longer."

****

She pulled discretely to the side of the road before she reached Juli's home. With the buffer of a couple of houses, she felt relatively anonymous. She needed a few minutes to think it out. To plan her first words.

How did one open such a conversation? Did one simply say, 'I think you are my sister?'

No, one didn't.

Maybe, she could say 'I think we're related. I believe Uncle Will figured it out. Do you mind if I tell you about it?'

That might be a better conversation starter.

She released the steering wheel and waved her hands. She'd never had sweaty palms before. Never in her life. Her anxiety was usually hosted in her tummy.

The file folder lay on the passenger side seat. It had the letter from Will's mom and the copy of the newspaper birth notice the detective had found. It also held Juli's birth certificate.

Juli, may I tell you about my father and his second wife, the woman I believed was my mother until a very short time ago?

She shook inside. With Juli's house so close, this was her opportunity. She placed her hands over her stomach. Don't betray me now, she begged. She closed her eyes and breathed deeply. She felt the muscles ease.

A brown dog trotted across the street, pausing to give her only a brief glance before moving on. Frannie scanned the street and saw no one, but people might be home and looking out their windows right now, and wondering why she was parked here.

This was silly, and potentially very embarrassing.

She put the car into gear and drove forward. She could turn around and go back. It might be best for everyone.

But she wanted family if there was true family to be had. How would Juli feel about it? To have this, whether sister or half-sister, thrust upon her?

Her eyes burned. She touched them with the back of her hand and found the lashes were wet.

Crying?

Maybe she wasn't ready yet.

Yet, life gave no guarantees. Tomorrow might be too late.

Frannie bowed her head and closed her eyes. She began, "Dear Lord, please hear my prayer," but the prayer had trouble coming together. She couldn't find the right words. Maybe because she didn't want to? Maybe because the response might not be what she wanted to hear?

She gave a great sigh and then blotted her eyes. She thought of the snippets of verses. Will's fortune cookies. Messages. She'd been getting messages since she'd stepped into Will's house. She needed to try to listen with an open heart before she moved forward solely on the basis of what she wanted.

As soon as she arrived home, Maia called, saying, "Meet me for lunch tomorrow?"

"Sure. What did you have in mind?"

"Everything all right? You sound funny."

"I'm good." She touched the handle of the tea steeper and spun it around on the counter. "Here or in Beaufort?"

"Beaufort, if that works okay for you."

"I'll be there."

****

She wore slacks. Funny thing was, they no longer felt quite natural to her, not in the fabric or cut. When she stood in front of the full-length mirror, her shoes looked wrong. Heavy. She needed some sandals, casual ones, not dressy.

Shorts, too. She pulled up her pants legs and stared at the mirror. She had the pairs of capris she'd purchased, but she needed more casual slacks. Maybe a few new tops, too.

Maia was waiting at the grill a few shops down from the gallery. She waved through the window. Frannie raised her hand in return and went inside.

"You've got a great table. A beautiful view." She pulled out the chair and sat. "There's a few more folks strolling around out there than the last time I was here."

"Spring arrives early in Beaufort. In a few weeks, this place will be hopping."

They placed their orders, and then Maia said, "Will you still be here when spring arrives?"

Frannie sighed. "Hard to say."

"At least that's not a 'no'. What's weighing you down?"

Maia asked.

"I don't want to think about any of it right now. I'm tired of dealing with my mother, of defending my sanity, of temperamental men. What else?"

Maia leaned forward. "I'm tired of mean people and bullies and...and..."

"And high heels."

Laughter really did help.

"Now, please explain the sanity part. Who's questioning your sanity?"

"Laurel. Sometimes me."

"You are one of the sanest people I know."

"That's nice, but you haven't known me long. Maybe I did inherit something from my mother. My birth mother, I mean."

"You told me yourself that you don't know what was actually wrong with her. It isn't necessarily genetic. Even if it was, there's no guarantee you'd have it." Maia stabbed a piece of lettuce with her fork. "As for your other mother, now that's a different sort of animal altogether."

"You only know what I've told you about her. I'm not objective."

"Brian, too."

"Brian? He hardly saw her. He doesn't know her."

"I thought he talked to her. He said she was too perfect to be normal. He must have noticed a lot in a brief time."

There wasn't much time for conversation between the time Laurel had walked in and she'd asked Brian to leave.

Maia said, "I hope you truly don't mind if I see Joel. He and I have a lot in common. I enjoy his company, but I don't want to tread on anyone's feelings."

"Not mine, for sure. I'll be delighted if you and Joel find something good together." Frannie sipped her tea. "He deserves it and so do you."

"What else?"

"What else, what?"

"I can still see it in your eyes. Like a shadow. Something

231

else is eating at you."

Frannie started to speak and then pulled it back. She shook her head. "There is, but I can't talk about it. It involves someone else. Without her," she broke off. "Without that person's consent, I can't discuss it."

"I understand. I respect your discretion."

"But it bugs you, doesn't it?"

"No. Well, maybe yes. Seriously, anytime you want to chat about anything whatsoever, you let me know and I'll be there. You can trust me." Maia looked curious, yet earnest at the same time.

"I know I can."

The waitress collected the salad plates. "Anything else?"

She said, "No," but Maia jumped in. "Chocolate pie, please." She looked at Frannie. "We'll each have a slice?"

"Sure."

Over pie, Frannie added, "You wouldn't believe how tempted I am to ask your opinion about it, but I can't."

"I can give you advice anyway. It's not always necessary to know the actual details of a problem."

"What does that mean?"

"Get away from people, and even away from the stuff that surrounds you. That's the only way to shut out the extraneous, distracting inputs. Take yourself outside. Stand on the beach, close your eyes, shut out the past and the present, and listen to what your heart tells you."

Chapter Twenty-Six

That pain-in-the-butt lattice had worked loose again. Brian knelt, prying a piece of the splintered white wood out from under the screw. He was a handy kind of guy all right, but a real handyman could have done a better job. Now, he was going to have to find lattice that matched the rest and cut it to fit and paint it. Might be easier to hire a real handyman to help this not-so-handy one get the job done.

How would he explain that to Fran? He was going to have to do that sooner or later. Probably sooner.

Actually, he had hired a very handy friend to do another project for him, but that project was a secret. He grinned. Just wait until it wasn't a secret. Maybe that would be a good time to clue Fran in about his lack of handiness.

He heard a noise on the porch. She must be home. He stood gingerly, but more easily than he used to. Physical therapy and healing took time and persistence. He'd said the same to Will.

It was virtually soundless to walk on the dry sand, that's why the guy on the porch didn't hear him. As soon as Brian was fully upright, he saw scuffed shoes and the skinny twerp who wore them. Through the upright rails, he watched the man press his face to the sliding door and cup his hands around his face, to better see through the glass, no doubt. Brian's surge of adrenaline cured his limp, at least briefly. He was up the short stairs to the crossover in a heartbeat and standing behind the creep before he knew he wasn't alone—that he'd been seen tugging on the door handle.

"What's up?" Brian grinned, but not in a friendly way, letting the man know his day had just taken a downhill turn.

He started forward, like he thought he might get around

him, but Brian moved faster, and with his greater size he easily pinned the guy back against the door.

"Don't move. You understand?"

He nodded.

"What are you doing here?"

"Nothing. Not doing anything. I was checking to see if anyone was home."

"Yeah, I saw that."

"It's not a crime to knock on someone's door."

"Not what I saw. Why don't you tell me what you wanted?"

Brian released the man's wrists, but stayed close. This guy smelled like he was living rough and he was up to no good, but as long as Brian didn't see a weapon, there really wasn't much to call the cops over.

He looked surprised and rubbed his wrists. He also put a smirk on his face.

Brian wedged one hand up against his throat. "I'm in the mood to bust someone's face. I don't really care who. You'll do."

The smirk vanished. "I wasn't going to hurt anyone. None of my business, anyway. I was paid to deliver a message."

"Hand it over."

"Not that kind of message. The lady who hired me wanted me to do a little something so the woman who lives here would know someone had been around."

"Intimidation? This isn't the first time you've been here."

The guy put up his hands. "I swear. First time. And I haven't done anything."

"Who hired you?"

No answer, so he shook him and pushed him back against the wall.

"A blond lady. I told you, it's nothing to me."

"Her name?"

"I don't know her name. My buddy told me she paid him, too. I don't know what he did. Hey, he didn't hurt anyone either."

Brian really did want to bust his face. It'd been a long time since he'd been in a real brawl, but this guy was too pathetic and this was Fran's front porch. He didn't think she'd be happy about blood spray on the deck boards. Then the thought of Fran and the potential for damage to her happiness made him even angrier.

"Did she say why?"

"No, she said to do a little somethin' to make her nervous." He waved his hands. "A practical joke, you know. Nothing big. Nothing like someone would call the cops for. Nothin' that would hurt anyone."

Brian held him by a fistful of grimy shirt. He could feel the guy's heart thudding against his fist. He smelled fear on him. It made him angrier, but in a different direction. He needed to think it out when he wasn't so pissed.

"I'm gonna give you a piece of advice. For free. When you leave—and yeah, I'm going to let you walk away—do not speak to that woman who hired you. You say nothing to her. Nothing. Got it?"

He nodded.

"Say it."

"You don't want her to know that you know. I got it. No problem. Like I said, it wasn't anything personal. A little joke."

Now the man's hands were almost in praying mode. Brian willed his temper to stay in control. He put his face close to the guy's and said, "You are never coming back here."

The guy shook his head. "No. Never."

Brian stepped aside, trying to keep his fists from doing their own thing. The guy didn't move. "What are you waiting for?"

"Can I go now?"

"Go. Fast."

Halfway down the stairs, he stumbled and fell. He scrambled back to his feet and was gone. Brian figured he'd earned a few splinters for his trouble.

Brian was still angry and there was no one he could take it out on.

Then he remembered he had Laurel's phone number.

He pulled out his wallet and searched for the slip of paper. With his temper still hot, still standing on Fran's porch with the ocean raging in front of him, he punched the keys on his cell phone.

Chapter Twenty-Seven

Frannie entered through the side door and, through the sliding door, saw Brian on the porch. His back was toward the house and he appeared to be speaking on his phone. She approached the door quietly, thinking to surprise him, but changed her mind by the time she reached the door because his posture was tense and his movements were abrupt. Whatever the conversation was about, Brian wasn't happy.

She stood at the glass, caught in indecision. Should she stay or go? Maybe pretend she hadn't noticed? Then he turned and his voice, loud and abrupt, came through the glass.

"You said to call if I was concerned about Fran. Maybe you thought I could be bought like the weasel I caught on her porch." After a pause, he continued, "No, don't even try. All you need to know is this: if anything happens to her, or around her, Laurel, we'll be having a conversation, possibly with the police."

He saw her. The moment his eyes caught sight of her there on the other side of the glass in the dim interior, his face went blank. He finished, "Remember what I said." Slowly, carefully, he put the phone in his pocket.

"Fran?" He reached for the door handle. "Let me in?"

Stunned, she shook her head.

"Fran, please."

She spoke through the glass. "Were you on the phone with Laurel? I heard you say her name."

"I can explain. Please."

She reached across, tugged the drawstring and the blinds closed.

"Fran? You're there. I know you are and you're listening."

237

True enough. She had paused a few feet away.

"Fine. You want me to shout through the door? I will. I promise I will. All of the neighbors will hear. But if you're okay with that, then so am I because I'm not going to walk away."

She faced the door and the closed blinds. Her feet felt stuck. Betrayal tasted like blood. Bitter. She wanted to run. Maybe to shut herself up in the bathroom. Forget the world.

"Fran. I called Laurel. I think I know about the noises you heard and all that crap. It wasn't you. Well, maybe some of it was you because you have that freaking crazy imagination... No scratch that, I didn't mean crazy. You have a strong imagination and you get all worked up over stuff. Stuff that doesn't matter. Sorry. I don't mean to say the stuff you care about doesn't matter. That's not what I meant."

She was having a hard time staying hurt and angry. There was something especially pathetic, yet incredibly adorable about a man like Brian groveling at her sliding glass door, trying so hard not to put his feet in his mouth that he sounded ridiculous.

"I found a guy on your porch earlier. Minutes before you got home. He was sneaking around. Up to no good. I beat... No, I got him to talk. Laurel paid him. When you came home, you heard me on the phone telling Laurel not to even think of doing anything like that ever again."

Frannie touched the blinds. She ran her fingers along the edge of the vertical slats.

"I know what you're going to ask next. How did I have her phone number? Laurel asked me to meet her. I did. Curiosity, I guess. She gave me her phone number. Wanted me to call if anything happened...you know, with you. I walked out on her. I was going to tell you. Not that there was anything to tell, but I was going to tell you, but when I got to your house you'd found Juli's birth certificate and I forgot. That's all. I forgot."

Silence. Did she hear him walking away? Anxiety gripped her. Was he giving up? Frantically, she scrabbled at the lock and slid the door open.

He stood there, his eyes wide as if he didn't think she'd give in.

She looked at him and asked, "Now what?"

He shrugged. "Whatever you want. Whatever you want to do about Juli, about Laurel, even about Will, I'll support you in your decision."

"That's nice." She stepped out onto the porch. "But it's not quite what I meant."

"No?"

She shook her head, slowly and deliberately. Brian moved forward and caught her up in his arms. He lifted her off her feet. She wrapped her arms around him and squeezed.

"Hey, not so tight."

"Oh." She pulled back. "I'm sorry. Did I hurt you?"

He laughed, low and warm. "No, just can't reach your lips. Now I can." And he did.

****

She dialed the phone with shaking hands. She breathed deeply, willing her nerves to settle, her stomach to behave.

"Hello?"

"Hi. Juli. Sorry to bother you. It's Frannie."

"Frannie? Hi, yourself. How are you?"

"I'm fine. I was wondering if I could stop by."

"Sure. When?"

"Well, whenever it's convenient? Maybe tomorrow?"

"What about now? I'm home. Danny's napping."

Now. She thought of a thousand reasons why not now, and none had any truth in them.

"Now is fine, if you're sure."

"I'll be here."

She was committed. No turning back.

The Winters' home, for all that it was a simple, brick house, felt imposing, like a wall to be breached, or a trespass about to happen. Either way, it would be an action she couldn't take back. Frannie held her purse tightly, all too conscious of the documents and the secrets securely tucked inside.

Chapter Twenty-Eight

"I have a question for you. It's personal." She shrugged. "It's delicate. I don't know a good way to ask this. But it's important. It has to do with my mother."

Juli led her out to the deck and motioned toward the cushioned wicker chairs. They sat. Juli leaned over and patted Frannie on the arm.

"You're so pale. Can I get you something to drink?"

Frannie shook her head. "No, please. You are so kind to me, and I hope you'll still feel that way after this conversation."

Her expression closed, becoming a bit wary. "I can't believe it's anything so awful. You know, Fran, sometimes saying something out loud has a way of defusing it, of taking away its power." She sighed loudly and with a rueful grin on her face, she said, "You didn't know me before. It took me a long time to learn to trust other people, to find value in trusting them even though they will surely let you down. They aren't perfect."

Frannie drew in a deep breath and then let the words out, "Can you tell me about your mother and father?"

Juli stared, but Frannie couldn't read her face. She put her hands together and gripped her fingers tightly. She hardly dared to breathe, afraid that Juli would change her mind, would reject the question. After all, who was she to ask such a thing?

"Her name was Frances. I don't know who my father was. Mama left that space on the birth certificate blank." She shook her head.

"Did you know her maiden name? Did you ever hear the name, Edward Denman?"

"Maiden name? I don't know. I presume it was Cooke

since that was the name on the certificate." Her eyes looked beyond sad and her voice was colorless. "I don't know anyone named Denman, or didn't until I met your uncle."

"I am so sorry. I don't mean to hurt you."

"Hurt me? No, it's just that I've never been curious. I was glad to be fed and warm." Juli closed her eyes. "I was five when they took me away. I don't remember much, but enough to prevent wasted sentimentality."

Juli pressed her fingers to her forehead. "I have a headache. It came out of nowhere. Will you excuse me while I go take something for it?"

Frannie nodded and Juli went into the house.

The visit felt over.

Her purse was on the deck next to her chair. She wouldn't be unzipping that bag today. With Juli unwell, it was better to wait.

Maybe Brian was right. Maybe what she wanted wasn't good for anyone else. Was it worth the angst? The risk of losing these new friendships? No one was going to thank her for upsetting Juli. Everyone loved Juli.

It wasn't too late. She stood, gathering her things. She turned. Juli was standing in the doorway.

"What are you doing?" Juli's eyes were red.

"I'm leaving. We can chat another time."

Juli stepped toward her. "You said this was important."

"Only to me, I think."

"Please." She took Frannie's hand. "Forgive me for getting emotional. I never was before, but since Danny was born...to be honest, even before that. I cried about the least little things during the pregnancy."

Juli sat, which effectively mandated that Frannie sit, too, or be rude.

"I meant what I said about mama, but now, having my own child gives me a different perspective on it." She hugged her arms. "Maybe that's why the memory has the power to overwhelm me."

She stared at the baby monitor with its bright blue light.

"He'll sleep a while longer. Why don't you tell me what's on your mind?"

"My mother's name, my birth mother, was also named Frances. Frances Anne. That's who I'm named for. She married Edward Denman, my father."

Juli's lips curved in an unexpected, unsuspecting smile.

Frannie had a panicked thought, Did she already know and hadn't cared enough to say. But that was silly. She drew the envelope from her bag. She removed the copy of her birth notice, which was photocopied on the larger piece of paper. She handed it, along with the envelope, to Juli.

"Please take a look at this."

Juli held the envelope in one hand while she read the copy of the newspaper clipping. "Frances C. and Edward Denman. Your parents? Frances Anne Denman, that's you, right?" She smiled at Frannie.

"It's a small world isn't it? I have 'Anne' in my name, too. My name is actually Julianne."

She opened the envelope to put the paper inside and found the certificate. She slid it out, unfolded it, and the smile froze on her lips. "What's this all about? Another Frances Cooke? She married Edward Denman? The Frances C. in your birth announcement?" She continued staring at the paper. "Why did you give me your birth notice?"

Juli's hands dropped to her lap, but she continued holding the paper. "What is this about?"

Her lips were frozen. Silently, she cursed the confidence that had brought her this far and then deserted her.

Juli persisted. "Your Frances, your mother, is dead, isn't she? Your father remarried that woman. What's her name?"

"Laurel," she gasped the word. "Yes, she did and he did."

"When did she die? You were young, I think."

"I was seven."

"I see." She refolded the paper and slipped it back inside the envelope.

The paper rustled. Juli was shaking though the movement was barely perceptible.

Suddenly anxious to spill it all while she had the chance, Frannie opened her mouth to speak, but was stopped by a slamming door and a crying baby.

"Luke." Juli stood as Luke appeared at the screen door.

"I'm sorry. Looks like I woke Danny. Shall I get him?"

"No, I'll take care of him." She turned to Frannie. "We'll get together another time, very soon. Okay?"

"Sure. No problem." She turned her back before her face could betray her.

"Frannie." Luke walked with her to the front door. "Are you all right? You look pale."

"I'm fine." Her face felt as if smiling might break it. "Time for me to get home."

****

She sat on the porch and rocked, focusing on the creak of the chair's treads and on the tall, ugly weeds growing atop the dunes. She wanted to think about anything, everything except her conversation with Juli, and she wanted to do it alone. Sometimes misery doesn't love company.

It had been the right thing to do.

That might be true, but what about the expression of desperation on Juli's face?

She closed her eyes and laid her head back against the rocker and listened to the swish of the weeds as they brushed against each other in the warmish breeze. The soft noises were faint against the backdrop of the ocean.

She sighed. "I've done it. I've really done it now. Messed everything up."

"Did you say something?"

Frannie's eyes flew open and she sat up, grasping the armrests. "Megan?"

"That's me." She tilted her head to one side. "Did you say something was messed up?" She plopped down into the other rocker.

How could she hide her deep disappointment from this child? She didn't know how to rearrange her expression, much less repair her heart. Where was Laurel's armor when she needed it? If Megan was here, then Brian wasn't far behind. He'd know by looking at her face that she'd done exactly what he'd advised against.

The child pulled some tangled yarn from a tote bag.

"What are you doing?"

"I learned to crochet. I have to practice."

Random chance—that was life. She'd screwed it all up, everything good she had going on here at Emerald Isle, and a young girl she hadn't known a few short weeks ago was sitting on her porch with a snarl of tangled yarn.

Megan shook the yarn as if that would fix the mess.

"Here. Hand it over."

Megan gave it up.

"Now, hold your hands like this. We'll fix this."

Random? How random was it to feel a bubble of something positive in her chest? Not only because of this child, but maybe the bubble included the child's father, too.

"Megan, are you an angel?"

Megan gaped and then giggled. "Mom and Dad don't think so."

"Definitely not an angel." Brian stepped up onto the porch. He was holding a white gift bag. "It's a perfect day."

"Almost perfect." She continued unwinding the yarn, rewinding it around Megan's two small hands. "I never cared much for the ocean, but I've changed, at least in that respect. The ocean, the sand, even the scents, mean something different to me now."

"Almost perfect?"

She laughed softly. "Except for those weeds growing on the dunes. I'd love to take a mower, well, maybe not a mower, but a scythe, to it. Still, while they're not pretty, I suppose even the weeds have a sort of wild charm. Sometimes they sing when the wind blows."

"Hold that thought." Brian walked over and stopped the yarn winding. "Megan, give us a minute. Fran, come with me."

She looked at Megan. "Be right back? Okay, Brian."

He took her hand and led her down the crossover, nearly to its end and to the bench where the view of the strand was all encompassing, like being in a panoramic photo. He was still holding the small white bag. "This is for you."

"From you?" She accepted the bag. More tea? No, it was too light.

"From me, yes, but Megan helped. She helped choose the color, so you know."

Frannie peeked inside, looked at Brian again and then pulled out the turquoise scarf. It was long and lightweight and seemed to keep coming.

"I know you're not much for bright colors."

"Oh, no. This is perfect." She meant it. "I have some new favorite colors."

"Those beachy colors?" Brian lifted the scarf from her hands and placed it around her neck.

She stroked the silky, crinkled fabric.

"Perfect." Brian touched her shoulders. "A moment ago you were saying something about the dunes and grasses being less than perfect."

"Like an eyesore, maybe?"

"Yeah. That." He used gentle pressure on her shoulders to turn her toward the railing. "Look at them."

"I see a paper cup discarded down there. I see tall weedy grass."

"Things are not always what they seem. You probably know that these dunes are important. Vital barriers. They protect what's beyond. The houses, et cetera. You know that, right?"

"Sure, the dunes protect the shoreline."

"The dune grasses you see are critical to the stability of the dune. Did you know that the growth of those grasses is the best indication of the health of the dune?"

"Those grasses don't look like much."

He took her hand, but waved his other arm to encompass all of their surroundings. "They are one part of this whole scene—one part—yet without them, the rest of this is nothing. It's only one big wave away from a big mess."

Maybe it was the viewing angle, maybe it was Brian's voice praising them, or maybe it was just getting to know them and to appreciate their purpose, but the grasses did look better.

"I understand what you're saying." She nodded. "One piece is dependent upon the other." She continued staring at the grasses, at the dunes, and her eyes strayed beyond to take in the strand and the waves rushing ashore. For a moment, it was winter again and the glass of the sliding door was between her and the scene, the living ocean. She almost reached out to touch the remembered door and then pulled her hand back.

It had changed. This had changed. Her perceptions had changed. Had she truly changed? A short time ago she'd discovered that Brian had met with Laurel behind her back, but she'd forgiven him in an instant. Her heart felt light.

Brian reclaimed her hand. "Without the grasses, the rest doesn't stand a chance."

"I won't call them ugly anymore."

He touched her chin and turned her face toward him. "I was going to add that, without you, the rest of us—me especially—don't stand a chance."

Her chest hurt. She thought the pressure might crush her heart. How could happiness hurt so much? She gasped for air. Brian slid his arm around her.

"Are you okay, Fran?"

She nodded. She leaned into him, resting her head against his chest. "I have a question for you."

"What?"

"Not saying I mind, but I'm curious. You are the only one who calls me Fran. Why?"

"Why don't I call you Frannie? Do you want me to?"

"Not really."

"Then I'll tell you." He dropped his arm away. He turned and leaned back against the rail with her, hip to hip. "Frannie. When I hear it I get a picture in my head. A girl who is polite, who does the right things. Someone sweet. With curls and dimples."

"I'm not sweet? Polite? Is that what you're saying?" She felt a little ticked off. He needed to explain this better.

Brian ignored her question. He grinned with a smug, satisfied attitude. "But then there's Fran. Fran is bolder. Not in a brash way, but she thinks for herself. She likes a good fight. Sometimes she's too stubborn, but she also doesn't give up. If she wants something, she keeps coming back until she gets it."

"That's me? I mean is that how you see me?" Wow, was he wide of the mark, but then, some of what he said resonated with her. The rest she might have to work on.

She reached out and touched his face. Gently, she guided his face toward hers and pressed her lips to his.

Voices came from the beach area. Suddenly, self-conscious and remembering they were in full view of anyone who might be nearby, like Megan, she looked over at the rockers, but Megan wasn't there. The yarn was hanging on the top knob of one of the rockers, blowing in the breeze, and the front door was wide open.

Had they upset Megan with their private conversation and the public embrace?

At the same moment that she whispered, "Megan," the wind rustled the grasses, a gust that grew in strength and slammed through the open doorway. It caught the vertical blinds, twisting them, trying to rip them from their fastenings.

Frannie ran.

Megan was in the living room, her face distressed. "I'm sorry, I'm sorry."

Papers had blown off the counter and flown around the room. Even the seascapes had gone cockeyed on the wall. A vase had crashed and glass shards littered the floor.

"I'm sorry."

"No worries, Megan." Frannie knelt and put her arms around the girl.

"I didn't mean to break anything. I only came in to go to the bathroom."

Frannie smiled. "You weren't upset?"

"Upset? About what?"

Impulsively, Frannie planted a kiss on Megan's cheek. "No harm done. Let's get this cleaned up."

She picked up the broken bits of glass. Megan gathered the loose papers. Brian straightened the paintings remarking on the quality of the picture-hanging workmanship that had prevented them from going airborne, too.

Megan asked, "Can I have this stamp?"

"What stamp?" Brian asked.

"This one. It looks old."

She handed the envelope to her father. He looked at it, frowned, and offered it to Frannie.

"What's this?"

The envelope was addressed to Will Denman. It looked modern and the postmark was relatively recent, only about a year ago, but a slip of paper and another envelope inside had slipped partway out. Will must have read it, then put it back together and stuck it in with his bills and correspondence, or at least someplace where the wind had found it.

Frannie pulled out the interior envelope. This one was older and had the stamp that had caught Megan's eye. The postmark was smeared. Folded around the envelope was a piece of lined paper. The spidery script read:

Brother—I found this in Mother's things yesterday. You can see it arrived after Marshall and Anne's deaths. So many years ago. I guess Mother meant to open it, but never did. I don't know what to make of it, but maybe you will. The note was signed, Penny.

Frannie held the envelope, addressed long ago to her grandparents, with a return address in Edenton—but, as Penny stated, opened only recently.

She didn't yet know what the letter said or who had written it, but her hands trembled. Her surroundings faded. Even Brian and Megan had fallen away. She didn't know why her hands shook, but her heart knew.

She held the letter close to her chest and breathed a silent prayer, then opened it and removed the paper. There were few words.

Mr. and Mrs. Denman—Edward doesn't know and I can't go near that house again, not with the new wife, but I did something I shouldn't have. Now I'm sick. I have another child, your grandchild. She's a sweet little one. Her name is Julianne. If you care at all, contact me at this address. Frances.

Did Frances ever realize that the letter hadn't arrived in time? That her former in-laws were already gone? Or did she go to her grave believing they hadn't cared enough to respond?

Brian cleared his throat. Frannie looked up at him.

"This is how Will knew. His sister, Penny, sent this to him." She handed it to Brian.

He whistled, low and soft.

She nodded. "Now what?"

His eyes were grave. "You have to make that choice, Fran."

"I already spoke to Juli earlier today. It didn't go well."

He frowned. "How so?"

"I tried to tell her, but she didn't want to hear it. As soon as an opportunity arose, she left me sitting there and," her voice dropped, "I gave up and left."

Brian shrugged. "At least you opened the conversation. It should make the follow up easier."

She hoped so. Because now she really didn't have any choice. Juli must be told. This was about her life as much as Frannie's.

When Brian left to take Megan home, she called Ron Hamilton. "Could you find out if Penelope Warren is still alive? I believe she lives in the Louisburg area." She read aloud the return address on the outer envelope.

"Sure. What else can you tell me about her?"

"She's my uncle's sister. About his age, I guess. Somewhere in her eighties. She's called Penny. Maiden name was Denman."

"I'll get back to you as soon as I know."

"Another thing. Could you get me the contact info for anyone at all who might have known, or might have information on Frances? I want to speak with them personally."

"It's a short list, but I'll see if there's anyone else I can add to it."

"Thanks."

After she disconnected, she continued standing there, staring into nothing. This was a winding road she was following. Tortuously winding, but with amazing scenery and some happiness and grief. At least, she was no longer standing still—at least not in the physical sense. No longer waiting, but instead, moving forward.

It was a crazy, adrift kind of feeling, but forward, definitely.

Frannie stood facing the fridge and thinking about Brian. Mrs. Blair had said "Name's Brian. His number is on the fridge." Or something like that. She touched the paper with Brian's name and number scrawled across it. Who could have known what a difference a few weeks could make, and a big part of that difference was Brian. All because of a piece of broken lattice for which she'd needed a handyman—Uncle Will's handyman. Now hers.

She'd left this mess of notes, cards and magnets untouched, as if disturbing them would irretrievably erase Will's life—the life he'd build for himself here at Emerald Isle and would want to return to, intact. So, she wouldn't remove them, but a bit of reorganization couldn't hurt.

She lined the larger magnets up and tucked the few business cards under the edges. Then she gathered the stray notes and secured them under the smaller magnets. It was interesting to see what Will had considered important to his life, important enough to keep front and center on the fridge.

A business card from an accountant. The Front Street Gallery. Will's attorney and a doctor's office. And one from "Odd Jobs and Handyman" that listed Brian. No, not Brian Donovan. Mr. Patrick Bryan.

Who the heck was Patrick Bryan? For sure, he wasn't her Brian.

A competitor in the handyman trade? Her brain twisted and turned trying to fit it all together in a comfortable, sensible way, but it couldn't happen.

So, who was Brian?

The phone rang. She let it go to voicemail. When the message light lit up, she punched the key to listen.

"Frannie? Frannie. I've been waiting for you to call me. I need to speak with you. I want you to know I've been thinking about you and about everything, and I want to help you."

There was a long pause, and then Laurel continued, "Call me, please."

Frannie disconnected from voicemail, then dialed her attorney. "Mr. Lloyd? I need to speak with you regarding my house. I've come to a decision and I want her out no matter what it takes."

****

It was still morning. Frannie had set her cup of tea on a small table next to the porch rocker, but today it failed to soothe her. She was tossed back and forth between anger and distress. She needed questions answered.

Maia came straight around to the back and climbed the stairs to where Frannie waited on the porch.

"Hey, there. I'm here."

"Thanks for coming over. I appreciate it. This was inconvenient for you. I could've driven over."

"It was no problem. I had to drop off something at Luke's."

Maia continued, "No one was home, so I left it inside the storm door and came on over." She dropped into a rocker and smoothed her flowered skirt and kicked off her low heels.

"What a gorgeous day. So what's up?"

"Would you like some tea?"

"Sweet tea?"

"A cup of tea. Hot tea."

"Oh. Maybe later. Thanks."

"Excuse me for a minute."

Frannie went inside, took a glass from the cabinet, and filled it from the pitcher in the fridge. She went back out with the glass in one hand and a napkin in the other. She put the napkin against the bottom of the glass and then smoothed it as she twisted it up the sides of the glass.

"Voila, Maia. For you."

"Look at you! You're one of us now. By the way, I love that scarf. It's a great color on you."

She almost answered, Brian gave it to me, but didn't want to invite that discussion. The more precious their relationship had become, the less she was willing to chat about it. Instead, she said, "I need to ask you about something."

"You seem so nervous. Surely nothing can be so dreadful on a beautiful day like this."

"I have several things bothering me, but this one, I think you can help with."

Maia stopped rocking and leaned forward, her feet flat on the porch. "Name it."

Frannie looked her straight in the face. "Will you be honest with me?"

"Of course. What's up?"

"It's about Brian."

Maia's face changed, going solemn, and her brows narrowed. Almost as quickly, her expression smoothed, but didn't quite return to the relaxed, cheery state she'd arrived in. She said, "Go on."

"Brian isn't my uncle's handyman, is he? What does he do for a living?"

She leaned back into the rocker. She put a finger to her lips and paused before answering. "This and that, I guess. I don't quite know how to answer you."

Her caution, the careful choice of words, worried Frannie. Maia opened her mouth and then snapped it shut again. Her face began to flush.

"Are you okay?"

Maia nodded, keeping her lips firmly pressed together.

In frustration, Frannie leaned back in her chair, too, and groaned. "Sorry. I shouldn't have asked you."

"Ask him." Maia said. "He'll tell you anything, but you know how he feels about gossip, even when it isn't really gossip, but only talking. I told him I'd try not to, you know, talk about other people's business. Anyway, ask him."

"You're right. I was too embarrassed. It must have started as a misunderstanding, but why wouldn't he tell me?" She stood abruptly and went to stand again at the rail. The rocker kept rocking. "But why should he be honest with me? I tried being candid and it went badly, believe me."

"With Brian?

She had a feeling that if she answered 'yes' Maia would dispense with caution and tell her anything she wanted to know. She said, "No."

"Not me, right?"

"Definitely not you."

"Oh, so it's Juli."

Her heart sank. Juli and Maia must have discussed what she'd told Juli. She felt like a fool. "So she told you?"

"Told me what?"

She heard sincerity in Maia's voice. "How do you know something happened between me and Juli?"

"I don't actually know, but I'm pretty sure you aren't talking about Joel. You aren't, right?"

"No."

"Whew. Good. Joel and I have been talking a lot and he's wonderful, so I'm glad. You mentioned 'she' the other day at lunch when you said you had something worrying you. Your mother might have been on your mind, but you were already troubled about her, right? Nothing new. Luke did mention you came by, but then left because Juli felt ill. Or, at least, he thought that was why you left, but I could tell he was concerned."

"I see." Juli had kept it to herself. Frannie found that reassuring. "You are one clever girl."

Maia giggled. "Not really, but I am intuitive. I pick up on moods and bits of info and they fit together sometimes." She looked down. "I'm not really a gossip. Or maybe I am. Brian is probably right about that, but I'm working on it."

"I'll ask Brian."

"Yes, please." Maia touched the corner of her eye.

"You aren't crying, are you?"

She shook her head. "Do you need help with Juli? I know she likes you."

From down the beach, a walker had approached, already nearly parallel with Captain's Walk.

Maia half-rose and squinted. "Is that Juli down there? Were you expecting her?"

"No." Frannie clutched the railing. "No, but I'm glad she came. I need to speak with her."

"I guess that explains why she wasn't home. Do you need my help?"

She almost wanted Maia for cover. Juli might be more receptive, or at least appear more receptive, with Maia present, but that wasn't fair to Juli and it was cowardly.

"I should speak with her alone."

"I'll run along then. Unless you need me to stay? To wait?"

"Thanks, Maia. I'll talk to you later."

She stood and waved at Juli, then slipped her bare feet into her shoes, grabbed her purse, and with a reassuring smile, she vanished down the stairs.

Frannie walked down the crossover. She felt like she was approaching fate.

Juli was here, dressed in rolled up jeans and carrying her sandals. Frannie touched the cotton capris she wore. Beach wear for a beach meeting. She descended the steps and asked, "Would you like to walk?"

"Maybe we could sit here?" Juli nodded toward the sand.

They sat, leaving about a yard of careful space between them.

"I'm not sure what to call you. I met you as 'Frannie' but Brian calls you Fran as if you've never been called anything else. Which is right?"

She dug her fingers into the warm sand. "Frannie." She laughed, but it wasn't a happy sound. "I might try on Fran for a while. I always wanted to be someone different, anyway. At least, I have since my dad died."

Juli arched one eyebrow. "Someone different? Who?"

One speechless moment, and then Frannie shook her head. "Who? You're joking."

"I am, but only sort of."

"You think I'm foolish, don't you? I have been blessed in many ways. I have so much. I've had it all of my life and yet I was never content being me."

"Why?"

"I never felt comfortable in my own skin. Complete. I felt like an imposter. Unworthy."

This time they shared the moment of silence, but Frannie was warmed by Juli's smile.

Juli leaned forward and picked up her water bottle. "I understand."

"You felt uncomfortable in your own skin, too?"

"No, not that. I felt comfortable as myself. In fact, I was self-reliant. I didn't need anyone else, until I discovered that I did. I thought I was content as myself, but I never belonged, not anywhere. I could carry it off as if I did belong, but I never felt it inside."

Juli's attention appeared to drift away. She tilted her hand so that the sand cascaded between her fingers. Frannie waited.

As she brushed the last grains from her palm, Juli said, "I worked all sorts of jobs. I was proud of my independence, but all I was really doing was hiding."

Frannie said, "From the first moment I saw you, you seemed to have it all—and to have it all together, too. Perfect family. Perfect life. Loving family and genuine friends. What could you possibly be hiding from?"

"From people and life. From having to trust, to depend on them."

"Because of Frances?"

Juli didn't answer. Instead, she shifted the conversation. "What about you, Frannie?"

"I'm hiding, too. Here at the beach." She shrugged. "There are worse hiding places, right?"

"No one can fault your choice of hideaway, but you aren't a hider." Juli looked away and then back. "You are a pleaser. You try too hard to please everyone."

"No, you're wrong. I always offend people, annoy them."

"Remember the old saying? Try to please everyone, and please no one, especially yourself." She stirred the sand with one finger. "Which, by the way, is not always true. Everyone here likes you very much. The important thing to remember is that people can like you or not. Ultimately, the only thing you can control is yourself and what you give to, and take away from, the exchange."

They let the words lie there on the sand between them for a few quiet seconds. When Juli broke the silence, her manner was sharper. "Why do you still live with your mother?"

"A few years back, I had some trouble in my life and also, I thought she needed me, but it hasn't been good between us in a very long time."

"So you came here?"

"I came to help my uncle. He asked me to manage his personal property, to keep an eye on things if he ever became ill or incapacitated."

"You could've done that from Raleigh, right?"

Frannie nodded. "I could have, but I've felt, for as long as I can recall, that I'm waiting for something. I decided to wait here. It's peaceful here. I can think better."

"What are you waiting for?"

She cast about in her brain. "Waiting for things to be right? For my life to start? Or maybe waiting to be the person I should be. Waiting to feel complete."

Juli shook her head. "I don't understand, after all."

"Waiting for what I was missing."

"I still don't understand."

"How could you? I didn't, either. But, finally, I think I do. For years, I awakened in the night to the sound of crying. Dreams or nightmares?" She shrugged. "When I found out about Frances, I thought it was me—the memory of the young me—long forgotten, crying for her mother."

"I can see that. It makes sense."

"Except now I know better." She dug her toes deeper into the sand. "When I found out about the second child, the one who was born when I was two, before I was returned to my father—that's when I understood." She pulled out her feet and the sand flew. "It's her cry that I remember."

She closed her eyes to banish the threatening tears and then faced Juli. "What about you? How do you feel about the subject we're tap-dancing around?"

"You mean Frances?"

Frannie nodded. "I mean our mother."

Chapter Twenty-Nine

Juli stared intently at her sand-covered toes, and Frannie watched her while a seagull loitered nearby, hoping for a tidbit.

Frannie dug her fingers into the sand. Perhaps seeking an anchor? Yes, she was. She closed her eyes and said a silent prayer. What do I do next?

She opened her eyes slowly and caught the glint of the sun catching on a tear as it slid along the curve of Juli's cheek. Instinctively, she reached out and touched her shoulder. Juli turned her face away.

"I'm sorry," Frannie said.

Juli brushed her hand across her cheek. "Sorry? For what?"

"For making you go through this."

"No." She shook her head. "I spent a lot of years telling myself that I was lucky. Lucky that the state took me away from her. That, even though it meant foster homes, still I was warm and my tummy was full. I told myself I was glad she didn't come back and get me."

Juli pressed her fingers to her temples. "Don't you understand? I came to terms with it and I was okay. More than okay—I made the best of it. I survived and made a life. This is opening the past back up, like a wound that healed. The scar faded, but the injury was never really gone. Now, I have to ask myself why she didn't come back.

"Do you understand, Frannie? Why didn't she come back? Because she couldn't? Because she... And I was glad she didn't.

"I have to ask myself what I didn't do that I should've. Not as a child, but when I became an adult." Juli paused for a breath. "How did she die? Do you know?"

"The death certificate says pneumonia, but what that means, I don't know. Pneumonia could be the result of something else." She took a breath and held it and then released it slowly. "I have reason to believe she was ill for some period of time before she died." She added, "I'm going to Edenton. That's where she's buried."

Juli gasped and shook her head. "I can't go. I have responsibilities."

"I understand. I didn't know if you'd want to go, but I wanted to tell you, in case."

"No, really. I have to consider Danny and Luke. I mean, even if this is all true… I'd go if I could. I can't."

"Not a problem."

Neither had yet uttered the word, 'sister', and it seemed almost anticlimactic to do so. Sort of stating the obvious. All of the fun stuff like figuring out how they were alike would be in the future, hopefully.

"I'll give you a chance to get used to this." Frannie stood up and dusted off the seat of her pants. Some part of her hoped that Juli would stop her, would want to discuss it more now, but she didn't. She continued huddling over her knees, as if she were grieving. Which, Frannie thought, she probably was. Finally, after all these years, Juli was officially grieving the loss of her mother.

"Frannie!"

She heard a voice in the distance, hard to hear with the ocean close at hand. She looked up and down the beach trying to discover who was yelling.

"Frannie!"

The crossover. A woman stood there, her arm raised, doing the queenly wave.

"Laurel." She groaned. "I'd better go speak with her or she'll come down here and get her heels mired in the sand." She added under her breath. "It would serve her right."

She remembered the paper in her shirt pocket. She held it out to Juli. "I want you to have this. It may be the last letter

Frances wrote. It was to her mother and father-in-law. Our grandparents. They were in a car accident shortly before she mailed it. They never received it and she probably never knew."

Without turning her head, Juli accepted the letter. She stood, brushing sand from her hands.

"One more thing. If Dad was still alive, he'd be devastated to discover he had a daughter he didn't know about. He would be delighted too. He would've loved you and you would've loved him. We would all have been the better for it—having you as part of the family. He wouldn't have let Laurel get away with what she did, and I won't either."

Juli stopped her. "Wait a minute. Don't be hasty. She might've made mistakes, but she's still your mother. She brought you up. She cared about you. You can't throw that away."

"You say that because you don't know what she's done to me, nor what she did to you."

"What did she do to me?"

Frannie looked down. "I wasn't going to tell you this." She swallowed, wishing she hadn't walked herself into this corner. "Frances brought you to the house. I think you were about five. I wasn't there, nor was Dad. Frances asked to see Dad and Laurel sent her away. She let Frances believe Dad would contact her, but she never told him."

She squeezed Juli's hand. "I found this out very recently, but don't worry, she'll be sorry."

She started to step away. Juli spoke her name softly, "Frannie."

Frannie stopped again, almost annoyed. She was ready to deal with Laurel. Now.

Juli said, "You've been to church. My church and I'm sure other churches."

"Yes, with Laurel, and for all the wrong reasons, so don't give her any credit for that."

Juli shook her head. Her eyes were stern, but her voice was gentle and persistent. "You know the Lord said vengeance belongs to Him."

Bitterness rose in her throat. It tasted of bile. She touched her stomach, asking it to stay quiet while she did what she had to do. She struggled to keep frustration out of her voice.

"Are you kidding me? Let's just say this is an instance of helping oneself. I'm cutting her out of my life."

"Maybe. What I'm saying is you can only control yourself. Make the decision to rejoice when things are happy, be patient when things are bad, and find your answers in prayer. You'll be amazed at how different the world will look to you, it will even feel different, when you find that peace within yourself."

She didn't want to hurt Juli and their brand new relationship, but this was ridiculous. This was the real world. She pulled away.

Juli looked at her with those deep blue eyes so like her father's that it struck into Frannie's heart like the point of knife. She breathed in and the air felt ragged coming into her lungs.

"Before you deal with your mother, promise me you'll read Romans 12:12. It's saved me more than once. Please."

"Juli, I wish I could, but this has to be done. You don't understand."

"I understand that harboring bitterness and anger is like poison in your body. You have to let go of it or it will destroy you."

"You aren't telling me anything I don't already know. That's why I have to deal with it right now, once and for all. Will you wait for me here?"

She left Juli standing on the beach. She was ready to deal with Laurel. She crossed the sand and walked up the steps to the crossover.

Laurel's eyes ran the length of the colorful Capri pants covering Frannie's legs before stopping on her bare, sandy feet.

"You look like you've settled in here." Her tone sounded ambiguous, but her face was flushed.

Frannie figured Brian's words were still ringing in her ears, and Laurel was probably wondering how much he'd told her. She saw no point in dragging it out.

"You sabotaged me. You did it before, too, didn't you? You drove wedges between me and my boyfriends and my other friends, then played games with my sanity. To drive me to return home? Why?"

Laurel looked up the beach and down. She settled her gaze on the dunes beside the crossover. "This isn't the place for that conversation."

"Shall we go in the house? Shall I make us a cup of tea? I've even got some of those special cookies you like so much. Is that what you'd like?"

As Laurel opened her mouth to respond, Frannie cut her off.

"In case you thought I was serious, understand we won't be doing that. Not now and never again. What I really don't get is why you worked so hard to make sure I didn't have my own life, didn't marry, and yet did your best to get Joel and me together. Why?"

Laurel's lower lip trembled. She lowered her voice. "So disrespectful. I never expected this of you, Frannie. I never wanted to hurt you. I was always there for you."

"Give it up, Laurel. Brian told me about the man you sent. Finally, I have the missing piece and the puzzle begins to make sense, except for the 'why' of it. It wasn't my companionship you craved. So, was it my money? Didn't Dad leave you enough?" Frannie spoke rough and low. "Why Joel and not the others? Did you really think he'd be so easy to control?"

"You would never have married Joel. I didn't blame you for wanting a boyfriend. You're young, so I understood. You could do far worse than Joel. In fact, you did. More than once. If somehow you did marry him, at least he would be kind and faithful."

"So selfless of you. Yet those household expenses have kept going up and up. I let it go rather than get into yet another argument, but now I'm beginning to see why you were so invested in keeping me close."

Laurel sniffled as she dug in her purse and pulled out a tissue. "It was never about the money."

"That's good to hear because I won't be paying any of the house or household expenses any longer. In fact—"

A swirling gust of wind kicked up the dry sand, flinging it up into the air. Frannie and Laurel both turned away shielding their eyes. In that moment, Frannie remembered something she'd heard: revenge is a dish best served cold. Shakespeare, maybe?

But as Juli had reminded her—God said, "Vengeance is Mine."

Perhaps she'd said enough for now. If more needed to be said, especially about the house and Laurel's living arrangements, then her attorney could say it for her. Now or later, it was up to her. So, for now, she'd leave it for later. Still, she wasn't quite done. Being clear in one's message wasn't the same as revenge.

"Do you see that woman sitting on the beach?" Frannie pointed toward Juli.

"I see her."

"You turned away a dying woman and with her, that child, and you condemned her to be an orphan, a foster child, separated from her father and sister."

Laurel was pale with only bright spots of red left on her cheeks. "I only did what I thought best."

"It's time for you to leave now."

"Frannie...."

"Maybe someday. Maybe when I'm no longer angry. Maybe after the relationship between my sister and me is as it should be, perhaps then we can have a reasonable conversation. Until then, respect my feelings."

Frannie walked past her, leaving her to stew alone. Inside the house, she closed the door firmly to be sure there was no misunderstanding about an invitation.

She searched in the dresser drawer and found the folded over sock. She pressed it to her heart. She picked up the photo of her father and Frances, holding it between thumb and forefinger for a few moments, considering. She wasn't likely to ever have one like it again. She should've made copies right away.

Her stomach twisted and she held her breath. She laid the photo back down on the dresser, but kept one finger on the corner, torn between what was the right, or the best, thing to do.

When she emerged from the house and reached the crossover, she was glad to see Laurel was gone, but the beach was also empty. No Juli.

She picked up her pace, jogging along the crossover, searching the beach strand as she ran along the boards. At the end of the walkway, she paused and looked up and down the beach. Juli was already a distance away. Frannie quickly descended the steps and stumbled through the dry sand. It kicked up behind her as she ran, the rough grains hitting her calves, until she hit a soft drift and her feet slid out from under her. She hit the sand on her knees and hands.

"Wait, Juli. Wait!"

Juli turned toward a path between the houses and headed in the direction of the road.

Perhaps she'd had as much as she could handle. Maybe she needed some time.

Had she, Frannie, said or done the wrong thing? Something that convinced Juli to not want this relationship?

Frannie stayed on her knees, the sock and photo cradled in her hands.

What was that first verse she'd found? The one about Jonah in the belly of the whale? She felt like she'd been spit out of a painful, tortured place to find herself on a sunny beach, a new world, never having realized she'd been trapped until she no longer was.

One thing she'd learned was that until you accept what must be done, rise above yourself, and move forward to do it with a whole heart, you were stuck. It wasn't enough to go through the motions; you had to be that new person. Until then, you couldn't go anywhere, not even back. You were doomed to be stuck, blind, mired in your own misery and self-doubt.

Frannie put one hand over her stomach. She was calm. Her stomach, that nervous, angry beast inside, was also quiet. She closed her eyes. What did she feel? Sadness maybe, but also something a lot like satisfaction. Regret? Maybe the tiniest twinge, but when it came to Juli, she still had hope.

****

Brian said he'd be there about noon. He'd made it a point to tell her it was important for her to be there. Some of her anxiety had returned. Not only did she wonder what he had on his mind, but she was going to ask him why he went along with the handyman-house painter charade.

Was he really a caretaker? Hah. Look at her—she'd certainly never made a go of a traditional job. It shouldn't be that difficult a conversation; however, she hadn't heard back from Juli since their beach chat yesterday, and those ugly little doubts were trying to worm their way back in to sabotage her hope, but now she recognized them for what they were.

As she carried her tea to the coffee table, she passed the sliding glass door and saw Juli standing on the crossover about halfway between the beach and the house. Her back was to the house and she faced the ocean with her hands in her pockets.

Frannie opened the door and received another surprise. Luke was sitting in a porch rocker. His hands were under Danny's arms and around his torso, while Danny kicked and tried to stand on Luke's thighs. Danny stretched his baby legs and gurgled, bubbles forming on his lips.

Luke looked toward her. "She's waiting for you."

She couldn't read his face.

He nodded toward Juli. Her hands were no longer in her pockets; her arms were now crossed tightly across her chest.

Frannie went back to the bedroom to grab the rolled sock. When she exited, she went straight to Juli.

"You're back."

Juli asked, "Take a walk?"

She nodded and followed.

"Did you work it out with your mother? How are you?"

"I'm better than I might have been. I read those verses in Romans. I'm not sure about forgiving her."

"Well, it's not really about forgiveness, is it? Deciding not to seek revenge or 'get even' and to leave it in God's hands, to trust Him to handle it, is more about acceptance and moving forward. When you do that, the anger and poison inside you will be neutralized."

"For a while maybe…until the next time."

Juli smiled. "That's true. As many times as needed." She leaned forward and caught Frannie in a hug.

The hug was brief and impulsive, but joy surged inside her, knocking out everything else. Even when Juli released her, Frannie knew they'd truly found each other.

"Here's the letter you gave me."

Frannie accepted it back. "You could've kept it." She put the folded paper in her shirt pocket and withdrew the photo. It was so small and fragile.

"Take a look at this."

Juli held the photo and stared.

"Edward and Frances Denman. About the time they married."

Juli looked up at Frannie and then looked back down at the photo. She shook her head.

"Maybe she looks familiar. Children see things differently, I guess. I don't feel a connection to them." But she didn't hand the photo back. As they walked across the sand, she kept looking at it.

"It's very small, I know."

"It's not that." Juli closed her eyes. "I've tried, but I can't remember what she looked like." When she opened her eyes, Frannie saw they were red and glittering.

"You've been crying. I'm sorry."

"I have, but you had to tell me this. I needed to know."

Juli had returned the letter to her, and when it came to the photo, she made it clear she felt no connection. Was it too soon to do this next step? It felt like a huge risk, one that if it fell flat, could put an end to the whole saga.

Frannie held up the sock.

Juli frowned. "Is that a sock?"

"Yes. It's Uncle Will's. I borrowed it." She held it up like a white, cottony, stretchy egg.

"I hope you'll accept this in the spirit intended."

"A sock?"

Frannie began to unpeel the sock. "Wait."

"It's a sock."

She paused before unwrapping the final layer. "Dad gave this to me on my sixteenth birthday. He would've given you the same, or something similar, if you'd been with us. Please hold your hands up."

She emptied the contents into Juli's palms. The deep blue of the sapphires in their platinum settings reflected the sun and the depths of the ocean. Juli gasped as an earring touched the edge of her hand and fell into the sand below. Frannie quickly retrieved it.

Juli said, "Are you crazy?"

She laughed. "So I've been told a few times."

"Is this real? Why are you doing this? I don't need your jewelry."

"Don't be offended. I know you don't need it. I need you to have it."

"No."

"Listen, please?" Frannie took the earring she'd picked up from the sand and held it alongside Juli's face. Satisfied, she held it next to her own ear. "See the color?"

"Yes."

"That was the color of our father's eyes."

"And yours." Juli sounded miffed.

Frannie put it back against Juli's cheek. "And yours."

"Mine?" She looked down at the jewels. "I guess so. Like mine."

"You don't have pierced ears, so I'll keep the earrings and the ring." She put the earrings on and slid the ring onto her finger. "Hold still." She reached around Juli's neck and fastened the necklace with the pendant.

The sunlight refracted off the jewels casting blue lights around them, dancing upon the sand and against their skin.

"This is crazy." Juli touched the pendant. "Like my eyes, you said." She started crying, the tears ran down her cheeks, as she laughed. "I'm crazy, too." She dabbed at the tears.

"Let's be crazy together?" Frannie laughed. "I hear it may run in the family."

They sat on the beach in their capris and sapphires, until Danny decided it was time to do otherwise.

They heard Danny fussing.

"Juli?" Luke called. "I think it's time."

"Why don't y'all come back for supper?"

"Supper?" Juli looked doubtful.

Frannie's mood threatened to tank until Juli added, "I'd like to keep it between the two of us for a while, before we involve others. It feels so new."

"I understand. Tell me when it's good for you. I'll try to be patient."

"Don't you want to take this back?" She touched the pendant again.

"No, that's yours. It's a gift from your father and your sister."

Juli nodded and brushed at her eyes again. "I'll call you later." She paused and then continued, "I have to tell you this. What I said about you being a 'pleaser'? I missed seeing the persistence. I admire determination. I have a feeling that's the real you." Juli smiled. "I have determination, too. More importantly, I have faith."

Frannie shook her head. "I think I'm a little short on that."

"I doubt it, but even if you are, don't worry." Juli smiled. "I have enough for both of us, for now, and I'm happy to share."

****

Frannie stood, at peace, watching the ocean. She'd done what she had to, including giving Juli space to absorb it all at her own pace. They'd parted with buckets of good feelings shared between them.

And she, Frannie, hadn't done everything she thought she had to do, specifically with regard to Laurel, and that was maybe a good thing.

"Fran!"

She turned toward the house. Brian was walking down the crossover with quick steps.

Her handyman.

She held out her hands and he took them in his own as he joined her at the railing.

"I have to ask you something, Brian."

"Anything. Ask."

His smile was so broad, she hated to risk dimming it.

"Why haven't I received an invoice?"

He tilted his head and frowned. "Invoice? Oh, for the painting and stuff."

"Yeah, that stuff."

"Must've gotten lost in the mail. I can send another."

"Liar."

He touch her chin and turned her face toward his. "Harsh."

"But true."

"Only in the sense that I didn't send an invoice." His words were playful, but his tone had lost some of its shine. "What's wrong?"

"Uncle Will's handyman is Patrick Bryan. His business card on the fridge gave your game away…except, what is your game? Why the charade?"

"Game? Charade? I'm a pretty handy guy and I did paint the house, didn't I? Most of it, anyway. And for what? You know, I'm beginning to think I've been played."

"What?" Her temper flared.

"That's right. You suckered me into painting that house. You were very clever. I'm still trying to figure out how you

269

managed it." He pulled her closer. "In fact, I think you do owe me, but I don't want money so I won't be sending an invoice. Nope, this bill gets delivered, and collected, in person."

His arms were strong around her. His dreamy blue eyes, eyes the fresh blue of robin's eggs, held her own.

"You're trying to distract me, aren't you? Why not just tell me? Admit it, you aren't a handyman. That's not how you earn your living."

"At first I was curious about you, and concerned about Will, but even that doesn't explain why I painted that house. I don't paint houses. I hate house painting."

"But you did."

"Exactly. Why is that?"

"How do I know?" She frowned.

"And I kept coming back. Why is that?"

"You are infuriating. You don't know how to have a simple, civil conversation."

"Why, Fran? Why did I keep coming back?"

"Because of me."

He dropped a kiss lightly between her eyes. "Because of you. You fascinated me in some way that I don't fully understand. Fate, I guess."

"Fascinated?" She started to frown, but couldn't. The touch of his kiss remained.

"What? You don't like that word?"

"It's a lovely word, but it's past tense."

In response, he picked her up and set her on the railing, then leaned forward so that their eyes were almost level.

"So, if I'm not an official, bona fide handyman, aren't you curious about what I do for a living?"

"You're a caretaker." Was he going to be sensitive about it? She touched his cheek. "And you've been recovering from the bike accident. If you don't mind, I would like to say that you need a larger place if you're going to give Megan a fulltime home. You are going to do that, right?"

"Yes. I'm going to come to an arrangement with Diane.

Something that benefits Megan more than the two of us. But I already have a larger house. I moved to the garage apartment after the divorce and the wreck. It was easier to manage on my own, without stairs, plus the big house had a lot of memories."

"You own that house? You aren't the caretaker?"

"Yes and yes. The marina down by the bridge, that's mine. Frankly, I lost interest for a while...lost interest in almost everything, but I've been going over there in the afternoons working my way back into it. Good thing, too, with the warmer weather coming fast." His voice softened, dropping as he spoke.

Fran had leaned toward him as his words grew fainter. Brian took advantage of the proximity and kissed her.

Chapter Thirty

Frannie leaned her head against his rough cheek. The clean scent of the breeze fresh off the ocean seemed to promise good things. Not cold, this was a spring breeze whose warm touch made winter an already fading memory.

"I feel drained, but in a good way." She draped her arms over Brian's shoulders. "I'm ready for whatever comes."

"How about lunch?"

"Lunch?" Trust a guy to think of food.

He looked at his watch. "It's lunchtime."

"Hard to believe. It's been a long morning. I'm not hungry. Too much emotion, I guess. I could stay right here with you and watch the ocean indefinitely."

"Not even a cup of tea? The kind you like? What did you call it? Chai?"

He was sweet to remember, even if he remembered incorrectly.

"Maybe in a little while."

He kissed her temple. "You have things to do."

"Like what?"

"Have you forgotten your uncle? You're overdue for a visit."

She sighed. "Yes, you're right. I have a lot to tell him, and a lot to thank him for. A lot to thank you for, too."

Her peripheral vision caught a glimpse of movement from the direction of the house. She started to turn that way, but Brian stopped her with a gentle hand to her cheek.

"Not so fast. I'll collect my thank you now."

She smiled and leaned forward with the intention of kissing him, but movement again caught her attention and she turned toward the porch.

"What's all that?"

Even from that distance, she could see people on her porch, but they were hard to make out because of the noon shade and the porch railing. A woman was standing and she was easier to identify.

Frannie grabbed Brian's arms. "What's Janet doing here?"

"Ouch. Your fingernails." But instead of drawing away, he slid his hands around her waist. "Looks like you have a couple of visitors. What are you waiting for?" He lifted her from the railing and, after a long, slow hug, he returned her to her feet.

Now she saw a hand, that dear, frail hand, waving.

She whispered, "You brought him home?"

"For an afternoon visit, that's all for now. A friend has an ambulance service. He coordinated it. I think, however, that we need to move forward with plans for the ramps and wider doorways. Looks like he might be needing them soon."

She placed her hand on his cheek, but couldn't find the words to express what she felt. She shook her head as hot tears filled her eyes.

"Fran? You okay?"

She nodded.

Brian touched a finger to her lips. With a grin, he said, "You can thank me later."

Frannie took his hand. Together they hurried along the crossover, past the dunes and the rustling grasses, to welcome Uncle Will back to his home, his Captain's Walk.

THE END

ABOUT THE AUTHOR

USA Today Bestselling and award-winning author, Grace Greene, writes novels of contemporary romance and inspiration or women's fiction with love, mystery and suspense, wth a strong heroine at the heart of each story.

A Virginia native, Grace has family ties to North Carolina. She writes books set in both locations.

The Emerald Isle books are set in North Carolina where *"It's always a good time for a love story and a trip to the beach."*

Or follow a Virginia Country Road and *"Take a trip to love, mystery and suspense."*

Grace lives in central Virginia. Stay current with Grace's releases and appearances. Contact her at www.gracegreene.com.

You'll also find Grace here:

Twitter: @Grace_Greene
Facebook:
https://www.facebook.com/GraceGreeneBooks
Goodreads:
http://www.goodreads.com/Grace_Greene

Other Books by Grace Greene

BEACH RENTAL   (Emerald Isle #1)

Brief Description:

On the Crystal Coast of North Carolina, in the small town of Emerald Isle...

Juli Cooke, hard-working and getting nowhere fast, marries a dying man, Ben Bradshaw, for a financial settlement, not expecting he will set her on a journey of hope and love. The journey brings her to Luke Winters, a local art dealer, but Luke resents the woman who married his sick friend and warns her not to hurt Ben—and he's watching to make sure she doesn't.

Until Ben dies and the stakes change.

Framed by the timelessness of the Atlantic Ocean and the brilliant blue of the beach sky, Juli struggles against her past, the opposition of Ben's and Luke's families, and even the living reminder of her marriage—to build a future with hope and perhaps to find the love of her life—if she can survive the danger from her past.

KINCAID'S HOPE   *(Virginia Country Roads)*

A quiet, backwater town is the setting for intrigue, deception and betrayal in this exceptional sophomore offering. Greene's ability to pull the reader into the story and emotionally invest them in the characters makes this book a great read.

This is a unique modern-day romantic suspense novel, with eerie gothic tones—a well-played combination, expertly woven into the storyline.

Brief Description:

Beth Kincaid left her hot temper and unhappy childhood behind and created a life in the city free from untidy emotionalism, but even a tidy life has danger, especially when it falls apart.

In the midst of her personal disasters, Beth is called back to her hometown of Preston, a small town in southwestern Virginia, to settle her guardian's estate. There, she runs smack into the mess she'd left behind a decade earlier: her alcoholic father, the long-ago sweetheart, Michael, and the poor opinion of almost everyone in town.

As she sorts through her guardian's possessions, Beth discovers that the woman who saved her and raised her had secrets, and the truths revealed begin to chip away at her self-imposed control.

Michael is warmly attentive and Stephen, her ex-fiancé, follows her to Preston to win her back, but it is the man she doesn't know who could forever end Beth's chance to build a better, truer life.

A STRANGER IN WYNNEDOWER

(Virginia Country Roads)

<u>Bookworm Book Reviews</u> – January 2013 - 5 STARS

I loved this book! It is Beauty and the Beast meets mystery novel! The story slowly drew me in and then there were so many questions that needed answering, mysteries that needed solving! …Sit down and relax, because once you start reading this book, you won't be going anywhere for a while! Five stars for a captivating read!

<u>Brief Description</u>:

Love and suspense with a dash of Southern Gothic...

Rachel Sevier, a thirty-two year old inventory specialist, travels to Wynnedower Mansion in Virginia to find her brother who has stopped returning her calls. Instead, she finds Jack Wynne, the mansion's bad-tempered owner. He isn't happy to meet her. When her brother took off without notice, he left Jack in a lurch.

Jack has his own plans. He's tired of being responsible for everyone and everything. He wants to shake those obligations, including the old mansion. The last thing he needs is another complication, but he allows Rachel to stay while she waits for her brother to return.

At Wynnedower, Rachel becomes curious about the house and its owner. If rumors are true, the means to save Wynnedower Mansion from demolition are hidden within its walls, but the other inhabitants of Wynnedower have agendas, too. Not only may Wynnedower's treasure be stolen, but also the life of its arrogant master.

CUB CREEK

(Virginia Country Roads)

<u>Brief Description</u>:

In the heart of Virginia, where the forests hide secrets and the creeks run strong and deep ~

Libbie Havens doesn't need anyone. When she chances upon the secluded house on Cub Creek she buys it. She'll prove to her cousin Liz, and other doubters, that she can rise above her past and live happily and successfully on her own terms.

Libbie has emotional problems born of a troubled childhood. Raised by a grandmother she could never please, Libbie is more comfortable *not* being comfortable with people. She knows she's different from most. She has special gifts, or curses, but are they real? Or are they products of her history and dysfunction?

At Cub Creek Libbie makes friends and attracts the romantic interest of two local men, Dan Wheeler and Jim Mitchell. Relationships with her cousin and other family members improve dramatically and Libbie experiences true happiness—until tragedy occurs.

Having lost the good things gained at Cub Creek, Libbie must find a way to overcome her troubles, to finally rise above them and seize control of her life and future, or risk losing everything, including herself.

Thank you for purchasing

BEACH WINDS

I hope you enjoyed it!

Please visit me at www.gracegreene.com
and sign up for my newsletter. I'd love to
be in contact with you.

Other books by Grace Greene

Emerald Isle, NC Stories
Love. Suspense. Inspiration.

BEACH RENTAL

BEACH WINDS

BEACH TOWEL (short story)

BEACH CHRISTMAS (novella)

Virginia Country Roads Novels
Love. Mystery. Suspense.

CUB CREEK

A STRANGER IN WYNNEDOWER

KINCAID'S HOPE

www.GraceGreene.com

37007058R00174

Made in the USA
San Bernardino, CA
07 August 2016